THE MISSING GIRL

JENNY QUINTANA

THE MISSING GIRL

MANTLE

First published 2017 by Mantle
an imprint of Pan Macmillan
20 New Wharf Road, London N1 9RR
Associated companies throughout the world
www.panmacmillan.com

ISBN 978-1-5098-3950-6

A CIP catalogue record for this book is available from the British Library.

Printed and bound by CPI Group (UK) Ltd, Croydon, CR0 4YY

Visit www.panmacmillan.com to read more about all our books
and to buy them. You will also find features, author interviews and
news of any author events, and you can sign up for e-newsletters
so that you're always first to hear about our new releases.

In memory of my parents
Joyce and Jack Quintana

PROLOGUE

You disappeared in the autumn of 1982, when the leaves switched their wardrobe from green to burnished brown, and our mother made great pots of jam from the fruit we picked in the garden. I was twelve, with clumsy clothes and National Health glasses. You were fifteen, crazy-haired and willowy.

I thought at first that you'd be back. I only had to wait, away in the woods where the birds were as silent as I was, as if they missed you too. I took to wearing your coat, my hands pushed deep in the pockets, playing with the bus tickets and the dust and the dried-up sweets I found there. Sometimes I thought I saw you, running ahead, weaving amongst the trees, but it was only sunlight glinting through the branches, or the wind brushing its fingers through the leaves. Other times I heard you laugh, but it was only water flowing over stones in the stream or birds suddenly finding their voices. It was as if you'd never existed, or else you'd disintegrated and scattered on the breeze.

That was one of my theories: that you'd self-combusted. You'd burst into particles and not one trace could be found. Or you'd been lifted upwards, taken to a different place, to heaven, like they said at church. But when I looked at the vast, dark sky, I couldn't contemplate you being lost there, so I came up with more elaborate ideas: you'd run away to be a dancer in Russia.

You were hiding out in a nunnery. You were a scientist in Antarctica.

I clung to each theory because it helped me reject what people said. You'd been abducted on your way home from school, raped and left for dead. You'd been decapitated, dismembered, bits of your body scattered across the countryside. Each day brought new horrors for me to dream of. Each dream made me wake sweating, screaming out your name. I wanted to tell these people to stop. You'd be back. You wouldn't leave me on my own forever.

But the rumours bubbled on, right through the community. Friends fell silent when I passed, though I heard their discarded words. I held my head high and kept my thoughts close, muttering them like incantations: you were in Spain, learning flamenco, falling in love with dark-eyed gypsy boys. Anything to avoid those creeping fears: a silent shadow swooping, gathering you up with its wings and bearing you away. Because if I thought about your potential captor, that was what I imagined happening to you: a cast-out devil tumbling from heaven, snatching his beautiful prize with indifferent arms, and keeping on going straight down to hell.

1

The train halted a hundred yards from the station. A voice announced a short delay. People around me were muttering, craning their necks at the window, wondering how long we'd be stuck there. Closing my eyes, I breathed deeply, distracting myself, flexing my fingers and blowing on my palms. They were sore and I realised I'd been balling my fists all the way from Paddington and the nails had made indentations in my skin.

Outside were familiar landmarks: Victorian houses with chaotic extensions; a narrow piece of wasteland that swept alongside. Boys had played chicken there once; vandals had set fire to the banks. Now the line was fenced off. Plastic bags clung to hedges and empty bottles littered the grass. It was autumn, yet there were none of the signs: no trees, no copper leaves, no pale golds. The place was stark. Depressing and still.

A few days before I'd been in Athens, drinking coffee in the October sun. My mobile had rung, a voice had spoken and I'd recognised Rita – my mother's best friend. It was the way she'd said my name, Anna Flores; the way she'd rolled the 'r'; the way she'd lowered her voice and explained how my mother had died. A stroke. When could I come home?

Rita had discussed the funeral, asking for my opinion: egg and cress versus salmon and cucumber; 'Lord of All Hopefulness' or 'Abide With Me'. Her talk had jarred with the smell of *souvlaki* drifting from a restaurant and the sound of a lone voice singing in a bar. Afterwards I'd sat for ages weeping and feeling as if the music was the most sorrowful in the world.

The train lurched, crawling forwards. Passengers shifted with mumbles of relief. I pulled on my denim jacket, fiddled with my bag, checked that everything was where it should be: purse, phone, lipstick, bottle of Givenchy, photo of my mother. Photo of Gabriella. A man in a raincoat reached for his suitcase. I followed his lead and retrieved mine.

A few people got off with me. I watched them rushing up the steps and across the bridge, scrabbling with their tickets and their bags. Dropping my case, I pulled out the handle and paused to look around me. Nothing much had changed. The empty waiting room. The broken bench. The CCTV. How long had those cameras been there? Too late to spot Gabriella leaving, or to confirm the difference between sightings and lies.

Three years. That was how long it had been. A pit-stop visit before I'd left for Greece, although I'd seen my mother since, when she'd made the journey to London, the day before I'd actually flown. Now, when I thought of that last meeting, in a cafe in Harrods, with my mother picking at her scone, my stomach wrenched with guilt. Three years. Only phone calls in between. Why had I assumed she'd go on forever? I should have known better than anyone how abruptly things changed.

A guard emerged from a doorway on the other side of the track. He looked across, his glance assessing me. I gave a half-smile, flexing my fingers as if my suitcase

4

was heavy and I'd stopped to take a rest. Straightening, I headed for the steps, trundling the shiny purple case behind me. I'd recognised him, although I'd pretended that I hadn't. He'd worked at the station for years. Then, he'd worn tight trousers short enough to see his coloured socks; now his trousers reached all the way down to the tops of his shoes with modest precision. That was the thing about this village: people stayed – except for me. I wondered if he remembered who I was.

Out on the street the sky looked damaged, bandaged with dark clouds. The trees wore bare branches like weapons, and the pavements were piled with leaves. Soon they'd be swept up by men in yellow jackets. Men like Tom. For a moment I held my breath and listened, half expecting to hear the trundle of his cart. On a day like this, he would have been out, head bent, focused on his task. Oblivious to the world.

I blinked and shook my head. It wouldn't do to think about the past. Instead, I concentrated on the walk, taking the back roads with their terraced houses and rows of parked cars, noticing a new takeaway, a pub with a name change, a building being renovated.

The streets widened and there was my mother's house, a rambling Victorian semi. I resisted the urge to stand still and absorb the moment, to pretend this visit was normal. Pushing on, I turned down the path, my stomach flipping at the creak of the gate. The door was black with peeling paint and a hairline crack across the glass. A peony sprawled against the wall and for an instant I remembered blood-red petals bursting from their buds; Gabriella, fixing a flower in my hair. I held the snapshot steady in my mind, until it blurred at the edges and faded, like a developing photo in reverse.

The door opened before I found my key and Rita filled the space. 'Anna,' she said warmly. Part of me had thought her beauty would have faded, that she'd resemble my mother: sparrow-like, with wispy hair and eyes clouded with cataracts. Instead she was buxom in a navy woollen dress, with light-coloured hair cut into a bob. Her face was lined, but she was still handsome, with high cheekbones and green wing-tipped glasses.

She took my hand – her grip was strong, and in a moment I was over the threshold parking my suitcase. And then she was leading me through the hall apologising and welcoming, offering tea, as if it were me who was the stranger in the house. We paused outside the living room. 'You mustn't mind the old ladies,' she whispered, leaning into me. 'They turned up this morning specially to see you.'

'Thank you,' I said. 'For all that you've done. I couldn't have managed without you.'

'Of course you could,' said Rita, squeezing my arm. 'Chin up, and come on through.'

The room, I noticed with a tightening of my chest, had hardly changed at all. My mother's sewing box, her knitting bag resting on top; the set of irons my father used to stoke the fire; the hard-backed chair where Grandma Grace liked to sit.

The old ladies, powdered and pressed, turned to look at me in one stiff movement. I smiled back, knowing I mustn't cry: I didn't want to embarrass these good people who'd come here for my mother. Straightening with the responsibility, I walked across the room, feeling uncomfortable in the black dress I'd dug out from my wardrobe and regretting my DMs. Perching on the edge of an armchair, I took off my jacket in compensation, trying to hide it away, bundling it into a ball behind my feet.

Rita took the hard-backed chair, her backside spreading out like a cake that had risen and expanded over the edges. She folded her arms and commented on the weather and the likelihood of rain. The ladies responded with nods and smiles and so did I. And when we reverted to silence, I fixed my eyes on the motionless pendulum clock, the empty grate, on anything but the sympathetic faces of the people in the house.

The doorbell rang and Rita leapt up before I had a chance to move. She came back with the vicar. Nicholas – a thin young man with a backpack and a motorbike helmet tucked under his arm. 'You must be Anna,' he said, leaning to take my hand. 'I'm so sorry. Such a difficult time.' I thanked him, aware my voice sounded choked. He settled at the end of the sofa as if he was accustomed to his place. And then he went on, speaking sincerely, openly. He hadn't been in the parish long, but he'd got to know my mother. 'She was kind, sociable, a popular member of the congregation,' he said.

Was that true? My mother was quiet. Withdrawn. Becoming more isolated as the years had gone on. At least that was how I'd seen it. I thought she'd stopped going to church years ago.

'Esther was a great believer,' said Rita, chiming in.
Until she decided God had let her down.
Nicholas looked at me earnestly. Had I said those

7

words out loud? If I had, he didn't respond. Instead, he felt around in his backpack and produced an order of service which he proceeded to take me through.

While he spoke, Rita made tea in Mum's best gold-rimmed cups. I took a lemon puff from the plate she offered and tasted childhood days. Sticky biscuits and cans of Lilt. Flashes of sunlight through autumn leaves. And there was Gabriella running ahead of me in the woods with her hair flying and her scarf catching as she weaved amongst the trees, leaping over broken branches and landing like a cat.

'Is there something you'd like to add?' said Nicholas, breaking into my thoughts. 'To the service?'

He leaned forward, his narrow face creased with concern. I shook my head and affected another smile. 'Everything's perfect. Thank you.'

Rita cleared her throat and looked at me. 'May I read a tribute?'

'Of course,' I said. There was a pause, an air of expectation. 'Although I'm not sure I . . .'

'It's fine,' said Nicholas, patting my knee. 'Most people find it too hard.'

After they'd gone, I wandered around the house, getting used to being back. The silence fell about me. I fiddled with the boiler in the kitchen and the heating spluttered into life. Going upstairs, I stopped at the first closed door. Gabriella's bedroom. Touching the wood, I felt the pulse of memory. I didn't go in, but I knew the room would be exactly as Gabriella had left it – ready for when she came home.

Mum's room was next and this time I opened the door. The bed was unmade. A pair of glasses rested on the bedside cabinet. A quilted dressing gown lay on a chair with maroon slippers on the carpet beneath. It looked as if she was coming back – to make her bed, to fetch her glasses, to slip into her nightclothes. I sat on the mattress. It wasn't going to happen. It was never going to happen. My mother had gone, along with the rest of my family, and there was no one left but me.

I breathed deeply to blot out self-pity and reached for the photo inside my bag. My mother: Esther. Grandma Grace had taken it all those years ago, on the day my parents met. 1966, when a summer storm had knocked off slates and dragged off branches; when Grace Button had looked at the adverts in the local newsagent's, traced her finger across the cards and stopped at Albert Flores.

In the photo, my mother was outside. Curls of fair hair blew across her face. She'd had a fragile beauty like Gabriella, but there was something more that was harder to identify, something lost in those wide, grey eyes. I spent time staring at the picture, searching the grainy image, wondering what it was my mother was missing, even then.

There was a clock on the bedside cabinet. It was gold, inset with mother-of-pearl and with hands that halted at midnight. I wound the key gently and set the clock back, letting my fingertips drift across the cherry wood of the cabinet and down to the single drawer. I drew it open. Softly. Empty save for a book. It was a scrapbook, like those I'd filled with postcards on holidays in Wales. I looked inside, still smiling from the memory, and a girl stared back at me. I took a breath and the lost air inside me grew cold. Gabriella in her school uniform, her eyes hiding laughter. I absorbed each detail, the secret smile, the dimple on her chin. I traced her hair and cheeks, the curve of her neck. It was a newspaper article: the story of the missing girl.

Grief crept within me, rising to constrict my throat. I closed the book, turned and lay down, pushing my face into the pillow. Lily of the Valley. My mother's scent. I thought of her cutting out pictures and stories, making a scrapbook of Gabriella. Scissors going around the edges. Pasting on the glue. Smoothing down the paper. I tried to dispel the images, but they wouldn't go away. And the story came back, as I knew it would. As it always did. And the pain and the loss slid through my consciousness in waves.

2

1982

When I heard that a man from Spain and his mad wife were moving to our village I was torn up with curiosity. They were buying Lemon Tree Cottage, a house near the woods, which had been empty for years. It was only a rumour that the wife was crazy, but the idea appealed to me. Mad wives belonged in books and now there'd be a real one on our doorstep.

They were due to move in on Saturday and I was planning to sneak out and spy. Mum had other ideas. I woke to the sound of her voice shouting to Gabriella. It was going to be a hot day – perfect for working in the garden. Grabbing my specs, I arrived at Gabriella's room in time to hear her protest. 'Do we have to?' she said, pulling the blankets over her head.

'Yes, Gabriella,' said Mum, sweeping back the curtains. 'And then you can tidy your room. It looks like a bulldozer's been in here.'

'But I've got homework,' moaned Gabriella. 'I've got O levels.' She emphasised the 'O' with a long, drawn-out groan.

'That's next year,' said Mum. 'Next year you're excused. This year you work in the garden. You too, Anna.' She left the room and we heard her tramping down the stairs.

'Jesus Christ and God Almighty,' said Gabriella, who had recently taken to blasphemy. 'What have I done to deserve this?'

I plonked down on the bed and crossed my arms, banging my chest with the force of it. Gardening wasn't my idea of fun either, and it had ruined my plans for the day. I surveyed the bulldozed room. The floor was a mass of clothes, make-up, ruined cassettes and records without their sleeves. Picking out a purple lipstick, I swivelled the tube and smeared it on my hand. With a glance at the bed, I closed my eyes and imagined wearing the lipstick. I was Kate Bush. Swirling in one of Gabriella's dresses, doing a windmill dance on stage.

'I know what you're doing,' said Gabriella through the covers. She sat up suddenly, eyes dark with yesterday's make-up, hair fanning out in electric waves. I grinned back sheepishly and held out the lipstick. 'Have it,' she said, with an exaggerated flourish. 'It's all yours.'

'Really?'

'Yeah. In exchange for the next chore.'

'Girls!' Mum's voice floated up the stairs. 'Breakfast doesn't make itself.'

Gabriella winked, reached for her Walkman and snuggled back under the covers, while I sloped out of the room, lipstick in my hand.

We spent the morning in the sunshine, yanking out weeds while Mum mowed the lawn. She wore a pink housecoat and a pair of Dad's brown boots to do the job. 'No sense risking toes,' she said. I watched her small frame shoving the heavy machine back and forth, leaving trails of grass in her wake. There was a Flymo in the shed that Dad had bought six months before. He'd set it up in the garden and the three of us had watched as Mum walked around, sniffing and saying she preferred the one she had.

Mum finished and disappeared inside, leaving us to rake the grass. We jumped up, glad to be away from the weeds and the worms, and took turns raking, collecting, covering each other in grass and shrieking with laughter before transporting the lot to the bonfire heap. Neither of us had dressed for the part: Gabriella in her boots and black dress with netted sleeves that captured the heat and caught on the brambles, and me in jeans and a thick yellow sweatshirt that Mum had bought at the jumble sale. Soon even laughing was too much effort as we scraped up the last bits of grass and shoved the mower into the shed hoping nobody would notice it hadn't been cleaned.

We lay on the stubby grass beneath the damson tree, eyes closed, hands crossed over our chests as if we were dead. The scent of mown grass and lavender hung heavy in the air. A small plane droned somewhere far away and an insect settled on my face. I felt the lazy stroke of its wings but couldn't be bothered to brush it away.

When I opened my eyes a red kite was wheeling recklessly, its wings outstretched, gliding in the endless sky. I watched until it dropped quite suddenly and disappeared from sight. Poor mouse. Or was the mouse already dead? Was it kites that ate carrion, or did they hunt live meat? I blocked out the thought of the bird tearing at a creature with its talons and turned to Gabriella.

She lay perfectly still, skin pale against her make-up and her dress. Like a fair-haired Morticia (or a vampire as Dad joked). Was her chest even moving?

'Gabriella,' I said. No answer. 'Gabriella.' I spoke loudly, my voice sounding urgent as I prodded her with my toe.

There was a long pause. 'Yes?'

My heartbeat slowed back down. 'Nothing,' I said, trying to sound normal.

She opened one eye. 'Did you think I was dead?'

'Course not.'

I looked away so she wouldn't see the truth on my face. I had this idea that if you imagined terrible things, they wouldn't happen. They *couldn't* happen because it would mean you were able to predict the future and nobody could do that. Now I tried to focus on something else. A vision of Lemon Tree Cottage popped into my mind and quietly disappeared. Gabriella would never agree to going there. Spying wasn't her thing. I suggested visiting Dad instead.

She groaned. 'Again? There must be something better to do.'

'Such as?'

'Listen to records, watch the telly . . .'

'Tidy your room.'

I counted silently. By the time I got to five she'd agreed to come.

The House of Flores was narrow, hunched up amongst the other shops on the High Street. I used to think it was an old man propped up like that, and inside were the old man's tumbled thoughts: the rickety tables and chairs, the cracked crockery and ornaments, the higgledy-piggledy paintings on the walls. One of the prints looked like Gabriella – without the messy hair. A Modigliani. It was a portrait of a girl with a narrow face and almond-shaped eyes.

Most days Dad would be at the counter, leaning over whatever item he was valuing, focused on his task. He'd describe it to us: age, purpose, material. Sometimes he'd make us guess. ('It's a portrait of a queen. They're pearls for a princess.' 'No, no. That's a duchess, and they're not pearls, they're paste.') Other times we'd parade, trying on clothes – velvet dresses and capes, silk scarves and hats – dressing up as people from the past.

Now when we pushed open the door and the bell jangled to announce our arrival, Dad was nowhere to be seen. We listened in the dusty silence, until the sounds came, shifts and groans from the back room, furniture scraping on the wooden floor, a sudden bang as something dropped. '*Madre mia*,' came his voice.

'House clearance,' mouthed Gabriella.

We both knew what that meant – Dad would spend hours sifting through a dead person's life. He'd be home late bearing gifts and bombarding us with tales of what he'd found: a leather-bound copy of *Paradise Lost*; a porcelain plate with a painted dragon; a pack of photos, somebody's life, childhood to adulthood, bound with a faded ribbon. A house clearance was a gamble. That's what he said. All those hours spent picking out stories. Usually the things he found were worthless to anyone other than him. Other times, digging deep, he found a fossil. Something valuable. And if we were unlucky, he'd haul us in to excavate.

Gabriella put one finger to her lips and we backed out, eyes locked, willing the chime of the bell to coincide with the noise Dad was making. 'Girls. Is that you?' his voice filtered through. The door slammed and we were off, running along the High Street and back up Chestnut Hill, while bubbles of laughter exploded inside me and a stitch grabbed at my side.

'Stop! Stop!' I said, turning into Devil's Lane and throwing myself onto the ground. Gabriella sat beside me and leaned against my shoulder. I listened to the sound of her breath and the stillness all around. Devil's Lane was a shortcut to the green. Dark and stony, hemmed in by high hedges, with a few houses backing onto the fields. No one was sure how it got its name, although one tale told of a boy whose sweetheart had died from a fever. He'd made a pact with the Devil: his soul for one more day with her.

Sometimes, when we weren't chasing shadows in the lane, we played *What would you do if you only had one more day?* Gabriella talked about hanging out in the music booth at Our Price, asking the boy with the drowsy eyes who worked there for a kiss. I found it more difficult to decide. In the end I thought I'd go wherever Gabriella went. There was nothing better than that.

Now she fumbled in her pocket and pulled out a packet of Old Holborn. I eyed it suspiciously. 'Is that Dad's?' I said.

She grinned as she piled up a Rizla, funnelling the paper round and licking the edge with the tip of her tongue. 'Problem?' I shrugged. I'd seen her smoke plenty of times, so it didn't surprise me. 'Don't worry,' she said. 'It isn't his.'

'Where's it from?'

'I bought it of course.' She lit the skinny roll-up with a silver Zippo that was definitely Dad's. 'Borrowed,' she said, her voice rough with smoke.

I watched her inhaling, picking out strands of tobacco from her teeth. She wore red lipstick. It stained the cigarette, making it seem it was lit at both ends. I imagined the two ends burning and crackling and colliding in the middle, exploding like a firework in her face. 'You shouldn't smoke,' I said.

'That's easy for you to say, small person. Wait till you're my age. Bet you'll try it then.'

'No, I won't, and anyway, you shouldn't encourage me.'

She put her head on one side. 'Little Miss Righteous.'

I turned away. I hated it when she called me that. She ruffled my hair. 'Only joking. I'm glad you care, really I am. I care too. If I ever see you smoking, I'll knock it out your hand.' As if to demonstrate, she pushed her cigarette stub hard into the ground and stamped on it with her boot.

At the end of the lane, we hopped over the rickety stile and mooched across the green, past the graffiti-covered playground. A few boys with spiky haircuts hung around, smoking and drinking from cans. They watched as we passed, their eyes stuck on Gabriella. I gave her a sidelong glance and could tell from her smile that she knew they were looking. She sucked up their admiration like I sucked up cans of Lilt and I had a sudden giddy sensation that she was slipping away. I put my hand on her arm and drew her to me. She didn't pull back. The boys were behind us and I felt the heat of her side against mine.

By the time we reached the edge of the green the idea of Lemon Tree Cottage had resurfaced and this time I suggested going there.

'Why?' said Gabriella.

'Because new people have moved in.'

'And?'

I shrugged, trying to think of an answer she'd like. 'There's nothing else to do, except help Dad with the house clearance, or Mum with the tea.'

'You can do that if you want.'

'I made breakfast.'

She narrowed her eyes. 'I gave you lipstick.'

I narrowed my eyes back. 'That was for *one* chore. And anyway Mum won't let you get away with it.' We both knew Mum was a stickler for turn-taking as well as preparing us for lives of domesticity.

Grinning as Gabriella gave in, I led the way out of the green and on to Chestnut Hill.

The road was little more than a single track at first, working its way through the village, skirting rows of cottages and weaving along past the church. Then it grew wider, and faster, as it burst out into the countryside and cars fled past, kicking up stones. Here the hedgerows ran like an unkempt fringe on either side of the tarmac, which was worn out, full of potholes, and dips. There was a solitary field where the cows lolled hefty heads against a five-bar gate. And a mass of churned-up earth, crammed with the rising skeletons of homes – part of the new estate.

At the brow of the hill, we turned onto a stony lane that led to the woods and passed a cottage, its roof ruined by patches of thatch stripped back and yellowed underneath. Pecked off by jackdaws. I remembered the story, in the local paper. They'd declared it the strangest thing to have happened in the village for years. Now smoke trailed from the chimney despite the heat. A woman pegged out washing at the side of the house while a small child scrambled at her feet. She stared as we passed. And then a man in dungarees came out and leaned in the doorway smoking.

The second house was Lemon Tree Cottage. The place had no story apart from being empty and next to the house with the jackdaws. But with the thought of a madwoman in the attic, I looked with new interest.

The building loomed like a shadow behind a mesh of dark green. From the gate, a gravelled pathway forced its way through the garden, pushing on and around a line of broken terracotta pots. A plant with purple flowers shaped like stars clambered across the doorway and cascaded down the walls. There was no sign of life, no people or sounds, only a broody stillness that pressed on the air, as if forcing out its breath.

I was looking at the diamond panes of glass when suddenly a shape flitted past a downstairs window. I stared, mesmerised. It moved lightly, and was quickly gone, disappearing into shadow.

'Upstairs,' hissed Gabriella, nudging me.

A girl. Framed behind a window. Fair hair floating around her face.

Footsteps crunched on gravel. A man about Dad's age rounded the back of the house. I froze like a creature snared in light. He was pale – his face and hair, even his clothes – and he looked straight at Gabriella. 'Let's go,' I whispered, grabbing her arm. For a moment, she resisted. I pulled harder until she gave in. And then I hurried her along the lane, turning once to see the man staring after us from the gate.

3

On the day of the funeral, I woke up with a feeling of dread, and a mind tangled with dreams. The weather matched my feelings: a single clap of thunder and then the rain came, sluicing down the windows. I listened to the sounds, feeling the weight of what lay ahead.

Downstairs I made coffee. Leaning against the side, sipping from my mother's cup, in the old-fashioned kitchen, with its tired lino and table, its chipped cupboards and sink, it occurred to me I was masquerading as someone who belonged here, the prodigal child returned, yet there was no one here to greet me.

In the living room, the feeling grew as I opened drawers at random. They were full of papers, letters and old address books belonging to my parents. There were photos too. I found one of Gabriella in Trafalgar Square, with pigeons dotted along her arm. My mind returned to the scrapbook. How many pictures of Gabriella had my mother pasted inside? How many articles and interviews had she kept?

Later, the ladies, led by Rita, filed into the house. They wore identical black skirts and shawls. Only Rita was different. I glimpsed a grey silk dress beneath her faux-fur coat. She'd always been elegant. And poised. Unlike my mother who'd been perpetually harassed.

Together, we waited for the cortège and when it arrived, we walked in silence to the cars, my heart dropping at the sight of the pale coffin and the respectful suited men. Slipping inside, I maintained my calm, but as the doors clunked and the car eased away, I felt as if my whole world glided with me, as if I'd lost control.

We drove down Chestnut Hill and out along the High Street. A child pointed and tugged her mother's coat; an old man raised his hat; a woman in a belted raincoat hurried into a doorway. I craned my neck as we passed the House of Flores but the shop was shut up as I knew it would be, the sign swinging in the breeze.

The church was packed. Looking around, everything was familiar: the stained glass windows and mahogany pews, even the embroidered hassocks with their crosses and doves looked the same, though they couldn't be, not after all this time.

Rita squeezed my arm as the pall-bearers settled the coffin and we took our seats at the front. Nicholas looked even younger in his starched surplice. He welcomed us all, saying why we'd come, to honour a loving wife, mother and friend. Rita stepped forward to pay tribute. She talked of my mother's loyalty, of her commitment to God and her stoicism in the face of tragedy. She spoke loudly and confidently, her voice trembling only once when she mentioned Esther's daughters.

More tributes followed. There was another prayer. A hymn. A baby screamed at the back of the church. I heard the crack of the door opening and the screams fading as the mother took it away. The organ played and

I sensed Gabriella beside me, tapping her foot to a different kind of rhythm; the one inside her head.

Afterwards, they took the coffin away and we spilled out into the churchyard. People came forward one by one, to take my hand and offer their hushed condolences. Faces with lines and wrinkles and familiar eyes, weakened and peering through thick lenses. I wanted to pull out my sunglasses to protect myself from their good intentions, but the sky was grey, and the rain was back, the faint drizzle turning to a downpour. I hid instead behind the mushroom of black umbrellas that sprouted in one synchronised click as soon as the coffin was lowered.

And then I saw her. Mrs Ellis. She was making her exit, scurrying along the gravel pathway towards the lychgate. Thin and hunched, there was no doubt in my mind that it was her, that forward lean, those quick, short steps, even the shopping bag, the raincoat, the flesh-coloured tights and the old-fashioned lace-up shoes.

The rain came harder as I stared after the retreating figure. The wind picked up, grabbing at my clothes. In the distance, there was the faint rumble of thunder. Mourners, forgetting etiquette, were surging around me and on towards the gate. I quickened my pace to match theirs. I needed to see her face, though I could picture it anyway: narrow lips, self-satisfied smile, skin stretched taut over the angles of her cheeks, her jaw, her forehead. I could see too her bony hands wringing as she spoke to the reporter, telling the story of Gabriella: the story of the missing girl. And I thought again of Tom trundling his road sweeper's cart, lips moving in conversation with himself. Mrs Ellis had spotted them: Tom and Gabriella. She'd been a witness, one of the last people to have seen my sister. And Tom – poor, befuddled, innocent – had been investigated. Although nothing had come of that.

My heart was thundering so fast I felt faint. But still I wanted to see her. I wanted to know how she'd changed. It was only as she passed through the gate, as I pushed forward and she looked back, that I understood. It wasn't Mrs Ellis. This woman was too young, in her forties, we might have been at school together, and then I realised that we had been. This was Martha. Not so far wrong: it was Mrs Ellis's daughter.

For a moment, the two of us looked at each other and the rest of the world dropped out of focus. There was only Martha, spotlighted. Martha Ellis who nobody cared about, who'd been bullied and ignored by everyone – except Gabriella.

I held Martha's stare, and she looked away, her forehead creasing, as if she didn't know who I was. And yet she must have. Her cheeks were sallow and sunken, her lips narrow strips. Her eyes darted about as though she had trouble seeing, until they stopped, quite suddenly, on me, and the cloudy look was replaced by recognition and something else. Fear. And I was glad. I wanted her to remember. I wanted her to feel the pain and the loss like I did.

She turned and hurried along the path, and the rain was dripping down my face, mingling with my tears, and Rita was pulling at my arm, and offering me a tissue, and urging me to put my jacket on. She marshalled me back to the house, speaking so fast my thoughts were left behind. And when we arrived, villagers, damp from the rain, stumbled in with their offerings: plates of triangular sandwiches and slices of cake.

I moved through rooms, greeting people, thanking them for coming. From time to time my mind flashed to Martha and I conjured up images: Martha perched on a doorstep; skulking in the woods; dragging after me on the green, telling tales in her whining voice.

Concentrating on the people around me, I braced myself for their sympathy. Time and again, faces loomed and words filtered. I held on to hard surfaces, to keep myself upright. I fixed my eyes on Rita and watched her making tea, offering sandwiches, bending to adjust an old lady's shawl.

'You look like Esther,' said a man with silver hair who stopped beside me. I smiled politely, but I knew that I didn't. I was dark, not fair; tall, but not elegant like my mother. The man stood for a moment, staring at me, examining my face. He too was tall, and looked straight into my eyes. 'I don't mean physically,' he said as if he was reading my mind. I shifted uncomfortably. What did he mean then? He didn't say.

The man moved on and I trailed after him, making my way to the kitchen. Rita and one or two others were busy washing up, but when I grabbed a cloth to help, Rita pushed me away. She gave me a cup of tea which was hot and sweet. I drank it quickly, impatient to help. Taking a knife from the drawer, I sliced a fruit cake into thick chunks. 'You might want to cut those smaller,' said Rita over my shoulder. I smiled, but kept the chunks the same. She'd always interfered in the running of our kitchen. Although Mum had thought she was indispens-able. *I don't know what I'd do without Rita*, she used to say.

Eventually, when the food was eaten and the clearing-up done, people left in twos and threes, helping each other exit. Rita was the last to go. She lingered at the door, doing up the buttons of her coat. I used to think she was like a film star, with her glamorous clothes and styl-ish hair. Now she offered to stay and keep me company.

'I'm fine,' I replied. 'Really, I am.'

She nodded. 'I understand, but I'm here if you want me and I'm more than happy to help.' She tipped her head to level our gaze and squinted through her glasses. 'The House of Flores. I know it's early days, but . . .' She stopped and produced a polka-dot scarf, tied it in place and patted my arm. 'Not now, dear. I realise you want to be alone. I'll meet you there tomorrow morning. Is that all right?' And she was gone, striding down the path, before I had time to reply.

In the kitchen, I poured a glass of red wine and drank half of it in one gulp. I thought of Rita taking things over, and the people who'd wanted to talk, and of Martha in the graveyard. Seeing her had been the biggest shock. That blast of memory. Her awful mother. What had hap-pened to her?

I finished my wine and poured myself another. Sipped and tasted plums. The purple fruit we ate in the garden. Damsons too. Colours and tastes. The red of Gabriella's lipstick. The yellow of her dress.

Three days. That was the longest I'd stayed whenever I'd visited my mother, and I'd kept indoors. Quick visits, avoiding people and places in the village. Any longer and the past would start rolling in like a carpet of thorns, inviting me to tread across it, searching for answers that never came. Already it was happening. I felt the spikes of memory stabbing at my skin.

I made an instant resolution. I'd explain to Rita. I had urgent things to deal with in Athens. The House of Flores and everything else would have to wait. Maybe Rita would offer to help and I'd pay her to sort things out.

Three or four days. And I'd go.

I nodded to convince myself. Drank more wine. Tried to ignore the voice inside my head. Challenging my thoughts. Telling me that no matter how often I thought I could resist the call, no matter how much I berated myself for considering it again, I would never stop asking the same questions that had haunted my whole life.

4

1982

'Where have you been?' Mum demanded, hands on hips.

'The House of Flores,' we said simultaneously, not daring to say we'd been roaming the village after that. Mum liked to know where we were. I imagined her charting our progress through the day, like a general moving troops across a board.

'Well,' she tutted. 'Your father should know better than to keep you so late.'

She would have gone on if Rita hadn't been there, sitting at the kitchen table with a cup of tea. Like us, Rita's family owned a shop – the butcher's on the High Street. She had a habit of bringing gifts – crime books for Mum and leftover meat. Offal was her favourite and today she'd brought a parcel of liver for our tea.

Now she winked through her green wing-tipped glasses and asked us how we were getting on at school. She always asked the same question. We always gave the same answer. 'Fine, thank you very much.' It usually put an end to anything else.

'Flour,' said Mum, getting out a nearly empty packet. 'We need flour to fry the liver.'

I groaned inwardly. Why did Rita feel the need to bring offal? It wasn't as if she ever ate it with us. She'd watch Mum cook and then she'd go home. I imagined her in one of her pleated skirts and perfectly matching blouses, tucking in to prawn cocktail and steak and chips, while we chewed tasteless strips of liver. It wasn't fair.

Gabriella sauntered out the room. 'Not too loud,' Mum called after her. A moment later, Siouxsie and the Banshees pounded through the ceiling.

I was about to follow, when Mum collared me. 'Anna,' she said. 'I need you to buy flour.'

'Do I have to?'

'Yes.' She grabbed her purse and handed me a pound note. 'Plain flour. And bring back the change.'

Making a face, I stomped off. This was injustice. Why did I always have to go on errands? Not only that . . . How could Mum tick me off for being late and then send me to face the dangers she was worried about?

As if to prove my point, a gang of boys were hanging around outside the phone box, smoking and sharing stubs. My heart beat faster as I passed, but they didn't call out like some of the boys in the village did and, when I glanced across at their ripped-up clothes and spiky hair, I guessed they were Gabriella's friends.

Three bulky women huddled by the shop door, handbags hoisted into the crooks of their arms. I dodged around them and headed for a shelf at the back. No plain flour. There was self-raising. Would that do? While I was considering, the women lowered their voices. I took a step towards them and listened.

Vandals had set fire to the railway bank. A boy had nearly died playing chicken on the line. A neighbour's son had been caught shoplifting in the off-licence: a can of Red Stripe and a packet of Discos.

I yawned. Not much of a story.

'Not much of a mother,' said one of the women.

I chose a bag of flour and heard the words Lemon Tree Cottage. Recognising the nasal tone, I looked across. It was Mrs Henderson, our next-door neighbour, her mean face eager with news. The woman was like an empty bottle of vinegar, that was what Mum said – sour-smelling and you could see right through her.

'His name's Edward Lily,' she announced. 'He's English. The wife was Spanish.' She paused. 'Killed herself.' A gasp. I moved a step closer, picked up a packet of custard powder and examined the label intensely. 'They say she was mad.'

So that part was right.

'And the daughter's much the same.'

The figure at the window.

'Daughter?' said the third woman. 'I heard it was his new wife.'

'Daughter,' said Mrs Henderson firmly. She didn't like to be contradicted. 'Lydia.'

A man came into the shop and the women stopped their conversation. I took the flour to the till and while Mrs Bloom was ringing it up, Martha Ellis, a girl in Gabriella's year, sidled in. She wore a thin dress and a drab cardigan. Her sandals were scuffed, her hair limp around her shoulders. I gave a grimace of recognition and concentrated on opening my purse and handing over the note.

Martha lived on Acer Street in a semi-detached house with a pebble-dash front and pots of flowers in the garden. I used to see her sometimes sitting on the door-

step with her school bag propped against her knees.
Other times she'd be trailing after girls in the playground until they told her to get lost. Martha was like
that, always going after people, not caring whether they
wanted her or not.

I took my change, pushed my glasses firmly onto my
nose, gave Martha one more grimace and a wide berth,
and left the shop.

At home, Dad was back. Siouxsie was still thudding
through the ceiling and was competing with the radio. A
newsreader was commenting on the end of the Falklands
War, but when Mrs Thatcher spoke, Dad leaned across
and switched it off. 'That's enough of that,' he said, heading to the fridge and pulling out a bottle of milk. Piercing
the top, he drank straight from the bottle.

I handed the flour to Mum who didn't notice that I'd
bought the wrong thing. She shook it onto a plate, sea-
soned and coated the liver pieces and heated up the oil,
before throwing in chopped onions and the liver. Soon
the meaty smell curled around the kitchen. Sitting at the
table, I wrinkled my nose and pinched it shut.

And still Mum was going on about us being late, bang-
ing down a saucepan on the stove, chuffing like an engine.
Dad rolled up his sleeves and waited until the steam had
evaporated. He was like that – as calm as Mum was fiery.
'You'd think it was her that had the Latin blood,' he said.
'Not me.'

Jasper appeared, sidling through the half-open back
door. He wound himself around the legs of my chair and
I smoothed his tawny fur. I wished I was as silent as a

cat. It would be easier to listen in, to find out all the things I wanted to know.

Dad had the newspaper and was scanning the headlines, reading out interesting snippets. Mum was yelling to Gabriella that tea was ready while Rita, who was off to a murder mystery at the local stately home, slipped on a coat with a collar that looked like a dead rabbit. She promised to come back the next day with news of who'd done it and a packet of kidneys for our tea. 'Or a pig's heart if you're lucky.'

Gabriella appeared. 'Christ,' she said, sitting down and prodding the meat with her fork. 'Do we have to have this?'

'Don't blaspheme, and yes, we do,' said Mum. 'It's full of iron.'

'Yeah,' said Gabriella, picking it up. 'Feels like it.'

'No need to be rude,' said Dad, flicking out his serviette and tucking it into his shirt. 'Remember. You're lucky to have anything.' His voice was firm, but his eyes crinkled like they always did when he didn't mean what he said.

'Eat,' said Mum, looking at me even though I hadn't spoken. 'You too, Anna.'

I cut a tiny piece of liver and stuck it in my mouth, while Gabriella dropped a slither down to Jasper. I grinned, waiting for my chance, keeping one eye on Mum who was eating her food with a solid determination and the other on Dad who was shovelling it in.

After Dad had finished, he fetched a can of beer and talked about the house that he was clearing. It had belonged to a rich old lady on the outskirts of the village.

'There's a library with books stacked ceiling to floor,' he said, rubbing his hands together. 'First editions galore. And a gramophone collection. You should see it.'

'Sounds like a lot of work,' said Mum, frowning.

Dad shrugged. 'Perhaps. But time is limited. Apparently, the son wants the house on the market as soon as possible. And that reminds me. I heard Lemon Tree Cottage has a new owner.'

'Is that so? They must be brave. That place has been empty for years. I wonder who it is.' I was about to tell them, when Mum clattered her knife and fork onto her plate and cast a long and significant look at mine. I took the hint and carved into the liver. And while Mum sorted out the rice pudding, I fed a chunk to Jasper.

'Talking of music,' said Gabriella, pushing away her plate and getting up.

'Who was talking about music?' said Dad.

'Gramophones. That's music, isn't it?'

He laughed as she moved behind his chair and dangled her arms over his shoulders. I narrowed my eyes. What was she after?

'There's a concert. At Top Rank.'

'Ah,' said Dad, taking both her hands.

Mum looked up from the floor where she knelt, hauling out the pudding from the oven. 'You're not going,' she said. 'You're too young.'

'But everyone's going. Bernadette's mum says she'll take us and we've only got to find someone to pick us up.' Gabriella paused. 'Dad?'

He looked across at Mum who was peeling off the foil from the dish. 'Esther?' he said. 'I wouldn't—'

'I said no. She's too young.'

'But it's not fair. *Everyone* else is going.'

'I doubt that very much,' said Mum, reaching in the cupboard for bowls. 'But I don't mind phoning around to check.'

Gabriella made a face. We all knew that it was only Bernadette who was allowed to do what she liked.

'Never mind,' said Dad. 'How about a Dad-and-eldest-daughter day instead. Trip to the flicks and a Wimpy?'

Envy prickled and I looked across at Mum to see how she'd taken it, but she had a funny expression on her face, a cross between disapproval and pleasure, and suddenly I felt left out, as if I was on the edge of my family looking in. It took a moment for the emotion to wash through me and then I shut it away, and let my thoughts drift across the day instead: the face with the cloud of hair in the window; back to the boys in the playground; onward again to the man who'd stared at Gabriella.

Next time I spied on Lemon Tree Cottage I'd go on my own. People were always looking at my sister. All kinds of men and boys. Just because she was beautiful didn't mean she was theirs.

Then I remembered how dark the cottage had been. What would it be like at night? Those shadows in the ragged garden and the jackdaws next door pecking at the roof. Imagine living there. Anything could happen and nobody would know. I shivered and held a final piece of liver down to Jasper who nipped my fingers as he snatched it away.

5

The bell jangled as the door pushed open and letters and papers shunted across the floor. Stepping forward, I closed myself in. The darkness fell about me like a shroud.

The House of Flores: a grandiose name for a second-hand shop. Dad had chosen it, proud of the business he'd built from scratch. He'd been eighteen when he'd begun, saving for a rusty van to transfer people's rubbish to the dump.

Now the place smelled of dust, closed-up rooms and the faintest whiff of tobacco. It smelled of my father and my sister; of lost dreams and grief. I drew up the blind on the door and the light pooled in. The place was cluttered as it always was; the walls a mosaic of paintings, hung haphazardly, with no attention to theme. The Modigliani was still there. Unsold. The girl with the almond eyes. For a moment the air shivered as my sister pirouetted past. I conjured her face and she was laughing as she danced, and Dad, watching from the counter, was cleaning an oil lamp with the greatest precision, treating it like a chalice.

Facing up to ghosts and demons and all the other hangers-on was the best way to exorcise them. So I tried it, gazing deliberately at every part of the shop: the counter with its out-of-date computer and out-of-date phone; the door that led to the back room; the antique-looking chairs stacked against the wall; the elaborate tables littering the carpet; the stuffed animals and gilt-edged mirrors. And the window displays with their dusty pieces of pottery and glass, tarnished silverware, cracked lamps and candlesticks. It was like being in a church or a crypt, and had the same stillness and hush.

Afterwards, I picked up the letters and placed them on the counter. I chose an envelope at random. And then I felt worse. It was an electricity bill. Red. Did that mean we'd be cut off? *We.* What was I talking about? There was no *we.* There was only *me.* I dragged out my reading glasses and ripped open more post and made piles: bills, junk, payments from clients.

A red and white mini stopped outside. Rita squeezed out and strode to the door. She looked ready for work and I had a sudden fear she was expecting me to open the shop, business as usual. 'Morning,' she said, coming in. 'Did you sleep well?' And before I answered, she grimaced, saying, 'Of course you didn't. Stupid question.'

Rita was the kind of person who'd camp on the sofa if she thought she was needed, so I told her I'd slept fine.

She seemed satisfied and turned to the post on the counter. 'Martin and Martin,' she said, tapping her fingers on the pile. 'That's who you want. Solicitors on the High Street.'

I felt the yoke of responsibility tighten: the will, the house, the shop and all its contents. How would I manage? The disarray, the sheer volume of stuff was colossal. I yearned for my simple flat in Athens, my uncomplicated job teaching English. The people who knew nothing about my past. *Three or four days*, I repeated in my head.

'In any event,' said Rita, picking up an envelope and turning it round in her hands, 'I thought I should tell you.' She stopped and frowned, glanced across and away before continuing. 'How things stand.'

'I have work in Athens,' I said quickly. 'Students. And a flat. I need to get back there. There's no question of my living in the village and keeping the shop open. No question at all. I'm definitely selling. In fact, I was wondering—'

'Of course,' she said, interrupting. 'I knew you'd say that. No. I was thinking more about . . .' There was a nervousness to her voice I hadn't heard before. 'The house clearance.' She put down the envelope and walked to the window.

'House clearance?'

There was a pause. 'Edward Lily.'

The light outside dropped. 'What do you mean?'

'Edward Lily,' she repeated, leaning forward to pick up a vase from the display. 'His things are due here in a few days.' She turned to face me, her expression at once apologetic and guilty. 'He died, you see, a few months before your mother. His solicitor asked for the contents of Lemon Tree Cottage to come here. Edward Lily's sister is dealing with it, apparently, although our point of contact is Martin and Martin. I believe she's picked out most of the things she wants and now the rest will be dealt with . . . by us. It seems your mother had already agreed it with Edward Lily. Before he died, I mean.' She stopped. 'Are you all right?' She looked worried now, behind her glasses.

I shook my head. No, I wasn't all right. Edward Lily.

Another name from the past. And, like Tom, another man investigated for my sister's disappearance. I'd been obsessed with Edward Lily for a while, spying on his house, his daughter. I'd even broken in one time. And Mum. She'd known he was a suspect. Why would she have taken his house clearance on? Why would she have wanted to relive those memories, because surely that's what would have happened, if she'd delved through his possessions? Besides, she'd always hated house clearances because they'd taken so much of Dad's time.

Rita was looking at me, waiting for an answer. 'I can't understand why Mum would have accepted this,' I said finally. 'And anyway, I'd assumed I'd be scaling down the House of Flores, not taking more work on.'

Rita gave a rueful smile that, despite everything, made me feel guilty. 'It's fine,' she said. 'I understand.'

I frowned, thinking back. Edward Lily had left the village a year after Gabriella had disappeared. Or had it been eighteen months? In any event, I hadn't known he'd returned. 'I thought Lemon Tree Cottage was empty,' I said, voicing my thoughts.

'Edward Lily moved away,' said Rita. 'But he never sold or emptied the cottage. He came back, about a year ago, to live there permanently.' She paused and fiddled with the vase. 'Look. I know it's a lot to ask, but it was something your mother wanted to do, and, well, I promised I'd help her.'

'But I can't understand why she cared.' I stared hopelessly at a broken grandfather clock as if it might speed up my understanding. The shop was full of broken things. What was I supposed to do with them all? And knowing what a house clearance was like, it would take far more than three or four days to complete. I could be stuck in the village for weeks.

Now was the time to ask Rita if she'd consider taking payment to oversee the whole thing, but she was staring back at me, her lips parted as if she was holding her breath, waiting for my answer. I doubted she'd say yes. And then it occurred to me, if my mother had accepted the clearance, the least I could do was to honour her wish. Rita obviously thought it was important. I spoke cautiously. 'I suppose if Mum agreed . . .'

Rita put down the vase with visible relief. 'Good decision. I'll let you know exactly when the things are due. Your mother would be pleased. She was very proud of you, Anna. She said you had a gift, an eye for beautiful things.'

'Well . . .' I stopped, unsure how to respond, but inclined not to believe it, and to wonder why my mother had never told me so herself.

Rita left, declaring she was off to an art class. I watched her from the window, revving the engine and waving as the car pulled away. Despite my warm feelings towards her, I questioned why I'd given in. Rita was like that. Decisive. Persuasive. In control. With a hint of emotional blackmail.

On the way home, I stopped off at the Co-op and bought a ready meal – chicken jalfrezi – and a bottle of red wine. It was only when I was at the checkout that I remembered Mum's old microwave had packed up years ago.

The house was chilly despite the heating. I dumped

my bags in the kitchen, turned the thermostat up a notch and headed to Mum's room. I might as well make a start on her things. Trying to avoid thinking about the scrapbook in the drawer, I sat at the dressing table and opened a jewellery box. I picked out things I recognised: amber earrings shaped like teardrops, a gold bracelet, a string of beads. A sapphire brooch.

There was a velvet pouch with an emerald pendant inside. Taking the necklace out and holding it to the light, I tried to think back. Had I ever seen Mum wearing it? I used to love watching her get ready to go out to special places, but I couldn't remember this. I sighed, wondering how many other things I'd forgotten.

Outside the light had darkened and even though it was only five o'clock, I went downstairs, heated the curry in a saucepan and poured a glass of wine. Eating rapidly, standing at the sink, I considered the house clearance. Lemon Tree Cottage. I tried to picture the house as it had been, but the memory, so long abandoned, was hazy. I closed my eyes and forced myself to remember, and slowly, slowly an outline and a background came. The ragged garden with its scuttling creatures; the broken pots; the stone cottage with its dark, shuttered windows and the sudden splash of orange. And then me, twelve years old, fleeing from the place. Feet pounding on the lane.

Later, I cleared the kitchen cupboards, taking out tins and packets and placing them on the side. There was a jar of home-made apple jelly right at the back. I stared at my mother's handwriting on the label until my eyesight blurred and the kitchen filled with the sound of bubbling and the earthy scent of fruit.

A rap at the door disturbed me. Peering through the spyhole, I saw Rita. Her face was serious and sad with her mouth turned down; she held her arms across her body, touching her elbows, holding herself in. And I understood. She was a woman who had lost a good friend, a woman who was grieving.

I opened the door and her sadness transformed into a smile. She unfolded her arms in a gesture of welcome as if it was me on the doorstep visiting her. 'I thought I should tell you the clearers have called. The first lot of Edward Lily's things will be at the shop in the morning.'

'Already?'

'I know. I'm sorry it's short notice.'

'It's fine,' I said after a moment's hesitation. 'I'll be there.'

'Are you sure?'

'Yes. Of course.' There was no going back on it now.

We stayed awkwardly for a moment more. Should I invite her in? A friendly face. A person who knew my past. Even as the possibility beckoned, I folded up my feelings and tucked them away. Besides, I was conscious of the three-quarters-gone bottle of wine, the fact that my head was blurring and one more glass could finish things off. So when she asked if I wanted company, I thanked her, but shook my head and watched as she trailed back down the path.

The night was sharp and cold, the velvet sky threaded with gold and silver. *The heavens' embroidered cloths.*

I smiled wryly as I remembered. I'd been keen on Yeats when I was young. I'd struggled to understand his poems, and then suddenly they'd made sense. If only everything worked like that.

There was movement beyond the path, a shiver amongst the leaves. I squinted, looking for a shape in the shadows. Was that a sigh or a rustling of branches? I called out. 'Hello?' No one answered. 'Rita?' The night was still. A bark. A fox. Foxes had been rampant in the past, skulking, looking for food. Mrs Henderson next door had had chickens until one night they'd got their throats ripped out. She'd come to our house screaming blue murder. Gabriella had whispered that Mrs Henderson had done it herself. She was a witch, wasn't she? Everyone knew that. I'd suggested it was Brian – her creepy-looking son.

I returned to the cupboards, keeping my mind closed as I worked, willing myself not to think of the enormity of the task. *Small steps*, Dad used to say when he had a house clearance. *Take a room. Divide it into sections. Take a section. Divide it into moments of a life.*

I dribbled the last of the wine into my glass and when that had gone, I searched until I found a half-empty bottle of Cinzano in the sideboard. I drank a glass, grimacing at the taste, but it worked. The edge of my discord softened.

Turning my energy to the cupboard under the stairs, I rummaged through, pulling out board games and videos, cassettes and reels of cine film. The projector was right at the back, along with the tripod and the screen

covered in plastic. On impulse, I hauled them out and
set up in the living room, hooking up a reel at random
and letting the silent films play. The shots were out of
sequence: one moment Gabriella was kicking her legs in
a silver pram, and then we were older, at the village fête;
we were in Trafalgar Square feeding pigeons and then
back at the green watching wrestling in a makeshift ring.
The camera jerked from my mother tucking a strand of
hair behind her ear to the rest of the crowd with their
soundless cheers.

I recognised faces whose names had long gone from
my memory. And there were Gabriella and me with our
arms wrapped round each other. Gabriella was grinning
and pouting, making a movement like a curtsy while I
stared awkwardly through my National Health specs.
Gabriella's hair was sleek and she wore no make-up so
it must have been before she fell in love with Siouxsie.
A year, or maybe two, before she disappeared.

The camera zoomed in, blocking me out of the frame.
Gabriella looked away and back again, her smile shy
and uncertain. And then Dad must have walked away
because the camera was wobbling and panning the
green. He carried on past the cedar tree, down the steps,
around the lake. A swan took off, slow beats. I watched
the silent flight, amidst the whir of the reel, until the film
abruptly ended.

I wandered through my childhood years playing and
replaying each scene, freezing the moment Dad focused
in on Gabriella. Was she looking at him, or beyond at
someone else? I leaned forward and scanned the people
in the crowd. I froze the film again and sat back in my

chair. The stillness of the house unnerved me. There was only the sound of the wind picking at the window latch, and the pipes gently sighing.

The curtains were open. I glanced across at the great slab of darkness outside. Anyone might come to the glass and see me sitting here curled up in my chair. The idea made me shiver. I should close the curtains. And yet I couldn't move. A heavy coldness was spreading through my body, weighing me down, keeping me in my seat. I looked back at the screen. What if someone in that crowd knew what had happened to my sister? What if, even then, they'd been planning to take her away?

The wind rapped on the glass, making me jump and stare. And a new thought gripped me. Here I was back in the village for the longest time in years. I had no choice about that. What if I stopped resisting? What if I allowed myself to start again, trying to find out what had happened? What if this was the moment when I was supposed to uncover the truth?

Over and over I asked myself the same questions. Over and over I rejected them, counterbalancing with the arguments I'd been giving myself for years. It was too long ago, all routes had been tried, there was no point in going back. Over and over the questions and answers came until I was exhausted by the contradictions. Until eventually, I stopped thinking. And, turning back to the projector, I watched the films once more.

6

1982

On Sunday we went to church. The only time we missed a service was when we were so ill we had to stay in bed. Gabriella faked it sometimes (with the thermometer in the Ovaltine trick) but she could never get past our mum. Dad was exempt on the grounds that his Catholic father from Chile had died when Dad was in the womb and Uncle Thomas was two; their Jewish mother, whose parents had escaped Russian pogroms, had allowed her sons to make their own choices.

Gabriella liked to bring this up. In an equal world she should be able to follow the way of her freethinking father. She posed a few of her favourite questions to demonstrate her feelings: what's the point of praying when God doesn't reply? How do you know God exists when you can't see him? How do we know we have a soul if it doesn't show up on an X-ray? Mum replied in much the same way as she did with anything that she wanted and we didn't. When Gabriella was an adult she'd be free to be ungodly. Now, she went to church. (And you too, Anna.)

As it happened, I didn't mind. Church was all right. I liked the scents: candle wax mixed with flowers and incense. I liked gazing at the stained glass windows and imagining the characters coming alive as the sun shone through. I pictured them clambering out of their tableaus and joining the congregation, telling their stories in languages we miraculously understood.

It was the usual scene before we left. Gabriella came down in a dress that fell off her shoulder, with black and gold make-up around her eyes. Mum told her she looked ridiculous and Gabriella replied that it was fashion. Then came the inevitable row. ('Why can't I dye my hair black?' 'When you're an adult you're free to ruin your looks. Now you do what I say.') And when that had ended, Gabriella appealed to Dad who suggested a compromise. This meant she stalked back upstairs and reappeared ten minutes later with a ripped sweatshirt pulled over her dress.

Finally, we were at church and three-quarters of the way through the service. The organist was playing and the vicar was conducting communion. Neither of us had been confirmed, Gabriella having threatened to go on a hunger strike if she was forced, but I trailed along to the altar, with everybody else, to be blessed, and amused myself afterwards by looking around at the congregation. I recognised people from school including Lucy Carlisle, who'd left in the fifth year and now wore a smock top.

On the way back from communion, Mum bent down and whispered to Lucy's red-faced mother whose cheeks burned brighter as people turned to see. Beside me Gabriella sat with her eyes closed, winding her hair round her fingers. I knew what she was doing, blanking out the service, filling in the space with music notes, tapping her feet to the rhythm. I nudged her. She opened her eyes. 'Lucy Carlisle,' I mouthed.

She shrugged and mouthed back. 'Who cares about Lucy Carlisle?'

Mum cared about Lucy Carlisle. It was written all over her face and I reckoned I knew what she'd said to her mother. She'd invited Lucy to the drop-in centre at church. The one for drug addicts, unmarried mothers and wives whose husbands beat them up.

When we got back from church, the house smelled of roast pork and boiled cabbage. Every week Dad was assigned to make Sunday dinner, and woe betide him if he didn't. Mum and her skivvies – Gabriella and me – prepared the food before we left in the morning. Once, Dad, too busy with his feet up, engrossed in a book he'd found in the shop, forgot to turn the oven on. We came home to raw beef and potatoes and Dad misquoting noble things from Dickens. ('It's a far, far better thing to read a book than do the cooking,' he'd said.)

Mum restricted saying grace to Sundays, and after she'd dished up and Dad had carved, she talked about being thankful for our food and all we had besides. I opened one eye to see what Gabriella was doing; she was looking straight at me with bug eyes and puffed-out cheeks. I stifled my laugh and focused on Mum who'd moved on to talking about the importance of forgiving transgressions.

Afterwards I asked what a transgression was. 'Ask Lucy Carlisle,' said Gabriella before Mum could reply.

Later, Dad said he was going for a stroll. I volunteered to go with him announcing the event as a Dad-and-youngest-daughter trip around the village. Gabriella rolled her eyes and I ignored her. I was determined to make the excursion last as long as possible.

Often when we were alone, Dad told me stories from his past and the special bond he'd had with Uncle Thomas. They'd been unstoppable – fighting back to back against the bullies who didn't like their foreign name. 'There's nothing so special as sibling love,' he'd say. And I'd nod vigorously, thinking of Gabriella and making up scenes in which I saved her from the bad boys in the village.

Dad stopped off at the House of Flores to fetch a vase he'd promised to an old lady who lived in one of the almshouses. And when we knocked, I waited in the doorway while he took it in and placed it according to her direction. I spent the time looking at my reflection in the downstairs window, admiring the latest lucky cast-off from Gabriella – a black bow that looked like a giant moth resting in my hair.

Eventually, Dad came out, having thankfully refused the offer of a cup of tea. Linking arms and walking slowly, I dragged him back to my pace. We passed The Eagle, where Dad drank on Friday nights and came home smelling of beer and tobacco, bearing gifts of Babycham for Mum, and chips for us all from the late night chippy.

'We haven't had chips for ages,' I said.

'You're right, Annie. We haven't done much of anything, have we?'

'Can we have them soon?'

There was no time to answer. Shouting spilled from

the pub. In an instant, Dad had told me to stay put, and disappeared inside. The shouting continued. I counted to three, and slowly pushed open the door and squinted through the smoke. A man was jabbing his finger in the face of the barman who held up his hands in a gesture of surrender. 'Sorry, mate,' he said. 'No can do.' I recognised the drunk – Mr Ellis, a short, stocky man in a brown leather jacket, with a square face and dark hair parted in the middle. I'd seen him before lurching in the street, yelling at his wife. Mum said he was a bully. And even though his wife had *little to recommend her* she didn't deserve *a man like that.* As for poor old Martha . . . Mum couldn't contemplate what life was like for her *with all that rowing going on.*

Now Dad walked straight towards him and I thought any moment Mr Ellis would swing around and punch him in the face, or pick up a bottle and crack it over his skull like in one of the police programmes I watched on the telly. I needn't have worried. In five minutes, Dad had quietened Mr Ellis, who then staggered out the pub. I watched as he zigzagged down the street.

The barman offered us drinks, on the house, but Dad was shaking his head and saying we needed to get home. I was disappointed. I would have liked to have spent another half hour there, drinking lemonade and eating peanuts, while Dad did tricks with the beer mats and told me stories – an extension of our outing.

'Some men don't know they're born,' he muttered on the way home. 'That one should spend more time looking out for his wife and daughter and less time doing that.' He gestured at the pub.

I hung on to his arm, proud that, apart from on Fridays, *my* dad spent all of his time looking out for his wife and daughters, and no time *doing that*.

The following Saturday, Mum announced we were delivering. I groaned while Gabriella protested, saying she had too much homework. We knew what delivering meant. It meant going to people's houses and shoving leaflets through their doors about church services, bazaars and jumble sales. Sometimes it included going inside and sitting quietly, while people – usually old people – droned on about their illnesses and holidays and hairdressers and the state of young people.

Mum pinned her hair neatly in a bun. She wore a beige dress and a beige cardigan, and a string of white beads. Beige was a good colour for church business, she said. It was neutral like our Lord. I wasn't sure what she meant by that since I thought the Lord wasn't neutral in the slightest. He had very clear preferences. Didn't He love sinners, and those who repented, best of all?

After the usual shouting match over Gabriella's clothes and Egyptian-style make-up (I went unnoticed in my jeans and yellow T-shirt with a picture of a Caribbean island on the front) we left the house.

We began as usual at the edge of the village and worked backwards, sweeping past the church, the school and the connecting streets to the High Street. Thankfully, we didn't go inside any houses, although by the time we reached Acer Street it was plain that Mum was twitching to entice an unsuspecting person to a jumble sale, a church tea or, if she was lucky, a Sunday morning service.

It was the way she walked that gave it away, striding purposefully and so fast I had to trot to keep up.

Mum needed an excuse, which she found at number twenty-five. Poised to put the leaflet through the letter box, the door opened and Mrs Ellis appeared, holding an empty milk bottle. 'Ah,' said Mum, her face lighting with the opportunity. 'I'm doing church visits today. Would you like a chat?'

Mrs Ellis blinked back at her. 'I don't think—'

'It would be lovely to talk through all our summer plans,' said Mum, smiling. She took the bottle from Mrs Ellis's hand and placed it on the doorstep.

Mrs Ellis opened her mouth, but nothing came out. Her hands fluttered to the scarf wrapped round her throat. The scarf was grey, the colour of her baggy cardigan, and she wore a grubby white apron tied at the waist, which reached down to the hem of a thick brown skirt. Reluctantly, she stepped back and we followed her in.

It was dark in the narrow hall. There were coats on a stand, shoes scattered below, and a pile of cardboard boxes stacked against the wall. The house smelled of damp clothes and something else, sweet and sickly. It reminded me of church.

For a moment, nobody spoke. I looked from Mum to Mrs Ellis to Gabriella. Gabriella was staring at the scarf. It had slipped and there were tiny bruises on Mrs Ellis's skin. Mrs Ellis must have noticed too as her hands were fluttering upwards, adjusting it back into place.

She led the way to the living room. It was small and crammed with furniture. And hot. A three-bar fire blazed against one wall. An old brown sofa and two matching armchairs faced a black and white TV set with the sound on low. The sickly smell was overpowering here. It came from dozens of pink flowers set in vases around the room. Mr Ellis lounged in one of the armchairs. He was snoring with his legs stretched out and his feet propped up on a battered plastic pouffe. His shirt was unbuttoned and the top of his trousers and the buckle of his belt were undone, showing a hairy white belly.

Mum stopped as if now she might regret the visit, but it was too late. Mrs Ellis was clearing a pile of red-tops from the sofa and dropping them on the floor. I saw huge lettered headlines and photos of warships on the front. Mr Ellis woke up with the noise. A line of dribble had run down the side of his mouth and the stubble of his chin. He scowled.

'We've got visitors,' said Mrs Ellis in a whiny voice. 'Isn't that nice, Charlie?'

He didn't answer, but carried on staring at the three of us. Mum sat on the edge of the sofa with a tight smile. Mrs Ellis offered tea and without waiting for a reply, hurried out the room, slippers flip-flopping on the wooden floor in the hall. There was silence until Mr Ellis levered himself up and followed his wife.

Raised voices. We looked at one another, but none of us spoke.

Mrs Ellis came back with a single cup of tea. She handed it to Mum who took it delicately. 'I've put in a sugar,' she said, sitting on the other armchair.

Mum grimaced as she took a sip. And then she cleared her throat. 'I was wondering if you'd like to come to one of our church teas. We hold them regularly on Friday

afternoons at two o'clock. There's no need to bring any-
thing, the ladies make lovely cakes – Victoria sponges,
Swiss roll, scones.' She stopped. No response from Mrs
Ellis.

Losing interest, I fixed my gaze on the picture on the
wall in front of me – a print showing multiple insects:
beetles, flies, ants, lined up in rows. I was counting them,
working out how many times each insect had been
repeated, letting the conversation float about me when
something Mum said made me look up. 'Everyone's
welcome at the drop-in sessions and they're very confi-
dential.' She glanced at the door. Gabriella reached for
one of the newspapers and flicked through as if she
wasn't interested in the conversation. I knew she was.
I knew she was listening to every word.

Self-consciously I fidgeted on the sofa. 'Do you need
the toilet, Anna?' said Mum quickly. I didn't. Mum
looked at me meaningfully. 'I'm sure Mrs Ellis will let
you use theirs.'

Mrs Ellis bowed her head as if giving permission.

'Upstairs, I expect,' said Mum, looking at Mrs Ellis
for confirmation. Again she nodded.

Having no choice, I stomped out the room and stopped
at the bottom of the staircase. At the other end of the
hall, the door to the kitchen was open. The back door was
open too; a breeze travelled through. It would serve Mum
right if I left the house and disappeared. I'd stay away
for a good few hours. That would make her think twice
about excluding me again. Instead, I climbed the stairs,
pulling my hands one over the other on the banister as if
I was in a tug of war. I hoped Martha wasn't home since

I had no desire to listen to her whinging voice. Worse, she might tell my friends I'd been round her house. I'd be the laughing stock of the school.

Three doors led from the landing, each of them ajar. Unable to help myself, I poked my head into the first room. It was Martha's. No sign of her, luckily. I inspected the miserable place with its blank walls. There was little more than a dull carpet, a single bed, a small chest of drawers and a wardrobe. Where were the records and cassettes, the books and the posters? I was tempted to look inside the built-in cupboard, but resisted.

The second bedroom was a mess. My eyes moved from the ratty sheepskin rug sprawled out like a dead animal by the wardrobe, to the unmade double bed and piles of magazines, and more boxes stacked up, like the ones in the hall. This room had a stale smell, like unwashed skin. Wrinkling my nose, I backed out, trying not to look at the rumpled nightclothes on the bed.

In the bathroom, a clothes horse covered with damp socks and pants stood spread-eagled across the pale pink bath. Here I concentrated on not sitting on the toilet seat, or looking at the stains on the carpet. There was a horrible queasy feeling in my stomach that I was trying to ignore and I said a swift thank you to God (and my mother) that our house didn't look like this. Finishing quickly, I pulled the chain and washed my hands with carbolic soap. I thought of Martha, standing where I was now, looking into the chipped mirror, getting ready for bed. It was a horrible house. Cold and dark and miserable. Drying my hands on my jeans, I came out as the front door slammed. Good. Mr Ellis had gone out.

Downstairs, the murmur of voices was still coming from the living room, so I snuck along to the kitchen to see what it was like. The sides were cluttered and the green-painted cupboards were splashed with stains. There was a pull-down tabletop with two chairs and the remains of breakfast – dirty bowls, a piece of cold toast in the rack. A threadbare mop in a metal bucket leaned against the wall.

I went outside. It was a warm day, hazy and hot. The scent of flowers was strong here too, around the trees and in the borders: lavender, honeysuckle and foxglove. I recognised them from the gardening books Mum read, only she could never make flowers grow, not like they did here. Next to the door was a hutch. I bent to see what was inside. A creature scampered and disappeared inside the straw. Startled, I stood upright, too fast, the blood in my head making me dizzy. I heard a noise. Mr Ellis was coming out of the shed with a toolbox. So he hadn't gone out as I'd thought, and now he stood on the lawn with sunlight catching on the buckle of his belt, and his bare feet like pale slabs of meat against the grass. He beckoned me across. I dragged myself over, wishing I'd gone straight back to Mum.

'Want a look?' he said, squatting and opening the box.

I stared politely at the jumble of tools, the rusty rolls of wire and broken plugs. Pulling out a pair of pliers and holding them out, he opened the crocodile jaws. 'Do you know what these are for?' He grinned.

'Fixing things,' I said. 'My dad's got some.'

He shook his head slowly, still grinning. 'Mine are for cutting off nosy children's noses.' He pulled out a hammer.

'And this,' he said, waving it around. 'This is for rapping their knuckles when they steal money from my wallet.' He held up the wire. 'And this is for tying hands and stopping the fidgets.'

I edged away, but he moved closer, leaning his head towards me until I smelled his stale breath. The back door creaked. Martha was there staring at the two of us. Mr Ellis noticed her too and gave another grin. 'Ah, Martha, just in time,' he said, scissoring the pliers. I took the opportunity and brushed past Martha, back into the house and to the living room.

'Pinks,' our mother said as we were leaving. 'Did you notice the pinks in the vases? Lovely, weren't they? Whatever you say about them, that family must have green fingers.'

On the way home, Mum walked fast in the way she did when she had something on her mind. 'What did they talk about?' I hissed to Gabriella as we dawdled along behind.

'Not a lot,' she said. 'Church.'

'Then why did Mum want to get rid of me?'

'You're paranoid.'

'I'm not. She sent me out to the loo. Why did you get to stay?'

'Cos I'm older than you, small person. I understand this stuff.'

'What stuff?'

She shrugged and picked a leaf from a laurel bush in someone's front garden. In the distance, Mum was nearing home. Mrs Henderson came out of the gate next door and I imagined how Mum would feel about that. She didn't like gossips. *People in glass houses*, she liked to say. *Nobody's perfect. Pot and kettle black.*

Gabriella had spotted Mrs Henderson too. 'Oh God!' she said, pulling at my arm. 'Let's wait till the old witch has gone.'

We sat on a wall. 'What stuff?' I repeated.

She sighed and tore a strip from the laurel leaf. 'Nothing.'

I narrowed my eyes. 'Why doesn't anyone tell me the truth?'

She narrowed her eyes back. 'You're just too young.'

I wanted to tell her about Mr Ellis and his toolbox, although I didn't know exactly what to say. He gave me the creeps with his small ugly eyes and weird smile and the strange things he said.

'What do you think of Mr Ellis?' I began. 'I don't like him. He's—'

Gabriella interrupted me. 'You don't have to like him. You don't live with him. Not like Martha.'

I frowned. The conversation had gone in the wrong direction. I knew I was supposed to feel sorry for Martha, but I didn't. Gabriella was much nicer than me, worrying about people's feelings. She even felt sorry for Mrs Henderson's son Brian whose eyelashes were so pale you couldn't see them and who was always staring at us from his window. Mrs Henderson said he was delicate and also *terribly bright*. I didn't understand that since he never spoke and had no opinion about anything.

I squinted down the road to see what was happening with Mum. The two of them were talking, although Mum had taken a few steps backwards as if she wanted to get away, and now she was tugging at her hair in that nervous way she had.

Eventually, Mum escaped and hurried into the house. I didn't move. I didn't feel like going home yet. I wanted to talk to Gabriella, but she was shredding the laurel leaf and looking into the distance and tapping her foot. She'd forgotten all about me. A song was stuck in her head and she was beating out the rhythm.

When we got back, Mum and Dad were in the kitchen and from the expression on their faces it was obvious something was wrong. Dad was slumped in his chair. Mum was pale and her hair where she'd been tugging it was loose.

'What's up?' said Gabriella, looking from one to the other.

'Nothing,' said Mum quickly. 'Nothing for you to worry about.'

She couldn't fool us. Something was going on. I ran through the possibilities. Jasper? No, he was in the corner lapping at his milk. Grandma Grace or Granddad? Were they ill? Granddad was always catching a cold, or taking to his bed, and Grandma Grace had arthritis. Maybe it was Uncle Thomas or the shop. I looked at Dad for a clue, but he didn't seem to even notice we were there.

Mum walked to the sink and leaned with her back against it. 'Go to your rooms,' she said in a strained voice. 'I'll call you when tea's ready.'

We knew better than to protest. We left the kitchen and as soon as we did, Mum and Dad spoke again, their

voices low and urgent, their words indistinct but growing louder as we moved up the stairs. I leaned over the
banister. 'It changes everything,' Mum said.

Instinct made me want to be alone. Walking across
the landing to my room, I ran through more possibilities. Maybe it was something to do with the Ellis
family. Mum had been uncomfortable when we'd left
their house. Gabriella had been cagey about what Mum
and Mrs Ellis had talked about. Or was it connected
with Mrs Henderson? Had she given Mum some news?
Maybe Brian had run away or was ill. I tried to feel
sympathetic and failed.

I sat on the bed, kicking my feet and chewing at the
edge of my thumbnail. *It changes everything.* That's
what Mum had said. But what was *it* and why was *it* so
important?

Shrugging away my questions as best I could, I pulled
out my latest Enid Blyton and got lost in Malory Towers.
An hour passed. My stomach rumbled. Why hadn't Mum
called us down for tea? Putting aside my book, I went
onto the landing and poked my head around Gabriella's
door. Still dressed, she'd gone to sleep listening to her
Walkman. Tiptoeing inside, I peered at the rise and fall
of her chest. Her eyelids were fluttering as if she was
dreaming. I reached out to touch her, but quickly changed
my mind. If I woke her, she'd be cross.

Downstairs, I pushed my ear against the living room
door and heard the murmur of my parents' voices. And
Rita's. When had she come round? And what was so
important that Mum had forgotten to feed us? I was
starving.

In the kitchen, I made two doorstep sandwiches, piling in Edam cheese and salad cream. On the way back, I listened at the living room again, but I couldn't make out what they said. A movement near the door made me jump. I scuttled away, dashing up the stairs. Depositing one sandwich beside my sleeping sister, I took refuge in my room.

Chewing slowly, spilling crumbs, I considered what was going on. More secrets. Between adults. Would they tell Gabriella? I doubted anyone would bother to tell me.

7

'Rita Saunders?' said the man, hardly looking up from his clipboard.

I shook my head. 'Anna Flores.'

His eyes flickered to the sign above the shop door and straight back to me. Holding my gaze, he spoke quietly. 'I'm sorry,' he said. 'And for your loss.'

'Thank you.'

'I'm David. In charge of the house clearance.'

He held out his hand and I took it. His palm was warm and rough from hard work. He proffered the clipboard and I read the details on the form. *Name: Edward Lily. Address: Lemon Tree Cottage.* My whole body tingled as I read the words and I closed my eyes, picturing the overgrown garden and the jackdaws pecking next door. David coughed. My thoughts receded. Scanning the information again, I signed, and after he'd taken the clipboard I peered inside the van. It was crammed with furniture, tipped up and fitted together like pieces in a puzzle. 'There's a lot here,' I said.

'And a lot more to come.'

With a sinking feeling, I put on a smile and indicated the shop door, telling him everything would be going in the back. David lowered his head in acknowledgement and now I looked at him properly. A few years older than me, he was slim, with strong, thin arms. Scruffy, in big boots and jeans, his dark hair was a shade too long and he had the shadow of a beard that suited him.

Two skinny young men in overalls, who looked like they'd rather be anywhere else, followed us into the shop. Rita and her nephew, Mattie, whom she'd hired for the job, took charge, while I shuffled paperwork, but it was impossible to ignore the shifts and grunts, the shouts of exasperation, as they organised the furniture into the space.

A dead man's life, I thought, each time the men traipsed through, their boots shedding mud and dried-up leaves. Eventually, when the contents of the van had been regurgitated successfully, the men took their leave. But not before I'd agreed to go to the cottage later to inspect what was left.

Mattie was slight and in his twenties, with a black quiff, and a habit of scratching his chin. After the last boxes had been stacked, he excused himself. He was off to a christening. 'Best friend's first baby,' he said, patting his quiff before blushing a surprisingly dark red. I supposed he thought it was tactless to mention birth so soon after death.

Rita was rolling up her sleeves ready to dive in. I looked from her eager face to the massive pile of Edward Lily's things and felt a sudden reluctance to start trawling through them already. I suggested we came back tomorrow instead.

Rita raised her eyebrows. 'Are you sure?'

I nodded. 'Mattie can't stay and I've got things I need to do at home.'

'All right. If that's what you'd prefer.' She patted my

arm and didn't comment further, only settled herself into her shawl, wrapping the ends close around her shoulders.

When they'd both gone, I considered the pile before me. How odd that once I'd been to this man's house and now his house had come to me. I tried to imagine Mum being here. It was hard to do. Uncle Thomas had taken over the shop after Dad had died, and Mum had avoided any involvement. And when Uncle Thomas had died too, she'd talked constantly about selling, or only opening up a few days a week. When I'd been home, she'd refused to even come here with me. Even stranger that she'd accepted this house clearance. What had made it so difficult to decline?

I looked around at the wilderness of belongings over-loading the room. The atmosphere seemed changed with all these things. It was quieter and more solemn than before. Personal too. I picked out the battered leather armchair, the chaise longue with its worn upholstery, the set of antique cups. Things which had been sat on, lain on, drunk from.

There was an oak desk at the front, with Queen Anne legs and a top that lifted. Now I sensed the thrill that my father had instilled in me as I touched the wood and felt the scratches beneath my fingertips. *An eye for beautiful things.* Had my mother really said that? If she had, it gave me a surprising quiver of pride. The desk was the kind that might have secret drawers. I ran my fingers around the edges and suffered a childlike disappointment at finding nothing: no buttons or levers. I lifted the lid to a mess of papers and rifled amongst them, picking out a scattering of photos.

They were portraits mainly: a prim middle-aged woman with hair scraped into a bun; a man with a prominent chin and moustache, smoking a pipe; a boy looking awkward, and the same boy as a teenager and later as a young man with round glasses, protruding ears and a long, fine-boned face. I guessed it was Edward Lily. I'd only seen him when he was middle-aged. Had his sister missed these photos? They were blurry, badly taken. Rejects maybe.

One of the photos was of a girl with light-coloured hair. Although the picture was out of focus, I knew who the girl was. She was standing self-consciously before a building with arched windows and railings. The place must be Spain where Edward Lily had lived before Lemon Tree Cottage and this was Lydia, his daughter – the girl I'd fantasised was mad. In the photo, she wore a long, flowing dress and held a wide-brimmed hat loosely in her hand.

I gazed at the picture and it drew me in. Was it the way Lydia held herself, or the distant look in her eyes, or the cloud of hair that fell about her face? Or the old-fashioned clothes? I wasn't sure, but as I stood there in the dusty room, staring into the photo, it felt as if her ghost was reaching out, winding its arms around my neck, dragging me closer, claiming me.

A clock chimed, a muffled sound at the back of the room, and a memory tapped in my head. The pendulum clock at home. When Gabriella disappeared, the clock stopped. The silence had been like an expression of her absence. One day, after my father had died and my mother was out, I'd taken a chair, climbed up and given the key a hefty twist, and as the ticking had begun again, it seemed as if my sister and my father might come home. After that, I wound the clock every night. If I wound hard enough, time might go backwards and we'd begin again. But of course, it didn't. The clock kept going forwards: endless hours of time passing, of loneliness and loss. Of time without Gabriella.

I took the photo of Lydia and a couple of Edward Lily into the main shop. It was gloomy outside, and the lamps cast shadows on the wall, yet I was reluctant to leave. It seemed safer here where there was no one watching me, no one expecting answers. Where the only questions were the ones I asked myself.

8

1982

A few days after our visit to the Ellis house, Mum and Rita were due to go on a shopping trip to London. They went two or three times a year and the event had been written on the calendar for weeks.

Since the day when Mum had forgotten to make our tea, the mood had been sombre in the house. My parents quiet, Gabriella and me wondering what was wrong. Mum became strict with us, insisting we came straight home from school and making us do our homework before tea. We wasted too much time, she said, wandering about the village or spending time at the shop. In the mornings, Dad began driving us to school. With the house clearance, he preferred a later start, he said. So instead of leaving home at six, he left at half past eight and dropped us off.

Now we were watching the evening news. A teenager from York had disappeared – a photo of a fifteen-year-old girl with blonde hair and a fringe and wearing her school uniform flashed up on the screen. The next shot was of her parents, holding hands and speaking into the camera. Mum switched off the telly.

'I'm going to call it off,' she said, addressing Dad who was sitting in his armchair.

He emerged from behind his paper. 'Call what off?'

'London on Saturday.'

He looked at her for a moment or two. 'There's no need.' He glanced across to where Gabriella and I lay sprawled on the floor. 'We'll manage, won't we, girls? Chicken kiev for tea?' We nodded vigorously. It was a treat when Dad was in charge of the kitchen. He didn't boycott the microwave.

Mum was tugging at her hair. 'I'm not sure.'

Dad folded the paper. 'I can look after them,' he said quietly.

Of course he could look after us. What was Mum worried about?

'We're not babies,' said Gabriella, retrieving her Walkman from the other side of the room and fiddling with a cassette.

'Nobody said you were,' replied Dad. 'Everything's fine. Mum's going to London.' He kissed her on the cheek.

My mood lifted; their argument was coming to an end. I exchanged glances with Gabriella who shrugged and shook her head. Noticing, Dad reached out to her too. She sat on the floor leaning against his legs, her hair static against his trousers. I watched them in their own world, as they talked about music. And Mum, instead of making irritated noises like she usually did when Gabriella enthused about the Clash and Siouxise and all the other bands she liked, sat back and listened.

Eventually, Mum disappeared. She was calling Rita on the telephone in the hall, planning their trip to London.

When Saturday came, Mum got ready – combing out her hair, painting her lips, clipping on gold earrings shaped like teardrops. Beige was for church. For London, she wore a lilac dress with butterfly sleeves, fastened with a matching twisted belt. 'What do you think?' she asked, turning in front of the triple-sided mirror and clamping a gold bracelet on her wrist. I stared at the transformation. No hint of jam-making, scolding or church. Mum was double-sided like one of those wooden jumping-jack toys, with different characters drawn on either side.

She rifled through the rest of her jewellery and pulled out an emerald ring. I'd seen it before: a thin gold band with a sparkling stone. She held it up to the light for a moment before putting it away. And when I asked her why she didn't wear it, she said she was dressed up quite enough. Was the ring so expensive she didn't dare put it on? More expensive even than the sapphire brooch Dad had bought her last Christmas which she was pinning onto her dress?

Later, we dropped Mum off at the station to meet Rita. 'Bread and lardy cake, Anna,' she said, opening the passenger door and leaning to pinch my cheeks. 'You will get them, won't you? Oh, and some of those waxy circles I put on the tops of jam.' She looked at Gabriella, opened her mouth as if to speak, but changed her mind. Turning to Dad instead, she said, 'Are you sure I should—'

'Yes,' he said as he pulled her across and they kissed goodbye.

I wound down the window and watched her sadly, missing her already.

Gabriella gave me a sharp nudge in the ribs. 'What's wrong with you?' I rubbed my eyes, mumbled about grit, and asked if she wanted to come with me to the baker's and afterwards to the green.

'Not today, small person,' she said, untwisting her Walkman as she got out of the car. 'Things to do.'

'Where are you going?' said Dad, opening the driver's door.

'Bernadette's,' Gabriella replied, looking surprised.

'Oh no you're not. You're supposed to be helping me with the chicken kiev.'

'I never said that.'

'Oh yes you did, young lady. Back in the car.'

'God. Are you serious?'

'Yes.'

'Is this something to do with Mum?' And when he hesitated, she rolled her eyes. 'Thought so.'

'Back in the car then, please.'

Gabriella made a face, but did as she was told. If it had been Mum talking, it would have been a different story. Dad always managed to get Gabriella to do things she didn't want to do. I, on the other hand, would have needed no persuasion to help him make the tea, and I wondered, as we drove home, why he'd chosen Gabriella and not me.

On the way to the baker's, I consoled myself thinking about the village fête. Every year, Mum made jam for her stall. Fruit from the garden: plum and damson, and apple when we went scrumping in the orchard and brought back a bagful, stomachs aching from too much fruit. Unable to resist, Mum washed and peeled, cored and chopped, let it all slide into her giant metal pot, where it mulched and broke down and reacted with the sugar, and the house smelled sweet for days.

At the baker's, I collected the jam tops and asked the girl behind the counter for a cottage loaf and a lardy cake with a thick crust of sugar on its base. She shovelled bread and cake into paper bags while I examined the glass display with its iced buns and cream slices and doughnuts oozing jam. I was thinking about buying a custard tart when a man wandered in wearing a light-coloured jacket and a panama hat. I recognised him immediately. It was the man from Lemon Tree Cottage.

Colour crept up my face and stained my ears, but instead of scurrying away, I focused my attention on a shelf of meat pies and listened to the conversation. The girl behind the counter was friendlier to him than she had been to me, giggling and blushing when he spoke. 'Can't get used to this weather,' he said in a friendly voice as she rang up the cost on the till. He patted his pockets and pulled out a handful of coins. 'Can't get used to the money either.'

Leaning forward and squinting at the pastry design on the top of a steak and kidney pie, I sensed rather than saw him stop beside me. 'Hello,' he said.

'Hi.' I straightened up and blinked back.

He looked at me for a few moments with blue eyes behind round glasses. His face was narrow and his nose thin and pointed. I guessed he was handsome since he made me think of one of the old film stars like Paul Newman, or maybe Frank Sinatra, someone Mum would like. I dropped my gaze to the bag of doughnuts he was holding. Noticing, he gave a smile and said, 'To tempt my daughter.' And added, as if he'd only just thought about it, 'Lydia. She's fussy.'

Flushing again, I pictured myself staring up at the window of Lemon Tree Cottage and I rubbed my face, trying to disguise the blush. Was I imagining it or had his expression changed? Was there the faintest sign of recognition?

'Well then,' he said, after a few seconds. 'Nice to meet you.' He shuffled away as if weary, or in pain.

I watched him, curious to know more. Edward Lily was intriguing with his fairy-tale cottage, doughnut-eating daughter and crazy Spanish wife. What other secrets did he hide?

'Goodbye,' I said suddenly, not wanting this encounter to go by without my saying something.

He stopped again, and blinked rapidly. I'd spoken more loudly than I'd intended. My skin tingled with embarrassment, but he nodded and grimaced and glanced across at the girl behind the counter as he walked out of the door, leaving me with a peculiar feeling in the pit of my stomach, a nervous kind of fluttering. I hadn't intended to draw attention to myself, and now I concluded he'd identified me as a spy.

Mum came back from London with her hair made dirty by the air on the Underground, and her dress crumpled by the crush on the train. She showed us what she'd bought, a pair of purple satin shoes, which she slipped on and off and promptly put back in the box. But she looked more cheerful than she had done before, recounting her adventures in Oxford Street while we ate the chicken kiev (delayed due to Gabriella having distracted Dad with a trip into town and to Our Price). Dad was relaxed too, teasing Gabriella about the boy with the drowsy eyes in the record shop. I watched them enviously, wishing I'd been with them, but my mouth was greasy with butter and garlic and we had jam roly-poly with custard for pudding, so I wasn't going to complain.

After we'd stacked the dishwasher and Dad had insisted on Mum resting while he scoured the pans, Rita arrived, banging on the back door. We retreated to the living room where Rita and Mum searched for records and Dad fetched three glasses, a bottle of Cinzano and a bowl of Twiglets.

We settled on the sofa ready to watch the adults embarrass themselves, which they did spectacularly, jiving to 'Jailhouse Rock'. And when Smokey Robinson came on, Rita sat down and Mum and Dad danced, smooching to 'Being With You', gazing into each other's eyes.

I leaned against Gabriella's shoulder, clamping her in place, thinking how everything was going to be all right. Whatever had happened to upset Mum and Dad was over. Things were back to normal. I was about to tell Gabriella about my encounter in the baker's, with plenty of embellishments, when the letter box clattered, and before anyone else moved, I jumped up and ran to see what it was.

A long white envelope lay on the mat. I stooped to pick it up. The name – Esther – was printed on the front in tiny letters. I held it to the light, scrutinising what was inside, but the envelope was thick, Basildon Bond, and revealed nothing.

'What's that?' asked Rita, appearing in the hall.

I jumped and thrust the letter behind my back. 'Nothing,' I said.

Rita raised her eyebrows and held out her hand. Caught out, I gave her the envelope which she studied for a moment and then, with no change of expression, slipped into the pocket of her skirt.

'I'll give it to your mother later,' she said, turning away.

'What is it?' I said, feeling a prickle of annoyance. I was the one who'd found it. Why shouldn't I give it to Mum?

She hesitated. 'Church newsletter.'

It wasn't. The newsletter came through the door folded into sections. I should know since I'd helped Mum fold and deliver hundreds of them. I watched suspiciously as Rita walked away from me. Why had she lied?

Back in the living room, Rita chose the hard-backed chair and sat with her hands on her knees watching Mum and Dad dancing. Gabriella was listening to her Walkman, so there was nothing for me to do but pick up a copy of *Smash Hits* and nibble on the Twiglets. I leafed through the pages, my eyes sliding over pictures of Fun Boy Three and Elvis Costello.

Mum came and leaned between us. Her breath smelled sweet from the lime in the Cinzano and her voice had the faintest slur. 'Gorgeous girl,' she said to Gabriella, kissing her face. She pinched my cheeks. 'You too, Anna.'

Looking up, I caught Rita staring at the three of us. She grimaced when her eyes met mine. I turned away. Rita had lied about the letter. Was she even going to give the envelope to Mum? I resolved that if she didn't, I would tell, so I spent the rest of the evening waiting for my moment. It wasn't necessary. As Rita was leaving, she slipped the letter into Mum's hand and patted her on the arm. 'Let me know if I can help,' she said quietly as she made her way out the door.

Mum dashed off to bed. Dad followed shortly after. And soon the fun of the evening was lost as they argued again, their raised voices bouncing through the walls.

9

The cafe was an antidote to the House of Flores. Minimalist. Although I wasn't sure if that was due to lack of funds. Surely they needed *something* on the walls. An old photograph of the village perhaps? A painting of the woods?

The lunchtime rush had gone. I ordered an espresso and a bacon sandwich from a young woman in a black dress, who had red lips and glossy black hair, save for one lock at the front, which she'd dyed purplish-blue like a magpie's wing. Too young to have been around in the eighties, perhaps her mother had inspired her dress sense. That was a thought. I was old enough to be this girl's mum.

Choosing a seat at the window, I laid out the photos on the table. I must have inherited my father's genes. Curiosity ran through our family like blood.

Edward Lily had been handsome as a young man. I wondered about his wife. She'd killed herself, hadn't she? At least that's what they'd said in the village. Why? I could guess: loss, disenchantment, grief. The precarious nature of life.

Outside, people walked quickly – heads bent against the wind, hands thrust inside their pockets. Martha appeared on the other side of the street. As I watched her, fidgeting along the High Street, pulling at her coat, hoisting up her shopping bag, I felt a return of the disquiet I'd experienced in the graveyard – that memory of Martha's mother as a witness, the investigation of Tom and his release.

Poor Tom. He'd been treated badly in the village. People had been so quick to proclaim his guilt; they'd stampeded on his life. The media had done that too, stirring things up like they always did, trawling through his business. It was only me who'd believed in his innocence. Me, I supposed, and Tom's mother.

Disquiet turned to pain. I allowed the emotion to take hold knowing from experience there was nothing else to do and soon enough the feeling drained and dulled to a bearable pang.

Across the road Martha stopped. Had she seen me? She hovered on the edge of the pavement, but changed her mind, switching direction, and going back the way she'd come.

Remembering my promise to go to Lemon Tree Cottage, I finished my coffee and took a few hasty bites of the sandwich. David would be waiting for me and there was no reason to let him down.

It had been thirty years since I'd taken the route, but as soon as I set off I knew I hadn't forgotten it. My feet carried me forwards, retracing the steps with certainty, through the village and up Chestnut Hill and out onto the main road.

So much was the same and so much was different. The neglected tarmac punctuated by potholes, the scruffy hedgerows and the fields stretching off to my right. All unchanged. But the building works on the left-hand side had sprung into a mini estate, an ordered labyrinth of identical houses and drives, with neat roads connecting them, and low walls and privet hedges, and conifers in need of cutting back.

When I reached the brow of the hill, and turned into the lane, it was as if time had stopped. There was the same stillness. The same feeling of being in another world. A tractor had made recent furrows on its way to the fields beyond. Copper-coloured leaves patched the hedges and shone in the afternoon light – the only bright splashes amidst the different shades of brown.

Walking slowly, I pushed down my unease. This was the emotion I'd always felt in the lane. It was a habit, I told myself. An involuntary reaction.

The first cottage looked abandoned, the thatch practically gone. A couple of the windows had been boarded up. In the garden, an old washing line drooped across the grass and a rusty lawnmower leaned against the wall.

The clearance van was parked outside Lemon Tree Cottage. The house itself seemed brighter, more defined, like places did when you hadn't seen them for a long time. There were certain characteristics I'd forgotten, like the lean of the chimney and the diamond panes of glass, but the garden was overgrown as I remembered it, with bushes and plants creeping too close to the walls. Through the open front door, I glimpsed the hall beyond and my fingertips tingled with the thought of going inside, of touching the furniture, the walls, of feeling the past on my skin.

In the distance was the low chugging of the tractor and the cries of a squabble of seagulls, in from the coast, wheeling over the fields where the farmer must have been churning up the earth. Apart from dog walkers, or the odd farm worker, you might see no one here for days.

David emerged from the cottage holding a standing lamp. 'You came,' he said.

'Of course,' and then, for something to say, 'Are your boys here?'

He made a wry face. 'One of them decided he was sick and the other was tired and had to go home.' I smiled and stepped to one side as he brushed past me to get to the van and manoeuvred the lamp until it fitted amongst the rest of the furniture. 'Shall we go in?' he said, slamming the doors.

I nodded as if it was of no real consequence, but my heart was pounding as we walked down the path, and when I stepped over the threshold, my breath stopped.

The cottage had a damp and woody smell. The carpet was patchy, and so were the walls, with lighter shapes where pictures had been. The living room was empty save for a rocking chair and a battered cushion. 'I always leave a chair until the end,' said David, following my gaze. 'It's a long job, clearing houses.' He looked at his watch. 'Shall I show you round, or leave you to it?'

'Leave me to it,' I said too quickly.

He raised his eyebrows, but didn't comment, only offered to come back and pick me up. 'Save you walking in the dark,' he said. 'I live out this way. A few miles up, on the main road, set back.'

I knew where he meant: a line of old cottages with long gardens and woods behind. 'How long have you lived there?' I said, making my voice sound casual. For all I knew, David might have been in the village for years. In which case he'd know about me. Not that I recognised him so I didn't think he'd been to my school.

'About six months. I was in Japan. And London before that.'

'Japan? What did you do?'

'Worked for a bit, odd jobs, anything really, just for a couple of years. It was . . .' He stopped.

'Exotic?' I offered.

'Cathartic,' he said at the same time. 'And accidental.'

There was a pause. It was a strange combination of words. 'How?'

'Accidental because Japan was the first place I thought of, and cathartic because it made me feel better. Is that what cathartic means?' He raised his hand. 'Don't answer. I'll leave you to get on. What about picking you up later?'

It was tempting, but I declined. 'I'd rather walk. I like the exercise.' The first bit at least was true.

As soon as the front door slammed, and the van drove away, the silence became absolute. The house dictated: no dripping taps, or clanking pipes; no sighing beams or scuttles in the loft. I clumped out of the room, if only to hear sound, and climbed the stairs more slowly, feeling the give of the boards. The fifth step creaked and so did the ninth. My limbs prickled. Above me a shadow moved. Was I following my own ghost, my twelve-year-old self, tiptoeing through the cottage?

Turning at the bend of the stairs, I continued to the top and sat on the musty carpet. The window ahead of me framed the trees. The afternoon sun was dropping, the grey sky turning slate, but still the light picked out the burnished golds and reds. A late swallow dipped across the sky. Two gulls appeared. Zigzagging, chasing. An aggressive flight.

The bookcase behind me on the landing had gone. Years before, the whole house had been crammed with books and ornaments. God, I'd effectively broken in. How had I been so brave? Twelve years old and determined to find out what had happened to my sister. When had I given up that fight?

Why *had* Mum taken this clearance on? I pictured the scrapbook lying in the drawer. What if she'd turned detective like I'd done once? She might even have done this before, taken on house clearances from people who had died in the village, and then gone through their belongings, looking for clues. I shivered. I was being morbid. My imagination was going into overdrive. It was this house. It had that effect on me. Mad girls. Men who locked people up.

Still, I explored the rooms. The bathroom was old-fashioned, the suite chipped with age. There was a toothbrush alone in a pitiful plastic cup, an electric razor next to that, a comb and a bottle of hair oil. One bedroom was empty. The other I'd been in before. Now the bed was covered by a grey counterpane with bags piled on top. I pulled open the wardrobe. Mothballs. There was no mistaking the chemical scent. In the drawer at the bottom, I found bundles of papers and a few more photos. The papers looked like invoices, or copies of them, sent out to customers. They were written in Spanish and headed with the name of a shop, La Plata, along with an address in Seville. Edward Lily's business, I supposed; the reason he'd been in Spain. I took the photos, thinking I'd put them with the rest.

Downstairs, the living room drew me back in. I sat down, grateful to David for having left the chair, and looked through the photos, recognising Seville: the Giralda, the Alcázar, and there was Lydia in the Plaza de España wearing a shawl covered in roses.

The front door opened, footsteps shuffled in the hall. I had no time to call out before a woman appeared. She screamed when she saw me. Lydia? Her mother? No. Lydia's mother was dead. And this was no middle-aged ghost, wearing a cardigan and clutching her heart. It must be a neighbour, or a friend. Too young for Edward Lily's sister.

Springing up, I leapt forward. 'I'm so sorry. I didn't mean to startle you.' The woman stayed where she was, hand gripping the door jamb. 'I'm Anna, from the House of Flores, the place where all this . . .' I stopped dramatically and swept my hand through the air, halting as I realised it was a futile gesture in an empty room. She looked around, eyes wide. She was short and solid with a mass of grey hair; her face white with shock. I panicked. Oh God, was she a relative who didn't know Edward Lily had died?

'You do know what happened?' I said, composing myself.

'Yes.' She passed her hand across her forehead as if trying to sweep it from her mind. 'Yes, of course. It was only seeing you . . .' She pointed at the chair and I turned automatically to look. 'That's where I found him,' she said, a little wildly. 'I think about it all the time. I thought he was asleep. I said his name and he didn't answer. I touched him, to wake him, you understand, but he was stone cold dead.' She paused, made the sign of the cross and then lumbered across the room, hands stretched out like a sleepwalker, the scent of something floral following in her wake. She dropped straight into the chair and set it rocking.

'There was a picture on the floor,' she said, jabbing her finger at the carpet. 'Right there. He was looking at it, I reckon, when he died. And there was a smell. I thought it was the rubbish. I never imagined . . .' She stopped, her voice tearful now. 'When I saw he'd passed away, the first thing I wanted to do was to phone my husband, can you believe. He's been dead almost three years. That's how upset I was.'

'How terrible,' I said, not knowing quite what else to say. 'Are you his . . . ?'

'Housekeeper. Dawn. I came to clean things up. The man, the one with the van, he said it would be all right.' She pulled out a handkerchief and blew her nose. 'I didn't want people to think I'd neglected the place.'

'How long did you know Mr Lily?'

'For years,' she said. 'Right from when he bought the cottage. Early eighties.' She sat forward, scrutinising me. 'How long is that?' She frowned as if reminded of something and took another look at me. 'Of course,' she said, her expression clearing. 'Aren't you . . . ?' She stopped.

I spoke quickly, avoiding the question with one of my own. 'Did you know Lydia? I remember when she lived here.'

Dawn glanced over her shoulder as if someone might

be listening and leaned closer, steadying the rocking chair with her feet. 'Lydia was . . .' She stopped and grimaced and tapped two fingers to her temple. 'You know what I mean?' I looked away, not wanting to respond. 'But then she would've been, wouldn't she, after her mother, you know . . .' She made the sign of the cross again. 'I didn't know Isabella. But I did feel sorry for Mr Lily looking after Lydia on his own. It was a shame. And she was a sweet girl. In her own way.'

I was curious now. 'What was she like?'

'Well, sweet, as I said, but quiet, very quiet. And so thin. I remember Mr Lily fretting and bringing treats to tempt her.' She looked away and made a face as if trying to decide whether to say more.

I didn't press her, although I wanted to know. I had a recollection that she'd stayed in England when her father had gone back to Spain. I wondered if she'd been to the cottage since he'd died.

'I don't think so,' said Dawn when I asked.

'Was she at the funeral?'

She shook her head. 'There was only myself and Mr Lily's sister and a few people from the village.'

'Do you think Lydia has . . .' I hesitated. 'Passed away?'

'No. The sister mentioned her, although she didn't say why she wasn't at the funeral. Mr Lily was cagey about Lydia, too – with me, at least.' She cleared her throat. 'To be honest, I always wondered if he put her in a place.'

'What kind of place?'

'For people who . . . you know, have that kind of problem.' She looked away as if embarrassed to talk about it.

'You mean a home?'

'Yes, or a convent. That's the kind of thing they have in Spain, isn't it?'

I had a vision of Lydia drifting through stone passageways or in a secluded garden surrounded by orange trees and bougainvillea.

'You really think he'd have abandoned her like that?'

'Well . . . that generation,' said Dawn, in the same conspiratorial tone she'd used before. 'They did that, didn't they?'

She was right. My mother had had a distant cousin she never spoke about. By the time I found out, both Grandma Grace and Granddad Bertrand had died as well as Uncle Thomas. I'd seen a letter on the kitchen table. It had come from a residential home in London and was asking my mother as the only remaining relative for permission to send on her cousin's things. Her name was Mary and it was obvious from the letter that she'd lived in the home for years. I remembered feeling angry about it, accusing Mum of being secretive, not mentioning her cousin before. 'It was different in those days, Anna,' she'd said. 'I don't expect you to understand, but there was shame in things like that.'

'In things like what?' I'd said. 'Mental illness? Family secrets?'

'Both,' she'd snapped back at me. 'That was how society worked. Your generation don't know anything about it.'

I'd tried to make her say more. I'd wanted explanations, justifications, but she'd tightened up her lips and no amount of prising on my part would extract any words.

Now there was silence as I searched for something more to say to Dawn. 'Mr Lily must have been glad of your help,' I said finally.

'I was glad of the work. Robert too.'

'Robert?'

'My husband. Well, he wasn't at the time.' She smiled. 'That came later. I suppose I should thank Mr Lily since he employed us both.' She stopped talking and seemed suddenly lost.

In the end, I suggested she came to the shop to choose a memento, and when she asked if she could set aside any of Lydia's things that remained in the cottage and pick out something of hers too, I agreed. I doubted Edward Lily's sister had left anything of sentimental value, and despite Dawn's clumsy way of speaking about Lydia, she'd clearly had an affection for the girl.

Dawn disappeared to do her cleaning and I took a stroll in the garden. The light was fading. It would be a dark walk home. Still, I stayed, wandering across the scruffy lawn, my mind swinging back to the idea that my mother had taken to foraging in other people's houses looking for evidence of a crime. The image didn't fit with the lost woman she'd become. Had the police even searched this cottage? I supposed they must have done when the investigation had been at its most intense, when Edward Lily had been a suspect. But how far had they gone? Had they lifted every floorboard, emptied every drawer? Had they looked in the shed, the water butt, the hollows in the trees? Was there a possibility that a clue had been missed either here or elsewhere in the village?

I looked back at the house. Slates were missing, the window ledges were peeling, part of the felt on the porch above the back door was hanging loose. The shutters downstairs were closed, making the place look gloomy and hostile. *Was* there something hiding here? *Was* it worth searching again, starting from where I'd left off?

A pigeon flew from a tree behind me, wings beating, making me jump. I spun around and watched as it stumbled, pecking at the ground. In the distance the tractor had stopped. Only the breeze ruffled the leaves, a creature stirred in the undergrowth. It was so quiet here. So lonely. Anything could happen in a place like this.

Had my mother believed that too?

What had she hoped to find?

I needed to look at things clearly. My mother's death, the return to the village, familiar names and faces had shaken me. I was thinking too much about the past.

And yet, as I stood gazing at the cottage, I felt something stirring, deep inside me, finding its way through the chaos of my mind. I felt it again as I rounded the path and set off down the lane. Distant now but marching closer, I recognised what it was. Persistence, the need to know, creeping back after all those years away.

10

1982

The last day of term ended with a dull prize-giving assembly in the hall. School was always dreary, with its concrete blocks and teachers who had nervous breakdowns. I'd wanted to go to the grammar school, where the building was like a mansion in a gothic novel, and the girls wore blazers and purse belts and learned Latin, and nobody called you four-eyes or a swot for listening in class. But tragically Saint Barnabas was in town – thirty minutes on the bus; Mum didn't like the journey and Dad despised selection. 'Jesus and Mary,' said Gabriella when I told her my dream. 'Latin is dead. D.E.A.D. And have you seen their uniform? Skirts down to their ankles.'

Now Mrs Green, the head teacher, droned on as she always did and dished out cups and shields. We sat in rows, our heads nodding, until Miss Pretty came onto the stage to declare the winner of the art competition. Then the school woke up. Miss Pretty was young. She wore flouncy dresses and big hoop earrings – exactly what an art teacher should look like.

The painting was concealed on an easel behind a cloth. With a great show, Miss Pretty pulled back the cover to reveal a painting of an old man. 'And the winner is,' she said, her arms wide as if to embrace the lot of us, 'Martha Ellis.'

Silence.

'Martha Ellis,' a boy in the row behind me said. 'She can't paint jack shit.'

But she could and there was the proof on the stage, and there was Martha climbing the steps to a patter of applause.

Afterwards, when the bell rang and we trooped outside, I searched for Gabriella. I found her with Martha. They were both looking at the prize – two tickets to an exhibition at the Tate Gallery in London. A dark feeling rose up and swept right through me. I tried to get rid of it. Why should I care? But Martha was fawning and smiling at my sister in that irritating way of hers and I gave in.

'Are you ready?' I said, my voice high and unnatural.

'What for?' said Gabriella, turning with a look of surprise.

'We need to get home.'

'Do we?' She frowned.

I fixed my face with a serious expression. I thought she'd resist, but she said goodbye to Martha and followed me to the gates. When I looked back, Martha was staring after us, her hand extended as if she was giving the tickets away. I gritted my teeth and hurried down the street, pulling Gabriella with me.

'Why do we have to get home?' said Gabriella.

'We don't,' I said. Although even as I spoke, I was looking around, half expecting to see Dad waiting in his van. He'd taken to picking us up as well as dropping us off. Or at least insisting we walk together to the House of Flores instead of straight home. 'You're as paranoid as

88

Mum,' Gabriella had accused him. While he'd claimed he only wanted to spend more time with his girls.

'So why did you lie?' said Gabriella now.

'I thought you needed to be rescued.'

She looked at me. 'Don't be stupid, Anna. What's wrong with you? Don't you feel sorry for anyone?'

My cheeks reddened. Gabriella's disapproval was like a blast of cold air and my stubbornness crumbled with its force. We walked the rest of the way in silence, my face burning with shame. Gabriella was right. I was stupid. I should have left her and Martha alone. Gabriella was only trying to be nice.

'Sorry,' I mumbled, when we arrived. I pulled at the peony by the door. The flowers were blood red and bursting from their buds. I picked one and held it out to Gabriella. 'Sorry. Really, really sorry. You can go with Martha to the exhibition if you like.'

'I wasn't actually going to offer,' she said, taking the flower and giving me another disapproving look. 'Now, if it had been tickets for Siouxsie . . .' She grinned. 'Forget it.' She pulled out a grip from her hair and fastened the peony in mine. Standing back, she admired the effect. 'You look gorgeous, Anna Flores. Like a flamenco dancer. I wish I had your black hair. I wish Mum would bloody well let me dye it.'

'Maybe you should just do it,' I said more forcefully than I intended.

She stared at me, her lips parted with surprise. 'What happened to Little Miss Righteous?'

I shrugged and smiled. We were united again, although this time against Mum.

Later, when I looked in the mirror, some of the petals of the peony had fallen off. How much better the flower had looked on the plant. I should have left it there. Guilt slithered inside my belly and joined Jealousy. But it wasn't the dying flower that was making me feel guilty; it was the memory of Martha's face as she stood with her hand out offering those tickets to no one.

The holiday began and we got used to our freedom. Mum took us on a trip to town and we argued over seeing *Rocky III* or *Annie* at the cinema. In the end, we watched both and had doughnuts in Debenhams afterwards.

On the first hot day, we decided to go for a picnic. Mum was lying down with a headache and a wet flannel laid across her forehead. There was no point asking for permission as we knew she'd make a fuss, so, helping ourselves to a packet of Scotch eggs, some sausage rolls and a Battenberg cake, we slipped out the door.

Tom, the road sweeper, was walking past. Tom had been around forever, always wearing a multicoloured scarf knitted by his mother, and pushing his barrow, with his spike, shovel and broom sticking out in unison like a trident. The perfect murder weapons, Rita said once, to pierce, to dig, to sweep away the soil.

Tom was only twenty-something, but to us he seemed older because he walked with a stoop. He had huge eyes but his gaze never stayed where it was supposed to, so you never knew whether he was looking at you, or even listening, which spoiled it for the teenagers in the village who liked to throw insults at him as well as stones. Now

Gabriella smiled and said hello as she always did; and he ignored her as he always did.

We trundled up Chestnut Hill planning to cut down the lane to the woods. The air smelled of mown grass and tiny flies buzzed in our faces. In the garden of the thatched cottage, a basket of wet clothes lay beneath the idle washing line. From inside the house came the thin cry of a small child. A lawnmower had been abandoned. One half of the grass was shaved, the other still long and untamed. Like a lopsided haircut.

'Human League,' I whispered to make Gabriella laugh. She clutched at her heart and grinned. Phil Oakey was the spit of the boy with the drowsy eyes in Our Price.

A dark red van was parked outside Lemon Tree Cottage. 'Dad,' we said at the same time and looked at each other. A delivery? It made sense. Everybody in the village bought furniture from the House of Flores.

'Shall we knock?' suggested Gabriella.

'What for?' I walked quickly past the gate and Gabriella followed. I didn't want to meet Edward Lily again. I was sure he'd recognised me in the baker's and would think I was spying. We'd gone a few steps further when a door slammed. We looked back. Dad was striding along the path. He opened the door of the van, jumped in and drove off down the lane, shaking up dust behind him.

We shrugged and wandered onwards through the woods, eating our picnic as we went. There was a route we always followed, a circular walk, using a lightning-split tree and a beech carved with graffiti as landmarks.

Voices ahead caused us to veer off in a direction we didn't usually take. The path here was a thin strip of hard ground that slashed through the trees like a pale, dry stream. The trees either side hooked up, making a gloomy passage that became denser as we walked until we reached a part where it was so overgrown, it was impossible to continue.

'Shall we go back?' I said, peering into the shadows, but Gabriella was already swerving off to one side. I watched her crashing through the undergrowth, her body disappearing bit by bit until she was submerged.

After a moment, I looked at my watch. It was silent in the shady woods, apart from the cry of a bird in the distance and a rustling in the bracken. I paced, kicking at roots and stones. I checked my watch again. Seven minutes had passed. And if you counted the minute that I hadn't looked that was eight. 'Gabriella?' I called. No answer and now the temperature had dropped. The sweat on my palms cooled. 'Gabriella?' I called again. Still nothing, but the whisper of a creature in the grass.

Feeling cold, I followed the way she'd gone. A mouse scurried across my path, making me step aside and stumble. Grabbing a bramble to right myself, I grimaced as the thorns pierced my skin and beads of blood bubbled to the surface. In a panic, I veered into the undergrowth. Fending off branches that sprang back into my face, I groped forward in the semi-light until a flash of colour halted me, and there, snagged on a bush, was a slither of material. *Like a necklace of rubies.* That's what Gabriella had said when she'd wound the scarf around her throat that morning, although to me it had looked like a trickle

92

of blood lacing her pale skin. I pulled the scrap loose and clutched it in my hands, my mind leaping with possibilities. She'd been kidnapped. A crazy person had taken her away.

A hand seized my shoulder. I gasped and turned, mouth open, ready to scream, but it was Gabriella. And now I wanted to yell and ask her why she'd left me on my own, but her finger was on her lips, and she was beckoning me. I took a deep breath and followed, my heart returning to its normal pace as we pushed through the bushes and reached the gap where she'd disappeared.

The forest floor stopped abruptly, dipping down to a clearing. All around the top of the dip, the trees formed a circle leaning across so their branches overlapped and shut out the light. There was an undergrowth of plants, a tangle of brambles covered in thorns, and bushes that gave way to a steep bank of dirt and stones that led to the dip itself.

'Look,' whispered Gabriella, indicating.

I blinked until my eyes were accustomed to the dark. A figure was kneeling by a fallen trunk on the far side of the clearing. It was Martha. She'd dug a hole in the ground and was lowering a shoebox inside. Now she was using her fingers to rake back the earth.

I gripped Gabriella's sleeve. Neither of us spoke. A crow called. Another answered. There was a stench of damp soil mixed with rotting vegetation. I expected a cloud of mist to rise, eclipsing us. I waited. Nothing happened. I shifted and a stone slid down the dip. We froze as Martha started and stared in our direction, searching blindly through the gloom, and we stayed silent, hidden,

93

watching as she pulled brambles over the place, and then scrambled upwards on the other side of the dip.

Now that Martha had gone the feeling of mystery went with her. I thought about my own shoebox, the one I kept hidden under the bed. It held nothing more than fossils and shells I'd collected from holiday, a few post-cards and pressed flowers. I doubted Martha's box was any more interesting than that.

'We could dig it up,' I said half-heartedly, and instantly regretted it when Gabriella laughed.

'What do you think you're going to find?' she said. 'This is Martha we're talking about. What do you think she's hidden?'

I looked away. I didn't want to say what was on my mind. A few months ago, Gabriella would have been the first to head down and take a look. I changed my expression, pretending not to care. 'I was joking,' I said, shrugging.

'No you weren't.'

'Yes I was.' I jumped up. 'Race you.' But she didn't run, she lagged behind while I pounded the path. And I realised that in future, I needed to be more careful with the things I said to Gabriella. She was changing and I had to adjust.

Mum was still in her room, sleeping, oblivious to the fact that we'd been gone. And when Dad got home, he dashed upstairs and the two of them remained closeted for an hour. Later, he heated curry and rice in the micro-wave and said us girls could eat in front of the telly for once watching *Top of the Pops*.

The novelty of the evening distracted me until I went to bed. Then, a vision of Martha crouching in the woods popped into my mind. What would someone like her hide? My mind dwelled on the possibilities: a diary, money, letters. It wasn't right to pry. And yet when I thought how Martha had tried to get Gabriella to go to the exhibition, I decided it would serve her right if I dug up her box. And besides, it was a secret and I didn't like secrets.

In the end I visualised myself sneaking back to the woods and executing my plan so strongly that by the time I closed my eyes it seemed as if it was done.

Early the next morning, I poked my head around Gabriella's door. She was sleeping on her side, one stripy pyjama-clad leg dangling out of the covers.

I left her there, and tiptoed downstairs, grabbed a trowel from the cupboard beneath the sink and left the house. Not bothering with breakfast, I crammed my pockets with ginger nuts which I ate as I made for the woods. I knew I might get into trouble when Mum found out I'd gone off on my own, but I didn't care. Besides, she seemed far more worried about Gabriella going out than me, even though I was the youngest. What did she think Gabriella was planning to do?

Lemon Tree Cottage sulked in silence as I hurried past. Nothing moved in the garden. No breeze stirred the trees or plants. I stole a look at the upstairs windows, but there was no sign of the mad girl staring through the glass.

Inside the woods, I moved quickly, flitting amongst

the trees, leaping over dead branches, roots and stones, sidestepping barbed-wire brambles, and clusters of fungi. After a few false turns, I found the pale path. The Pale Path. I liked that name. The ring of trees would be the Common Circle. The dip would be Devil's Dip. I teetered at the edge, crouched low and clambered down. At the bottom it seemed even darker than before, as if the canopy had thickened overnight. I waited for my eyes to get used to the gloom, and then headed for the place beside the fallen trunk. There was a pile of stones marking the spot, like a mini-tombstone.

Martha hadn't buried the box deep. I soon dug far enough to find it. Prising it out, I laid it on the ground. It was an ordinary shoebox like mine and for one moment I felt the weight of my conscience, telling me to put it back. I brushed off the dirt, my fingers scraping the lid. Around me the dark shapes of the undergrowth seemed to take a step closer as if urging me to go ahead. Quickly, before I changed my mind, I flicked the lid upwards.

The smell hit me first: a sweet, rotten stench. I covered my mouth to stop myself from retching. Inside the box was a brown twisted body covered in dried blood. I stared at the mangled creature and swallowed hard. I'd always suspected Martha was weird and now I knew for sure. Here was the proof. She'd killed her own guinea pig. She'd taken a hammer and smashed its skull. There it was with bits of bone poking through the fur. Nausea came back.

Controlling myself, I picked up the lid with finger and thumb, dropped it in place and shoved the box into the hole. The grave I'd disturbed gaped back at me. I should fill it in: Martha might come back. But my head was swimming and I leaned to one side and was sick.

Standing shakily, I wiped my mouth with the back of my hand and backed away. I couldn't touch it again. Besides, Martha should know she'd been found out. Why should she think her secret was safe? I clambered to the top of the dip wondering what Gabriella would say if she knew. Would she despise Martha as much as I did?

11

When I unhooked the trapdoor, the ladder came easily enough. The loft was lit by a single bulb that swung precariously from a length of thin wire. Clambering inside, I stepped gingerly across the boards to a pile of crates that I recognised as mine.

Opening one of them, I found books: Poe, Wilde, Brontë, Collins – tales of ghosts and madness. *King Lear*. *Macbeth*. My friends from university – closer than the students I'd liked but always kept at a distance.

It had been a relief the moment I arrived in London. Walking down the Mile End Road and into the gates of the college, I felt the freedom. People hadn't remembered the Flores case, or if they had, they hadn't connected it with me. I'd shed my role as the missing girl's sister, shuffled off the claustrophobic mantle of the village. I'd taken my place amongst the others on my course and become what I strived to be: unremarkable. And since nobody had truly known me, it had been easy to say goodbye when I left, easy to pick up new friends and lovers who knew even less.

Now, as I rifled through my books, and unearthed *Hamlet*, I imagined the loft brimming with voices of insanity and passion. I could add mine and nobody would hear.

The second crate contained the remnants of childhood: scruffy teddy bears and broken dolls; a menagerie of china animals and a scribbled diary that had fizzled out and become a book of poems, copied in my best handwriting.

My memories unwound. And like my father's old cine film, the images jerked and skidded and froze in a moment of action. Two girls hand in hand, running into the sea. Rolling down a hill. Feeding ducks. On swings. A serious face with loose light hair. A darker child with bandaged glasses.

I found an exercise book. Here were my notes, my list of suspects, a young girl's clumsy search for truth. I scanned the names: Edward Lily, Charlie Ellis, Stuart Henderson, Rupert Sullivan. How far was that a litany to the dead? And what about Tom? Poor Tom. Sacrificed and kicked out. Accused of taking my sister and even when he'd been exonerated, the label had stuck. He'd been branded a pervert, driven from the village. Who knew where he was now? And the women and the girls. Each of them were catalogued in my notebook, their movements cited, their connection with Gabriella there in black and white. Every person in the village had been a suspect. Every one of them, dead or alive, still was.

There was a metal trunk on the other side of the loft. I stepped across the floorboards still gripping the notebook. Inside were clothes, old dresses and shawls, a pair of frayed satin shoes. I pictured Mum wearing them, taking surreptitious looks at her feet. Beneath the clothes was an envelope of documents and a wooden box. I tried to open the box, but it was locked and there was no key. Intrigued, I took it, together with the envelope, and made my way back down the ladder.

Settling on the sofa, I studied the documents first, unfolding each one carefully. The life of my mother's parents, Grace and Bertrand Button, laid out on thin and yellowed paper marked with spots of mould. Their story seemed complete. Birth and marriage and death. All their certificates were pinned together. In comparison, there was hardly anything on Dad's side, which wasn't surprising since neither of his parents had been born in England. Much of his history had been lost.

Mum and Dad didn't appear to have been vigilant either. The only document I found of theirs was Mum's birth certificate. I rummaged around for a while looking for more before I gave up. I'd come across them eventually and it would be interesting to piece everything together, to create a family tree. I considered researching online, ordering the certificates, completing the set, until I remembered there was no Wi-Fi. Mum hadn't owned a computer.

I tugged at the lock on the wooden box again. It didn't budge. When Dad found a cupboard or a door he couldn't open during a house clearance, he'd picked the lock using a paper clip and a pair of pliers. Now, with an edge of guilt, I fetched the tools, tried his trick and the lock gave a satisfying click.

Inside, there was a christening bracelet wrapped up in blue velvet. The bracelet was beautifully made, with two tiny hearts each set with a minute green stone and *Gabriella* engraved on the front. I held it to my lips and let my breath mist the metal. Had Gabriella known it was hers? Had I been given one too? I didn't think so.

I sat there, trying to remember, chasing away my

resentment. Had my parents thought more of Gabriella than of me? No. I dismissed the thought. I was being petty, selfish and mean. What did it matter if they'd bought a bracelet for her only? They'd loved us both the same. And I was the second child. Everyone knew that the second child got less attention.

Later, I went to the cafe. The cars drove past with their headlights on and even though it was only two o'clock it felt like an early dusk.

It was raining and a woman pushing an old-fashioned pram stopped to fix the hood. She looked behind her, eyes searching anxiously, until a girl in a buttoned-up coat appeared and then she smiled with relief.

The bracelet was in my pocket. I took it out and cradled the tiny circle. It was wrong to be jealous, I told myself again. My parents had bought this gift for their first child; a daughter taken from them after fifteen years. Now they were gone and I was the only one left to care.

The rain grew heavier. A man in a suit barged through the door and collapsed his umbrella, opening and closing it to get rid of the spray; behind the counter came a hiss of steam, a clatter of crockery, loud laughter from the waitress as the two of them talked.

David appeared with a folded newspaper under his arm and gave his order at the counter. 'Sit in or take away?' the waitress asked. When he answered take away, I felt a drop of disappointment and drained my coffee.

On his way out, he spotted me and came across. 'I'd have offered if I'd seen you,' he said, glancing at my empty cup. 'Espresso?'

I smiled. Why not?

He put his plastic cup and paper bag on the table and came back with coffee and a Danish pastry. I raised my eyebrows when he put them in front of me. 'I thought you looked hungry,' he said, sitting down and smiling awkwardly. He turned to the waitress and lifted his cup in a questioning gesture. When she waved and nodded permission, he prised off the lid, blew on the liquid and drank.

'How's the clearance?' he said.

I considered for a moment before saying, 'Intense.'

He laughed warmly. 'That's exactly the right word.' He glanced at the half-done crossword in his newspaper. 'I could do with a few more of those. Three across: *The capital of Italy, supposedly*. And the answer isn't Rome.'

I made a face. 'Don't ask me then. I'm useless at crosswords, especially if they're cryptic.'

'This is the quick crossword – supposedly.'

'Well, it could be anything. Ancient, touristy, holy.'

He smiled, opened the paper bag and inspected its contents. Pulling out a pie, he held it up to the waitress. She shook her head, amused, and wafted her hand to show she didn't care.

'Seven letters. Fifth letter N.'

'Is that all you've got?'

He shrugged. 'I'm useless at crosswords too. Don't know why I do them.'

'Brain food.'

'Maybe.'

There was a lull while David ate. He wore a checked shirt and had missed a button. I stopped myself from pointing it out and focused on his face instead. Stubble suited him. He was definitely more attractive than I'd given him credit for. Funny too. Was he married? Picking an almond from the cake and nibbling the end, I took a quick glance at his left hand. Single then. Although you could never really tell.

The woman with the pram was coming back. The little girl had opened a huge umbrella and was being blown along by the wind. I watched as they made their way along the road, and when I turned, David had paused mid-bite and was studying me with an enquiring expression. I realised I was smiling. 'She reminds me of someone,' I said and felt my stomach grip as I thought about what I'd said. Which one: the woman or the girl? Gabriella the child that was, or Gabriella the mother that would never be?

Tears threatened and I hoped David hadn't noticed. I didn't get away with it so easily. He put down the remains of his pie and spoke quietly beneath the sounds in the cafe. 'I'm sorry about your mother. It can't be easy doing things alone.'

The unexpectedness of his comment caused the tears to come again. 'Thank you,' I replied, blinking hard.

He started on about the clearance again, predicting how long it would take to finish, offering advice and extra help, from him and his lads. He had plenty of contacts, he told me, and more importantly a van. 'A man with a van,' he said, finishing his coffee, 'can shift anything.' He glanced at his watch. 'Fancy a drink?'

For a moment I was taken aback. 'It's a bit early,' I said.

He grinned. 'It's never too early.'

What was I supposed to say since I pretty much thought the same? Casting about for a proper excuse, I told him I'd been planning to go to the library. It was partly true since my intention was to go there in the next day or two to use their Wi-Fi. Why not bring it forward?

He waved his hand in dismissal. 'Library? Pub? Is there a contest?'

I gave a smile. 'Maybe another time.'

He didn't move, only smoothed out the paper bag and folded it into squares. 'I'd like that,' he said finally.

And suddenly I realised I'd like that too.

After he'd gone I sat for a few more minutes gazing out at the passers-by. An old man trudging along, hands in the pockets of his greatcoat. A couple of teenage girls, arm in arm and giggling as they passed. A boy. Moody. Kicking at the pavement. A never-ceasing stream of people. It was endless. Perpetual. Eternal. I smiled at the answer to David's crossword clue. And then I saddened: so many people; so many different lives. No wonder some of them went missing.

12

1982

The image of the guinea pig stuck in my head. At tea-time, I gazed at the slices of tongue on my plate and asked to be excused. Mum let me go without question. She and Dad were quiet, so I guessed their problem hadn't been resolved.

I slept badly, waking several times through the night, each time remembering the broken, bloodied body. I lay in the darkness, desperate to go into Gabriella's room to tell her what I'd seen, but each time I convinced myself to confess, I thought of her slow, reproachful gaze and her words: *Don't you feel sorry for anyone?*

The next morning, when I went downstairs, Gabriella was still in bed. Mum was in the kitchen on her hands and knees, scrubbing the oven. She'd already scoured the racks that now stood gleaming on the draining board and I noticed she'd emptied out a cupboard of pots and pans ready to be cleaned.

'Can we go into town today?' I asked, trying to be casual and taking a piece of cold toast from the rack.

Mum pulled her head from the oven and wrung out a cloth in a bucket of soapy water. She pulled at the fingers of her Marigolds with a plop and, ignoring my question, asked me to sit down.

'I've been meaning to have a word,' she said.

I had a vision of the dead guinea pig and my stomach clenched.

'It's only . . .' Mum stopped. Maybe I should confess before she spoke again. 'She's of a certain age.'

I stared at her. 'Who?'

'Gabriella.' She tugged a lock of her hair. 'She's of a certain age when she does things.'

'What things?' Now I was certain she wasn't talking about the guinea pig, I took a bite of toast.

Mum spoke rapidly. 'Look, Anna. I'm worried about your sister. I think she might be doing things that we – me and your father – might not like.'

I couldn't think of anything Gabriella had done wrong – apart from smoking. Had they found out about that?

'Can you help me, Anna?'

'How?'

'Let me know if you see her talking to anyone . . . I mean, anyone we don't know.' She smiled brightly. 'Is that all right?'

I opened my mouth to say that it wasn't, but the words disappeared with my breath. It was the way Mum looked at me – intense and sad at the same time. The feeling that something drastic had happened swept through me. I sighed heavily and nodded, chewed my toast half-heartedly. I was lying. I had no intention of spying on my sister, or at least I had no intention of reporting back to Mum.

Later, Mum finished the oven and the pots and pans, and cleaned the bathroom, bleaching every tile on the wall, scrubbing the bath as if she'd take the colour off.

Gabriella didn't emerge from her room until lunch-time. She wandered sleepily into the kitchen, still in her pyjamas, while Mum was making sandwiches, cutting the bread with fierce jagged strokes. She barely looked up when Gabriella appeared and although I was expecting Mum to yell about wasting the whole morning, she didn't say a word.

Belinda Stock's parents had got divorced last year. She'd described in detail the rows they'd had, the plate smashing and yelling and clothes thrown from windows. Nothing like that had happened with my parents, but there were other scenarios to consider. Jane Taylor's dad had gone to buy a packet of Silk Cut from the corner shop and disappeared for three months. Her mum had cleaned the house from top to bottom and side to side until finally he'd come home.

The cleaning was familiar enough, so in the evening, after tea, I followed Dad into the garden. I found him leaning against the damson tree smoking. For a few moments, we stayed in silence. I was reluctant to ask my question. In an instant *yes* or *no* could change my life.

Finally, I spoke. 'Dad. Is something wrong?'

He looked at me. 'Why do you say that, Anna?' And when I shrugged, 'There's nothing for you to worry about. Nothing that will affect you.'

I took a breath. 'Is it because of Mum? Are you . . .' I hesitated. 'Are you getting a divorce?'

He threw away his cigarette, swung round and grabbed my shoulders. 'No,' he said, lowering his face until it was level with mine. 'Your mother and I would never do that. Whatever happens, we love each other. And we love you too. You and Gabriella. Nothing can alter that.' I nodded. I wanted so much to believe him. I wanted it so badly, I didn't move. I didn't tell him how much he was hurting me, his fingers digging into my flesh.

In the morning, despite Dad's promises, nothing seemed to have changed. Mum's face was white, her eyes glittering. Dad was unshaved and late for work.

He roused himself when I appeared and stood unsteadily. Mum followed him out the room and they talked in low voices. I strained to catch what they were saying, but all I heard was Mum telling him to stay away. Stay away from what?

Mum stopped cleaning and moved on to clearing out the cupboard under the stairs, making piles of old raincoats and broken toys. I offered to help, and she accepted, holding up each item for my opinion: a deflated space hopper, a set of plastic Wombles still in their packets. Her mood lightened until she found an old pair of sandals that had belonged to Gabriella.

My chest tightened as I watched her crying. I fetched a tissue from the box in the living room. And when I gave it to her, she touched my hair. I leaned against her hand, wanting to ask her what was wrong, but I was too afraid to hear her answer, so I stayed silent, waiting for her to speak. She drew me against her chest, and I breathed in the scent of her perfume, Lily of the Valley, the one she always wore. Dad had said there was no divorce. How honest had he been? Why else would Mum be so upset?

Mum sighed and blew her nose. 'I'm sorry, Anna. I'm being silly. It's these sandals. Look at them.' She tried to smile. 'Wouldn't it be lovely if things stayed the same?'

I volunteered to go and fetch Dad, but Mum shook her head, and when I suggested finding Gabriella, she only cried again.

By lunchtime, Mum had bagged up the unwanted items from the cupboard and was in the kitchen making chutney. I decided to give her a test, asking questions about weekends and holidays and scrutinising her response. She answered fully and with no suggestion that our future as a family was about to be cut short. I concluded Mum had a secret, but not necessarily plans for divorce.

The trouble was, now I had two secrets of my own: Martha's shoebox and Mum's request for me to spy. I badly wanted to share both with Gabriella.

She was in her bedroom, dressed up and spraying her hair with a can of Harmony. I asked her where she was going and when she replied, 'Nowhere', my stomach dropped. It was the kind of answer she gave to my parents, not to me.

'Can I come?' I said in an optimistic voice.

She knotted a yellow scarf and laced a studded belt. 'Not today. People to see.' I sniffed loudly, and as if to recompense, she threw me a bangle. I took it and slipped it on my wrist. 'And don't tell Mum I've gone out,' she said. 'You know what she's like. Especially recently. Tell her I'm doing my homework and don't want to be disturbed.'

'She's not going to believe that.'

'Tell her I'm in the garden then. Anything.'

I agreed to do as she asked, but as soon as the front door closed, I followed. I'd spy like Mum had asked me to, though I wouldn't tell her what I found. At the gate, my plan took a tumble. Mrs Henderson and Brian blocked my way.

'Is your mother in?' said Mrs Henderson primly. 'I'm here to offer my services for the fête.'

Beside her, Brian shifted awkwardly. Neither of us were looking at Mrs Henderson. We were both gazing after Gabriella disappearing down the street.

'Well?' Mrs Henderson's face loomed in front of mine. She was waiting for an answer.

I took one last look along the street, empty now of Gabriella, and reluctantly opened the door. Mum appeared, her face dropping when she saw who it was, but she invited them through to the kitchen anyway. Good manners. Another of her rules. And hospitality. Although in their case it didn't extend to a seat in the living room.

The code of conduct didn't apply to me. If Brian thought I'd entertain him, he had another thing coming. I flounced off, leaving him no choice but to follow his mother. And I passed the time watching telly and flicking through magazines, waiting for them to go.

Eventually, the front door banged. Mum was muttering to herself about not needing any help from *that woman* as she poked her head around the door and asked about Gabriella.

'She's upstairs,' I said, not taking my eyes away from

Danger Mouse who was saving humanity from Baron Greenback's plan to flood the world with custard.

Mum nodded but didn't comment. As she left again, I wondered if I could persuade her to let us have jam roly-poly again for tea. With custard.

The credits rolled. I yawned. Most of my friends were on holiday. They were lucky, especially the ones who'd made it abroad. Even our usual trip to north Wales had been cancelled. 'Your father says we shouldn't go this year,' Mum had said when I'd asked her why. 'He thinks we need to save our money.'

'What for?' She'd shrugged and looked away. More secrets.

Still, as far as I knew, Belinda Stock was home, so I let myself out without telling Mum. Not that she'd be bothered about *me* going out. She only cared about where Gabriella went.

The day was baking hot and I quickly regretted my tight jeans and long-sleeved Snoopy top (fifteen pence from the jumble sale). Belinda lived near school in a modern house with a dormer window. There was no answer when I rang, but I stood in the porch for a good five minutes anyway, pushing on the bell and thinking that if I stayed there long enough, she'd come.

Eventually, I gave up, strolled to the end of the road and then on to the top of Acer Street. Tom walked by on the other side, the wheels of his cart rumbling on the pavement. He stopped beneath a tree and looked up. A bird was singing in its branches. I listened too, identifying a blackbird. I was about to move on when a door slammed. I glanced idly down the houses to see who it was. Gabriella was coming out of Martha's house. I gaped as she fixed on her Walkman and sauntered off in the direction of home. As if visiting Martha was the most natural thing in the world.

A few seconds later, the front door opened again. This time Martha appeared with a shopping bag. She walked towards me. It was too late to hide. Fiddling with my glasses, I took a step as if I'd been moving all along, but it didn't fool Martha and she gave me a sly smile as she passed.

At home, I stomped upstairs and into Gabriella's room. 'What's up?' she said, putting down her copy of *NME*.

Biting my lip, I tried to ignore the worm of jealousy trapped inside my belly. I put my hand there to still the feeling, but it wouldn't go away. 'You didn't tell me you were going to see Martha,' I said accusingly.

Gabriella frowned. 'Why did I need to?'

'Because I always tell you what I do.'

'Do you?' She stared back at me.

For a moment, I regretted asking, but it was too late now. And besides, I was bitten with curiosity. 'So when did you arrange it?'

'I didn't. I was going to Bernadette's but changed my mind when I met Martha.'

'You met her?'

'Yes, but I didn't mean to. She was just there.'

Martha was never just there. Gabriella knew her reputation as well as I did. 'Where?'

'On the street. Sitting outside her house. What is this? I told you before, Anna. I feel sorry for her.'

Gabriella rolled her eyes and started reading again. Knowing I was being stupid, I hovered by the window, chewing my nails, desperate for more details.

'Was her mum there?' I said.

'No,' said Gabriella, her eyes not moving from the page.

'Her dad?'

Now she looked at me. 'No. He's gone away.'

I was glad about that. I didn't like to think of him being with Gabriella. Still, I wanted to know. 'Where?'

'No idea. I didn't ask.'

I scowled. 'He was probably in the pub. He's always there.'

'Well, he wasn't in the pub today. He'd gone off somewhere with his work. Martha said. And their car was gone.'

'What? The Morris Minor?'

She rolled her eyes. 'For God's sake, what's wrong with you? Why do you care?' Fumbling under her pillow, she pulled out a handful of sweets and threw me a Bazooka Joe. 'Forget it, Anna. I don't like Martha more than I like you. I feel sorry for her. That's it.'

Glumly, I unwrapped the pink slab of gum and stuck it in my mouth. A few months ago, we'd have sat down and gone through every move Martha had made. Now I was ignored. On my own. I contemplated how I was going to get through the rest of the summer holidays with no friends and no sister to be with. If only I could whisk Gabriella away to the middle of nowhere, like the cottage in Wales, and have her all to myself. It would solve everything.

At teatime, I brought up the question. Why weren't we going away this year like everyone else in the village had done?

'We're saving money,' said Dad, wearily sawing his pork chop. 'I thought your mum explained that.'

'Yes, but what for?' I looked at Mum.

'Nothing you need to worry about,' she said quietly.

I sighed, thinking about all those times I'd complained about our trips to Wales. Now there was nothing I wanted more than to sit on a stony beach with Gabriella in the rain, eating sandwiches and waiting for the sun to come out. The two of us, away from annoying people like Martha. Away from the miserable atmosphere that was taking over our house.

I was about to start complaining again when Dad cleared his throat. 'This might be a good time to tell you . . .' He glanced across at Mum and then back at us. 'We're thinking about moving house.'

I lost my ability to speak. *Moving house*, my lips mimed. I'd lived here all my life. 'Why?' I said, finding a word at last.

'We're thinking of making a change.' He looked down at his plate.

'But where will we go?'

'Maybe London – near to Uncle Thomas.'

'But London's expensive. You always say that.'

'Not all of it . . . and we might stay with your uncle for a bit, until we get sorted out.'

Gabriella was staring at Dad now, fork suspended halfway to her mouth, face etched with disbelief. 'You aren't serious,' she said.

'What about school?' I chimed in.

'We might get you into a grammar,' said Dad.

'But you hate grammar schools.'

'If it makes you happy.'

'It won't make me happy. And what about the House of Flores? We can't leave that.'

Dad looked at me sadly and shook his head. 'Sorry, Anna. But you'll see, it'll be for the best.' He turned to Gabriella. 'How does it sound to you?'

'Rubbish. I've got O levels.'

Dad rubbed his chin. 'I know that, but—'

Gabriella dropped her fork. 'I can't change school now, can I, Mum?'

Mum shook her head, but didn't reply to Gabriella. Instead she spoke to Dad. 'It's not feasible, is it?'

'We can make it—'

'No, we can't, Albert. And what's the point? It won't solve anything.'

Gabriella's chair scraped on the floor as she stood. 'I'm not going anywhere,' she said, giving Dad a deadly look. 'You can't expect me to leave my school now. Or my friends. I won't go.'

She left the room and I held my breath as my parents exchanged a glance I wasn't supposed to understand.

13

The library was an old building that perched on the edge of the village. I recalled the librarian prowling the narrow aisles with one finger pressed perpetually to her lips. The place had been dark and atmospheric with corners perfect for skulking children to swap sweets and secrets. Perfect for me to pick out tales of adventure set in boarding schools, in jungles or on seas; and then to slide into the adults' aisles to find poetry and Poe.

Now the place was brighter and had the addition of several computers and a young male librarian with a beard and a cheerful manner. I settled down and googled an ancestry site, paid a temporary subscription on the first one that came up and typed in Albert Flores. There were three results: birth, marriage and death. I tapped my fingers on the keys and found my grandparents. Hannah and Luis, married in 1932. And their first child, Thomas Flores, his birth and death. For Gabriella Flores, there was one result – birth.

'Anna.' I jumped at the tap on my shoulder. It was Rita, clutching a book.

I minimised the screen. 'No Wi-Fi at home,' I said, pre-empting her question.

'I'm not surprised. Esther wasn't one for computers. Next time, come and use mine.'

'Thanks.' I gave her a smile.

'How about I check this in and we walk out together?'

She dropped her voice. 'It's a week overdue, but I'm hoping he won't notice.' She nodded over at the librarian and I looked at the title of her book. *Dead Man's Folly*. Still reading crime.

While she was busy negotiating her fine, I ordered copies of Dad's birth and death certificates and my parents' wedding certificate and joined her at the entrance. 'Which way are you going?' said Rita.

I cast about for a destination. 'The churchyard.' I hadn't been there since the funeral. I should go and check the flowers.

'Perfect,' said Rita, as if she'd been planning the same. 'I'll come with you. There's always something to do in the church.'

We set off. The rain had stopped, but there was a chill in the air and as we walked I dreamed of a balmy autumn in Athens and wondered when I'd get back there. My return to England had already been far longer than I'd anticipated. What would happen to my job? I'd asked for a leave of absence, but how long would they wait?

Rita interrupted my thoughts. 'I've been doing my family tree for years,' she said and gave me a sidelong look. 'I find it best to focus on one generation at a time.' There was a pause and when I didn't respond, 'What are you looking at first?'

'I'm not sure,' I said vaguely. 'I've only just started.'

'Well, I don't know if you've considered this, or how important it is to you, but . . .' She stopped as a woman in a tea-cosy hat approached, smiled at Rita, and glanced curiously at me. Rita waited until she'd gone. 'As far as I know your mother never applied for a death certificate.'

117

'What do you mean?'

'For . . . Gabriella. She didn't apply for death *in absentia*. So, she's not on the register.'

Why was she telling me this? I'd guessed that Mum wouldn't have done that. 'I didn't think she was,' I said.

Rita nodded and folded her shawl tighter. 'I thought I'd mention it just in case.'

We continued in silence although I had the feeling that Rita had more to say. Whatever it was brooded between us until we reached the lychgate where she stopped and straightened her glasses. 'There's something else.'

I said nothing as we stood beneath the entrance to the graveyard, with the grey church looming at the end of the path. The organist was practising, the music reaching a crescendo and fading away. A red kite wheeled overhead.

We watched the bird as it was joined by another, and the two of them swooped simultaneously in the field beyond. 'Poor thing,' I said out loud, thinking of a field mouse being ripped to shreds.

'Carrion,' said Rita. 'They eat carrion.'

There were a few beats while the two of us kept our eyes fixed on the empty sky, both putting off, I supposed, whatever it was Rita wanted to say. I might have helped her out, prompting her to continue, but suddenly I didn't want to know.

I had no choice because she began again, speaking in a rush as if she'd been storing her thoughts and had memorised them. 'Sometimes our parents don't tell us things for a reason, well-founded, or ill-founded. If we pick through their lives, we have to take the consequences. Be forgiving, Anna. That's all I'm saying.' And she looked at me with an intensity I hadn't seen before.

What did she mean? What would I need to forgive? What might I discover? It wasn't as if I was trying to catch my parents out. 'I don't understand,' I said at last. 'I'm not looking for anything in particular.'

'Aren't you?' She fixed her gaze on me and then relaxed. Patting my hand, she said, 'Don't worry. It'll be fine. Mark my words. Come and see me if you need anything – computers, advice, anything.' She strode towards the church, waving her hand as she went.

I stared after her, confused by not knowing what she meant and the feeling that I should. Steadying myself, I made my way to a bench on the opposite side of the graveyard beneath a line of beech trees. Here a mass of gravestones spread out before me. So many lost people scattered underneath. Some of the gravestones were broken and cracked; others were elaborate with carvings of angels, some so small they made your heart constrict. After a few moments the church door creaked and Rita reappeared with one of the ladies. They bustled out and disappeared around the side of the building.

Two minutes more and they returned with a watering can, and this time, Rita gave me a wide wave. I waved back and dwelled again on what she'd said. Had she been talking from experience? Maybe she'd discovered a terrible secret when she'd been searching her own family tree and that was why she'd warned me about mine. But no, it had been more specific, more personal than that. More deliberate. What did she think I'd find?

Once the church door had slammed, the graveyard fell into silence again. I stood, stamping my feet for warmth, and wandered past the spindly trees and bushes, the unkempt grass and tombs, to a better kept area, where the more recently buried lay. The stone on my parents' grave had been taken away to add my mother's name and in the meantime had been replaced by a simple wooden cross. I spent time clearing the dead flowers. I needed to lay down fresh ones. What else did people do to tend a grave?

I looked around for inspiration. The other graves had bunches of tulips and roses, while a few were covered in heather. Low maintenance for people who couldn't or wouldn't visit. That would be me once I disappeared to Greece. I should speak to Rita, ask her to look after my parents' grave for me.

I moved on, making my way through the criss-cross of paths and reading the headstones. There were familiar surnames: Henderson. Stock. Sullivan. Past generations – parents and grandparents of children from my school. Here a younger brother, or an older sister. The tragedy of sibling loss.

Nearby, a grave covered in blue and grey stones caught my eye. Leaning down, I read the name: Edward Lily. Of course his grave would be here. There was no mention of his role as husband or father, only the dates of his life and death.

In one corner, a group of headstones clustered together. They might have been well looked after once, but now they were choked with nettles and long grass as if there was no one left who cared. Here was a cracked pot, there an upturned metal vase. And all of the stones were engraved with the same family name. Ellis. I peered to look. The family had been in the village for generations. Was there no one left to tend their graves – apart from Martha? Perhaps she didn't think about it. Some people didn't. Soon I wouldn't. Unless Rita agreed to my request, my parents' graves would be as neglected as these.

How miserable it was here. A host of forgotten people. Their bodies mouldering, their minds gone. And how morbid I'd become. What had brought me to this place, wandering around graveyards thinking about the dead? Once I'd played hide and seek here with Gabriella while we'd waited for our mother to finish in the church. It had been a happy place. A playground not a graveyard. We hadn't known that Life transformed into Death, that Loss was a menace that sneaked up without warning.

One of the graves was damaged. I bent down to examine it more closely and instantly recoiled. The stone bore an inscription I could just about read: Charles Stanley Ellis and Dorothy Maureen Ellis. There were no other words, but it was the state of them that shocked me. Letters half scraped away, as if someone had tried to gouge them out, and the rest of the stone was punctured with holes, like a frenzied stabbing.

An engine starting made me jump, but it was only a man pushing a mower on the other side of the churchyard. I considered telling him about the grave, or perhaps I should mention it to Rita.

Nicholas appeared at the lychgate with his motorbike helmet under his arm. I hadn't seen him since the funeral, although he'd suggested I came for a chat or to a Sunday service any time I was free. So far I'd avoided it and now, since he hadn't seen me, I wouldn't attract his attention. He'd know about the state of the graves anyway. Vandalism was a common problem. It always had been in this village. In the past.

The church door cracked open and shut as Nicholas stepped inside. A gloom had settled on the graves. I'd hardly noticed how quickly the afternoon had gone and how fast the temperature was dropping. The cold crawled right through my clothes. I shivered, buttoned my jacket tightly and blew on my hands.

There was movement at the side of the church. Was it a shadow, a tree shaking in the wind, or Rita, back to collect water, or something else? I shivered again.

Bored teenagers, I told myself as I walked back to the lychgate. They would have desecrated the grave. And no one had liked the Ellis family. Charlie Ellis was a bully. And a drunk. Mrs Ellis might have been a victim, but she'd been unpleasant too. For a short time, she'd redeemed herself as a witness, but her story had been inaccurate and then it had become nothing more than an archive file. If she'd been alive, I would have found her. I'd have made her tell the story once again. The fact that she was dead like so many others from the village made the whole possibility of truth slip backwards even further.

Shaking off my thoughts, I passed through the lychgate. Behind me the wind sighed. I looked back. And the light at the side of the church darkened.

14

1982

The last few days of the holiday were made miserable by the threat of moving house. Gabriella refused to discuss it. 'It's not going to happen,' she kept saying. 'They always say we'll do things and we don't.' I listened but I didn't agree. In my opinion our parents did the opposite. If they made a decision, it happened. Maybe not this year because of Gabriella's exams, but next.

I convinced myself moving was a good idea, listing the things that were bad about the village and imagining instead being in London and finding the grammar school Dad had talked about. I imagined a grand new church for us to go to, like St Paul's Cathedral. I might even learn to play the organ. I wasn't sure why London would be able to offer me that, but I liked the idea, so I kept it.

On the first day of the autumn term, I stepped into the concrete school block and comforted myself with the thought that I'd be leaving soon. I was an alien jostling along with the rest of the reluctant kids, through corridors that already smelled of sweaty PE socks and the fear of first years trying to blend in.

Lessons were my refuge as I hid between the pages of the textbooks. In English we had a new teacher, a thin woman with dark hair and pale skin who had a passion for Joyce, Shaw and Yeats. Her name was Miss O'Dell and she was *as Irish as they come*, or so she told us when she'd come into the classroom and found the words *IRA scum* scrawled across the board. She introduced Shake-speare: 'Hath not a Jew eyes? Hath not a Jew hands, organs, dimensions?' she recited, fixing us with her needle stare.

The following Saturday was the day of the fête and for that I was happy to be in the village. I woke up and ran downstairs to the kitchen. Mum and Rita were packing jam into cardboard boxes ready for Dad to load into the van and transport to the green. There were jars all over the kitchen table: glossy yellow, red and black, each topped with different-coloured chequered hats according to its contents.

I waited for instruction. Mum seemed harassed. She shoved a packet of Rice Krispies in my direction and told me to sit down and eat. I sat quietly, one eye on the pro-ceedings and the other on the poetry book lent to me by Miss O'Dell. At least Mum had forgotten the rule about no reading at the table. Upstairs, the thud of Gabriella's music signalled she was awake.

Mum glanced at the ceiling, but didn't comment. She closed one of the boxes. 'Where's Albert?' she said. 'He should be here by now.'

Jasper made an appearance instead, sliding around the open back door, leaping onto the table and licking his paws. Rita pushed him down. 'Sorry, puss,' she said. I narrowed my eyes and finished off my cereal. It was all right for one of us to do that, but Rita? Surprised and disgruntled, Jasper leapt onto my lap. I stroked him,

trying to make him stay. Every now and then he made a
bid for freedom. I knew Rita would give him another
push if he jumped up again, so I clung on hard and
coaxed him into submission with quiet words I read
from my book. 'Tread softly because you tread on my
dreams,' I said as Jasper kneaded my thighs.

They carried on packing the boxes while Mum fussed
about the time and Rita told her to stay calm and that
getting worked up wouldn't help. 'It's only a local delivery,' she said.

'If that's where he's gone,' muttered Mum.

Looking up from my book, I caught the two of them
exchanging glances. Where would Dad be if he wasn't
working?

At last the boxes were sealed and Mum sat at the
table with an exaggerated thump. She twisted her wedding ring, taking it off, putting it on again, while Rita
tried to distract her, talking about her latest murder
mystery evening. 'You'd never have believed it,' she said.
'Stuart Henderson with the lead piping in the library.'
I believed it. Mr Henderson was squat and hefty. If his
wife was a vinegar bottle, he was a flagon of beer.

The front door opened and slammed. Heavy footsteps
in the hall. Dad marched into the kitchen, straight to
the sink, turned on the tap and stuck one hand under the
water.

'What have you done?' said Mum, rushing forward
while Jasper leapt down with a yowl as my hands automatically gripped his fur.

Dad was breathing heavily, his back rigid as he leaned
across the sink. 'Nothing I shouldn't have done before,'

he said. His voice was tight as if his mouth was full of things he didn't want to say. He didn't sound like Dad. He didn't look like himself either when he turned to face the room, his eyes sparking anger. My heart thumped. What had happened?

'I told you to stay away,' hissed Mum as she grabbed his hand and examined the back of it.

He didn't answer. I glanced at Rita. She was standing too, her lips pressed closed and her hands clasped. She didn't speak, and yet, the way she looked, her eyes full of knowledge, I thought she knew exactly what my dad had done. Had he had a fight? Was that possible? Dad was the negotiator, the pacifist. That's how Mum always described him.

Now Mum was wrapping his hand in a tea towel. Both of their faces were white and Mum was swallowing, trying not to cry.

'We need to go,' said Dad abruptly. 'Anna, fetch Gabriella.'

I got up, my legs trembling as I walked to the door.

'We should stay at home,' said Mum. I stopped.

'No, Esther. Damn it, no. Why should we change what we do?'

'We've got no choice. We need to speak first.'

'Not yet.' Dad stopped and looked at me. 'Anna. I asked you to get Gabriella.'

I stepped into the hall and, leaning my forehead against the wall, took a breath. They were still talking. Dad's voice low and insistent. Mum's uncertain and afraid.

'Nothing's going to happen,' said Dad.

'You don't know that. You don't know anything. Everything's changed. We need to speak first.'

'No. Trust me. I've sorted it out.'

'With a threat? With violence? How's that going to help? It will make things worse. Rita, tell him.'

Rita said something I didn't catch. Dad ended the conversation. 'All right. Tonight. Now, we'll carry on as usual. Please, Esther. One more day.'

I peered through the gap in the door. Mum nodded briefly before taking off her apron and placing it on the side.

It was warm for September and the green pulsed with people. Women wandered about in loose print dresses; men in shirtsleeves stood in groups; children weaved amongst the tables and the bunting. The noise intensified as we pushed our way through. People yelled above the jangling of the merry-go-round and the music from the stalls. 'That's the way to do it,' shrieked Punch from the puppet stand.

I grabbed Gabriella's arm, afraid she'd slip away. Mum had told us to stay close and now, after what had happened, I intended to obey. We talked about the incident with Dad. I described the scene, but I could tell that Gabriella wasn't taking me seriously.

'Have you ever seen Dad get angry?' she said. 'Let alone punch anyone?'

She was right, it was difficult to believe. And by the time I'd been through all the people in the village he might have had a fight with, the idea was wearing off. Gabriella wasn't even listening. She was too busy looking around to see if the boy with the drowsy eyes from Our Price had come. I hoped not. There were enough boys hanging around as it was. Not surprising. Gabriella looked amazing, like she should be on an album cover, in her black and yellow polka-dot dress and boots, a slash of red on her lips.

We arrived at the centre of the fête as the brass band struck up. Men in red uniforms and peak hats marched in formation, playing trumpets and trombones. A group of Gabriella's friends appeared and tried to call her away, but she shook her head as I clung on. And I was grateful for that.

The band stopped and was replaced with a troupe of country dancers. We moved to the sweet stall – jars of rhubarb and custards and pear drops and aniseed twists. We chose a selection and crunched our way to where the tug of war was assembling: beefy men rolling up their shirtsleeves, leaning backwards in red-faced unison.

At around three o'clock, Dad, who'd been walking alone, doing circuits of the green, caught up with us at the jam stall. He was going to the beer tent. Mum gave him a look and opened her mouth as if to protest, but he stopped her. 'We do the same every year and this year will be no different.' He turned to us, 'Stay together, you two.' As he moved away, Gabriella rolled her eyes.

It was true that the men, including Dad, always escaped to the beer tent – a few lone stragglers at first, and then crowds of them, piling in. There was shouting and lots of laughter; the occasional argument that slid up the pole of seriousness as the afternoon wore on, like a game of ring the bell.

Now we bought candyfloss and ate it next to the coconut shy. I'd persuaded Gabriella to go on the merry-go-round when a figure appeared. The sun was behind her, but I knew it was Martha. It was the way she stooped low as if trying not to be seen.

I hoped Gabriella would ignore her. Instead she chatted, offered candyfloss, asked her to go on the ride. I gritted my teeth waiting for Martha's reply. Luckily, she shook her head and refused, although she stayed anyway, fiddling around with the pocket in her dress, looking like she wanted to speak, even though she had nothing to say. Finally, she mumbled about meeting her mum and disappeared. Gabriella gave me a look as if it was my fault, but for once I didn't care.

It was the same merry-go-round as last year, and the year before that and probably the year before that. I recognised the red and yellow dome criss-crossed with bright coloured bulbs, and the column in the centre decorated with organ pipes and golden cupids. It was the same boy in charge too. Black-haired and dark-eyed with a wide grin and a wink for Gabriella. We paid and I got on first, choosing a blue and white horse with startled eyes. In front of me a small girl with a short white dress and frilly knickers was scrambling onto a pink pony. Her mother was hovering, jumping off at the last minute as the music came on and we started to rotate.

The pace picked up. I swivelled in my seat, searching for Gabriella. A man in a cap sat behind me, quietly smoking a pipe. A boy in shorts was beside him, clinging to the twisted silver pole. I looked about me anxiously.

Where had Gabriella gone? And then I spotted her standing at the side chatting to the dark-haired boy. I swallowed hard and held back my tears. She'd changed her mind, or else she hadn't wanted to get on in the first place.

The ride spun faster. The volume of the jangling music grew. Gabriella disappeared again. I craned my neck to see where she'd gone and caught a glimpse of her figure walking across the green, back the way we'd come, to look for the boy from Our Price, I guessed. She was always leaving me on my own. Like the time she'd gone off to Martha's.

And now the music jarred. The horses were shabby and seemed smaller than they'd been the year before. The spin was sluggish. The merry-go-round was childish. No wonder Gabriella hadn't bothered. And when the ride finished at last, I peeled myself off the horse and stumbled to the edge of the platform, pushing past the anxious mother. I was stupid. The ride was for babies and their parents.

The mood of the fête had changed. Young women paraded past the beer tent waving at the young men inside. Older women and children sat under trees on blankets, delving into picnic hampers for last-minute treats. Off to the side, a group of boys were playing football. Teenagers lay on the grass listening to a ghetto blaster: 'Come on Eileen' full blast. The band had come to a standstill; its members shading beneath the stretch of the cedar tree, hats off, instruments resting beside them. Even the merry-go-round had stopped and a man in overalls crawled between the horses.

I spotted Dad in the beer tent, showing no sign of his earlier rage. I wandered closer. Martha stood to one side of the entrance, with her back to me. I scowled. Did she know where my sister was? I didn't want to ask, but I had no choice.

'Have you seen Gabriella?' I said.

Martha turned. She seemed different somehow. Her hair was tied back awkwardly with a scarf. She reached up self-consciously, took a strand that had fallen loose and wound it around her fingers. I recognised Gabriella's gesture and my anger ignited. 'So, where is she?' I snapped.

'How should I know?' she said, glaring back resentfully.

I looked away, trying not to give Martha the satisfaction of thinking she had information that I wanted. Clenching my fists, I counted in my head. I wouldn't ask again.

Shouting came from the beer tent. The sound rose as a glass smashed. Women were gathering nervously, standing on tiptoe, pushing closer to the entrance. Mrs Ellis appeared, her grey dress hanging on her broomstick body, her face pinched and white.

The argument spilled out. A thin man came first clutching a bloody nose, his glasses knocked askew. He staggered and fell on the ground. Mr Ellis followed, his hands clenched in two great fists. A dark-haired woman rushed forward with a handkerchief and dabbed at the victim's face. 'You should be ashamed,' she yelled at Mr Ellis, her small face defiant. Dad stepped into the arena and spoke quietly to Mr Ellis. Others came forward, remonstrating. Women were involved. 'He's not worth it,' one of them yelled. I wasn't sure who she was talking about.

Next to me Martha watched the scene with her father at its centre with no change of expression. I was about to move away and carry on my search when she spoke. 'You should take care of your sister,' she said. 'He could be a pervert for all you know.'

'Who?'

She was silent for a second as if deciding whether to reply. 'The one she was speaking to.'

I waited a beat and said again, 'Who?'

She glanced away and then back as her face hardened. 'It's none of your business.'

'It's more my business than yours.' I tried a different tack. 'What did he say to her?'

'I don't know. I didn't hear, did I?' She paused and now a sly smile crept across her face. 'But he gave her something.'

'What?'

She leaned towards me until her breath was hot on my neck. 'A letter.'

I stared at her, open-mouthed. 'A man gave my sister a letter?' She nodded and I scowled. Martha was a liar. Everyone knew that. I made a great show of shrugging and looking around as though not interested before I said, 'It's probably someone from church.'

She laughed. 'No, it isn't.'

I flushed. 'Well then, it's our Uncle Thomas. He's visiting today.' It was a stupid thing to say and Martha was bound to know it wasn't true.

'Why would your uncle give Gabriella a letter?'

'Because that's what he does.' I was burning to know who she was really talking about, but I didn't want to show it. And now she was staring over my shoulder as if she saw the man right there. I wouldn't look. I wouldn't give her the satisfaction. Instead I gave her one more glare of contempt and strode away.

A few minutes later, I scanned the green. There were no suspicious men, of course, although how could I tell since I didn't know who I was searching for? Maybe the letter was from the boy from Our Price, or someone from school. Or else Martha had written the letter herself – a pathetic note telling Gabriella how much she liked her.

At the jam stall Rita was busy packing up. Mum was standing alone, shading her eyes as she searched the green. I skirted her vision and kept on walking, in the direction of the lake, hoping to find Gabriella.

She was standing alone beneath the cedar tree. Relief surged through me. There was no letter. There was no man. Martha had invented him. Martha with her stupid dirty clothes and her stupid hairstyle. When had she ever worn a scarf? A scarf! Heat rose until my cheeks burned. Realisation struck. Gabriella had given it to her. She'd taken it from her own hair and given it to Martha. And Martha had been trying to make me jealous, flaunting it. I bit my lip. Gabriella was no better. Why did she have to feel so sorry for everyone?

Stepping closer, I called out Gabriella's name, but she looked across and her eyes were blank. I wasn't sure she even knew I was there. I stayed anyway, frozen by her indifference, waiting for acknowledgement, until finally she set off across the green without a backward glance.

Feeling helpless, I watched her walking, arms loose at her sides. And then my throat went dry. A sheet of paper dangled from her hand. It was the letter. Martha had told the truth. And if she'd told the truth about that, why would she have lied about the man? I looked around uneasily. The crowd was thinning out now, people traipsing away from the green. I followed slowly, my mind whirling. Who was the man?

That evening, Gabriella stayed in her room. Mum went to church, to pray, she said, and Dad shut himself away in the kitchen.

I grabbed my book of poetry and lay on the rug, reading and not understanding 'Leda and the Swan' until the doorbell rang. When Dad opened the door, Rita's voice filtered from the hall. I crept across the living room and listened.

'They were together at the fête,' said Rita.

There was a pause. 'How do you know?'

'Mrs Henderson. The old gossip. I heard her talking about Gabriella to her cronies.'

'Well, she can't know anything.' Dad's voice was sharp.

'No, she can't. But . . . you must realise what this means.'

Back inside the kitchen, they closed the door.

Frowning, I returned to Yeats, but now the poem seemed even more confusing. I tried reciting the lines out loud, and from memory, but my concentration had gone. Throwing the book down, I switched on the telly. The news was all about the funeral of Princess Grace. It was too sad to be thinking about death, so I switched it off and paced the floor until, at last, the front door opened. Rita was leaving. Tiptoeing back into the hall, I peered into the kitchen.

Dad was trying to light a cigarette, but the flame wouldn't catch. He stopped when he saw me and gave a small smile that didn't reach his eyes. 'Was that Rita?' I asked awkwardly.

He nodded and tried the flame again. 'Rita. Yes. She was looking for your mother.'

'Is something wrong?' I said carefully, seeing how his hands were shaking.

The flame caught and he inhaled. He met my gaze and looked away. 'Nothing for you to worry about, Annie,' he said. 'Nothing that affects you.'

It was the second time he'd said that to me, and this time I definitely didn't believe him.

As soon as Mum came home, she and Dad disappeared into Gabriella's room, closing the door and shutting me out. I stood at the foot of the stairs yearning to follow, but not daring to interrupt. Sinking onto the bottom step, I hugged my belly, trying to unfreeze the ice that had formed there. I was an outsider. An orphan. A changeling. Different somehow. Shut out from my family. I closed my eyes and imagined the three of them connected by a cord that didn't include me.

It was quiet in the house for a long while. The pendulum swung. Jasper appeared and mewed for his food. I took him into the kitchen, opened a can of Whiskers and spooned out chunks into his bowl.

Silence exploded. A door banged. Feet stamped on the landing. 'She had no right,' yelled Gabriella. 'It's nothing to do with her. Who does she think she is?'

'She was trying to help,' said Mum.

'She was telling tales. You're all against me.'

Dad spoke. His words inaudible.

'For Christ's sake. How can you say that now? For Christ's sake. Leave me alone.'

Silence came back. It was Mum's turn to shout now, to tell Gabriella not to blaspheme, but she didn't say a word. There was only Dad again, speaking quietly, trying to keep the peace, like he always did.

I crept up a few steps, ears straining to hear. 'Nothing's changed,' Dad was saying. I imagined him taking Gabriella's hand, pulling her close and stroking her hair. 'We'll talk. We'll work things out.'

'No we won't,' said Gabriella, her voice breaking as she spoke.

'Of course we will. You know we will. Come back inside.'

The door clicked as he persuaded her. And once again, I was left alone, standing on the stairs, feeling dizzy as the carpet seemed to shift beneath my feet. Gripping the banister, I raked through my mind trying to understand.

Gabriella didn't come down for tea. Mum laid the table and ladled out stew – meat and vegetables, dumplings on top – but she spilled sauce on the cloth and then played with her food, pushing it around with her fork. Eventually, she cleared her throat. 'Were you listening, Anna?'

Shaking my head, I speared a dumpling that wasn't cooked properly and tasted of grease and salt. A piece lodged in my throat.

'You must have heard something,' she said, fixing her gaze on mine. I shook my head again.

'Now's not the time,' said Dad, intervening.

'That's what you said before.'

'It's different.' He spoke quietly.

'Different how?'

'One thing at a time.'

'Is that the best you can say?'

I held my breath, wanting them to tell me what was wrong. Dad remained motionless, with only a pulse throbbing at his temple.

Mum cleared the table and took the plates to the sink. 'Anna,' she said. 'We need to—'

'Esther. Stop. That's enough.'

'No, it isn't. If we don't say, Gabriella will.'

'No, she won't,' said Dad, suddenly shouting. 'I've told her not to.' He turned to me, his face white, his jaw clenched. 'Leave us, Anna, please.'

I was glad to, walking heavily up the stairs to find Gabriella.

She was kneeling on the floor, stuffing clothes into a suitcase. A hot wave of panic moved through me as I grabbed her arm. 'What are you doing?'

'What does it look like?' She shook my hand away.

'You're packing,' I said, but my voice was raw.

'So what?'

'You can't leave me. What's happened?'

She shook her head, but her shoulders slumped. 'Nothing's happened.' She pushed another jumper into the case.

My tears welled. Gabriella had secrets. She'd never had them before. But instinct told me if I kept on, she'd never tell me anything again. 'All right,' I said miserably. 'But you won't go, will you?'

Gabriella sighed. 'I will, one day.'

A tear slid down my face. She came across and slipped an arm about my shoulders. 'But I won't forget you, small person,' she said. 'You're my sister. Nothing changes that.'

I stared at her, taking in her words. 'Then stay,' I said. 'Sisters stick together.'

'Yes,' she said quietly. 'I told you. Nothing changes that.'

I nodded and rested my head on her shoulder, but in a moment she'd moved away and gone back to her suitcase, squeezing shut the lid and shoving it under the bed.

The days stumbled forward. Each morning, Gabriella missed breakfast and instead of protesting, Mum didn't speak. Dad insisted on taking us to school, until the day that Gabriella screamed in his face that she wanted to go alone and if he didn't let her, she'd leave home for good. I listened with my heart thudding, thinking of the suitcase tucked under her bed. Dad froze for one moment at the onslaught before he gave in and let us walk.

At school, I hardly came across her. And when I did, she barely acknowledged me, surrounded as she was by spiky-haired boys who jostled for her attention. Martha was there too. Snapping up Gabriella's smiles, grabbing titbits of affection. There was nothing left for me.

In the afternoons I waited at the gates, rushing to get there early before Gabriella disappeared. Sometimes she talked, answering questions about her day, or letting me chatter, exaggerating stories to make her laugh. Most times she was silent. And the atmosphere was dense with a layer of sadness I couldn't pass through.

On those days, when we got home, Gabriella stayed in her room, refusing my attempts to persuade her to come down for tea. I yearned for Mum to yell and make her. Instead, she'd take up a plate of sandwiches that she'd later fetch untouched. I watched with a mixture of resentment at the special treatment Gabriella was receiving and sadness for the absence of my sister.

Dad's birthday came. It was Saturday and the family were invited. It was a tradition and although Mum grumbled as she busied herself in the house, cleaning, checking there was enough food, the visit wasn't cancelled. Uncle Thomas and Donald arrived first. 'Surprise!' said Uncle Thomas when I opened the door and he produced an egg from behind my ear. It was a trick I'd seen him do a hundred times before, but I laughed anyway as he chucked me under the chin and strode off to the living room to join my parents.

Donald stepped past, chewing his pipe, stopping to press an object into my hand. An ammonite. I grinned.

He was a geologist. He was also Uncle Thomas's closest friend. At least that's how my parents described him. I followed and watched them settle on the sofa next to Dad. 'This is nice,' said Uncle Thomas, pushing off his shoes. He had a big hole in one toe of his sock.

Grandma Grace was a large woman with a robust frame, who moved clumsily, in a direct contradiction of her name. She sat on the hard-backed chair, leaning heavily on her stick as if it were a staff and she was about to go on a pilgrimage. Granddad Bertrand, who was as large as she was, shuffled in behind, plonking himself into the armchair, sinking downwards, letting his arms hang over the sides, as if he'd melted.

Gabriella was absent, as I knew she would be. I'd tried to prise her from her room, but she'd refused and given me the listless look I'd grown accustomed to. Surely Mum and Dad would insist she socialised – family was important, Mum said, the mainstay of society (along with church) – but still Gabriella didn't appear.

Settling on the rug in front of the fireplace, I watched Mum, with a painted smile, handing round fish paste sandwiches and fruitcake on the best plates, along with English tea in gold-rimmed cups. The conversation ranged from Uncle Thomas's magic shop in north-west London – an Aladdin's cave of whoopee cushions, loaded dice, and fake beards – to the Falklands War. Even Dad, who'd been as brooding as Gabriella over the last few days, roused himself and joined in the discussion. 'The *Belgrano* might be a Thatcher triumph now,' he said, 'but next election . . .' He waved his hand. 'For whom the bell tolls, all right.' Meanwhile Granddad Bertrand dozed and Donald, apart from sending the occasional wink in my direction, remained aloof, refilling his pipe.

'You'd think,' said Grandma Grace, thumping her stick down as if to put a stop to the conversation, 'they'd have had enough of wars and suchlike.'

The adults noisily agreed with her. There was a lull and I think we all knew what was coming next because we couldn't have a family gathering without Grandma Grace telling the story of how my parents met. Mum cleared away, banging plates together, stacking them unevenly. Dad stood and fumbled in his pocket, muttering about tobacco.

'Love stories are so much nicer,' said Grandma Grace as both my parents left the room. 'It was 1966.'

I stifled a yawn, looking away and shoving my fist against my mouth, and only then realising that Gabriella had come in. She sat next to me and I nudged her, hoping to get a reaction, but she didn't smile. She wore a ripped T-shirt that dropped from one shoulder, a crumpled black skirt and purple make-up. Her hair was backcombed. Electric. Donald, I noticed, was glancing at her curiously. Uncle Thomas, who was busy scratching his stomach, had adopted a glazed expression, preparing for the story to come.

'There was a summer storm in London.'

I closed my eyes and pictured an exaggerated version of the scene with the wind snarling through the Button family's garden, ripping out plants, dislodging parts of the shed and the roof.

'We had to find someone to get rid of the rubbish, all those fallen branches and suchlike. I went to the newsagent's and there was the card: Flores Rubbish Removal. It sounded so nice. Flores.'

Such a lovely name, I mouthed to Gabriella, but she wasn't looking. She was picking at a thread on her skirt, winding it round her finger.

'Such a lovely name,' said Grandma Grace. 'Esther was poorly that day. She had a stomach bug. So when Albert came along in his little van there she was waiting for him.'

'Hardly,' said Mum, coming back into the room. 'I happened to be there, that's all.' She noticed Gabriella and took a hesitant step towards her. They looked at each other, a silent communication that excluded me. Donald glanced across. He must have realised something was wrong, unlike Uncle Thomas who was still scratching his belly, his head tipped back, eyes closed.

'Well, you hurried down to the garden fast enough when you saw how handsome he was,' said Grandma Grace, carrying on her tale.

Mum shook her head, picked up an overflowing ashtray and, with another glance at Gabriella, left the room.

'The truth is, your mother was miserable until she met your father,' said Grandma Grace. 'She was going through a phase, wasn't she, Bertrand?' No reply. 'She was staying in her room, making excuses not to go to work. She did the accounts for a business. A foreign business. Note that, accounts. She wasn't just a copy typist. Still, it wasn't a good place to be, was it, Bertrand? That place. Central London. Too busy.' She nodded as if agreeing with herself. Uncle Thomas scratched his shoulder. Donald reached for the newspaper.

London. How serious had Dad been about living there? The more I thought about it now, the more I wanted to go. Things would be better if we moved away. There were so many things to do. We'd been on a day trip a few months before. Visited the National Gallery and fed the pigeons in Trafalgar Square. We'd bought seeds from one of the stalls and stood like scarecrows, counting the birds that landed on our arms to see who attracted the most. Mum had taken a photo. Click. The birds had flown away.

I looked across at Gabriella, but she didn't notice me, too busy with the thread. She'd wound it so tightly round her finger the skin was bulging and red.

Grandma Grace had stopped talking and was smiling, trying to remember. 'Do you recall, Thomas?' she asked. 'Esther was transformed when she met your brother.'

Uncle Thomas was pulling at his jumper. 'Is it hot?' he said, ignoring her. 'Or is it me?'

'It was a fact,' said Grandma Grace, taking up her tale again. 'Esther mooned about like a sick child from the day she fell in love.'

Snap. The thread gave way. Gabriella kicked out her leg. She caught the coal scuttle, which crashed against the irons.

'Dear God,' said Mum, coming in as Gabriella jumped up and ran out of the room. The front door slammed. There was silence as Mum looked around at the five of us.

'Hormones,' said Uncle Thomas, his voice muffled as he pulled his jumper over his head.

And then everyone was talking again as if nothing

had happened. I knew better. I saw the pain on Mum's face. What had upset Gabriella now? Was it something Grandma Grace had said? I tried to think back, but it was the same old boring story she always liked to tell. I studied Grandma's face for an answer, but she showed no sign that anything was wrong, too busy instructing Donald to take the cup and saucer from Granddad Bertrand's drooping hand as he nodded off to sleep.

Uncle Thomas was folding his jumper. He placed it to one side and exchanged a look with Mum. A tingling sensation shot through me as I realised. Uncle Thomas knew exactly what was going on. He was as much a part of the secret as I was not.

15

Martha was in the street when I came out of Martin and Martin with the word 'probate' resounding in my ears. She carried a mop with a shaggy, ropy head and the handle wrapped up in plastic. I nodded at her, hoping she wouldn't want to speak, and as a precaution, took a detour into the butcher's – Rita's old family shop.

The place was traditional with sawdust on the floor and chalkboards advertising the bargains of the day. Pheasants and rabbits swung from hooks. There was a whole side of an animal on the work surface, a pig or a sheep. The place was clean, the glass counter polished, but nothing hid the stench of old blood, the flesh and bones of dead animals.

While I was considering what to buy, a woman in a headscarf came in. I gestured for the butcher to serve her first and stepped to the window to see if Martha had gone. She hadn't. She was standing on the other side of the road, as if she was waiting for me to come out. How irritating she was. I didn't want to speak to anyone in this village, let alone Martha. Not only that but the sky was purple, suggesting rain, and if I wasn't quick I'd get soaked.

The woman in the headscarf was looking across at me. She was in her late sixties, and I was sure I knew her. No surprise. Everybody was familiar in this place. Even the butcher, muscles bulging through his overalls as he sharpened his cleaver, looked like somebody I knew. 'Anna Flores,' the woman was saying in a loud voice as if announcing my entrance. 'Mrs Henderson. Live next door. Sorry to hear about your mother.'

The vinegar bottle. The village gossip. She must have been at the funeral and the wake. I hadn't noticed. Or maybe I'd made a subconscious point of avoiding her. The woman had always been vile. I smiled tightly, irritation buzzing.

She smiled back, a lizard smile, lips puckering. 'If there's anything I can do—'

'Thank you,' I said quickly. 'You're very kind, but I can manage. Rita's helping—'

'Oh yes, Rita. The woman's a diamond.' She addressed the butcher. 'Isn't that right, Peter? Your aunt's a diamond. Do you remember when my Stuart passed away? Rita was very good to me.'

'Absolutely,' agreed Peter, hacking into the carcass on the work surface.

Stuart. Her unappealing husband. Squarely built, always standing behind Mrs Henderson like a wall she never quite leaned on.

'It must be difficult, though,' she was saying now. 'To understand, I mean, when you don't have—'

'Was it two chops or three?' asked Peter.

Taking my chance as she repeated her order, I sidled towards the door, but she was still talking, her eyes never leaving mine. 'When you don't have a husband,' she said, finishing her sentence. 'Or anyone else close.' Her eyes glittered with interest. I was silent. I knew what she was trying to do. She wanted to talk about Gabriella.

Peter was wrapping the chops and putting them on the counter. 'I hear there's a house clearance,' said Mrs Henderson as she handed across a note. 'Maybe I can help with that. Or else Brian can. You remember my son, don't you? He's very obliging.'

My God. Did Brian still live at home? Wasn't he older than me? Colourless and sly. That was how I remembered Brian. Mrs Henderson's Achilles heel, the way she doted on him. 'Thank you,' I said. 'But it's all in hand.'

'That's good to hear.' She paused. 'Isn't it Edward Lily's house?'

'That's right.'

She looked at me curiously. 'How interesting.'

'Yes,' I said, determined to draw the conversation to a close. 'House clearances are always interesting.' I took another step towards the door.

'This one particularly, though, don't you think? There were so many rumours about Lemon Tree Cottage.'

Rumours created by you.

'I rather wondered why your mother would . . .' She let the rest of her words hang between us like a string of silent accusations. What was she trying to say? My mother shouldn't have taken on the clearance. Why? Because Edward Lily had been a suspect? There'd been rumours he'd locked his daughter in the attic? He'd been an incomer? The latter was most likely. That fact would offend Mrs Henderson far more than anything else.

'Mum took on the clearance because she was a kind person,' I said firmly. 'The job needed doing, so she accepted it.'

147

Mrs Henderson raised her eyebrows, a hint of surprise at my tone. She turned to take her parcel, mouth already open to speak again. But I took my chance and slipped out the door, calling to Peter that I'd come back later.

Martha was gone. Good. I wrapped my jacket about me with icy fingers. The sky had changed colour. Even in the few minutes I'd been inside, purple had become black. I headed for home feeling frustrated that I'd wasted time with Mrs Henderson and now was going to get wet. Had she believed my explanation about my mother? I doubted it since I hardly believed it myself. For a moment I regretted not letting her speak. If anyone in the village knew about Edward Lily and the house clearance, it would be her. Perhaps next time . . . I dismissed the idea. I'd had enough of listening to people like Mrs Henderson years before. I didn't need to listen now as well.

Head down, I walked fast and just as I got to the House of Flores, I saw too late that Martha was standing in the doorway. I stopped. There was nowhere for me to go this time, no excuse to ignore her. Anyone would think she was following me the way she was always there. Footsteps in the dark. Shadows in the graveyard. I must be getting paranoid.

We faced each other. There were dark marks beneath her eyes and I felt the same old merging of pity and contempt. 'Hello, Martha,' I said.

She looked steadily back at me. 'Anna.'

I shifted uncomfortably and cleared my throat. 'I saw you at the funeral,' I said finally. 'In the churchyard, but I didn't see you in the church. Were you there?'

She shook her head. 'I don't like funerals,' she said, and her voice was low and scratchy, as though the cords were out of practice. 'I'm not equal to them.'

Who the hell is? I wanted to reply. I moved to indicate I wanted to go, but she didn't take the hint, and in the awkward silence that followed, I said, 'Are you still at number twenty-five?' She nodded. 'I'm sorry about your parents. I noticed . . .'

'Yes,' said Martha, abruptly. 'They're dead.' She spoke as if it was of no consequence, as if she was talking about a pair of distant relatives she'd never met, or a set of unloved pets. I wanted to ask if she'd been to *their* funerals, or if she hadn't been equal to that either, but I clamped my mouth shut. However much I disliked Martha, it wasn't her fault she had such awful parents.

For a few more seconds I struggled to think of a reply. At last, in an effort to show sympathy, I said quietly, 'I'm sorry to hear that.'

She opened her mouth to speak, but seemed to think better of it as she shrugged and looked away.

'Well then,' I said, straightening and trying to give an air of conclusion. 'I should get going.'

Martha lowered her gaze. She looked so thin, standing there, like a reed. The wind might blow her away. And so tired. I softened towards her. Not sleeping I understood. Since I'd been home, I'd lain awake trying not to slip into my dreams – old nightmares of demons that sidled along walls and hid amongst branches and grabbed my sister while I watched from a distance, frozen, unable to intervene.

'You look tired,' I said to Martha now, my voice

begrudgingly kind. 'It's lonely in a house after everyone's gone. Do you find that?' Her eyes were watery and pale. I spoke quickly and awkwardly, not wanting to see her cry. 'Especially when it's your childhood home. I've found that. I can't imagine what it's like for you. Your mother was . . .' I stopped and struggled to think of a good quality.

Martha was frowning and I could see the muscles in her scrawny neck moving as she swallowed.

I tried again. 'Do you remember when I came to your house? I sat in the living room with your mother and asked her questions. It wasn't long after Gabriella disappeared.' Gabriella. The name rested heavy in the air. 'What happened to her?' Martha's eyes widened. A new emotion. A flicker of loss or pain?

'Tell me,' I said gently. 'What happened to your mother?'

Martha jerked as if I'd hit her and I realised, with a sudden rush of air inside my chest, she'd thought I'd been asking about Gabriella. Breathing out slowly, I counted to ten. 'Your mother,' I said, stumbling over my words now, trying to compensate for the mistake. 'I only wondered what happened to her.'

'She fell,' said Martha at last.

I flushed and lowered my voice. 'I'm sorry. Was it at home?'

'No,' she said, looking behind her, as if someone was listening. 'On steps. She slipped.' I waited, not wanting to press her now. 'It was on the green. By the lake. You know?'

Of course I knew the lake with its putrid smell of rotting reeds submerged too long in stagnant water.

'Were you there?' I touched her arm.

'Yes,' said Martha, pulling away.

I had an image: early morning mist and Mrs Ellis descending the mossy steps, clutching the rail for support. She would have done that, Mrs Ellis. She was always grasping at things: Martha's hand as she dragged her home from school, her husband's arm when she wanted him to leave a confrontation, the reporter's elbow to show her sincerity. I pictured her falling, tumbling, turning in slow motion, down the steps and then, fierce and violent, striking her head on a stone. I saw the blood spreading, staining the ground. *Did you push her?* I wanted to say to Martha.

I shivered and pressed my palm against my damp forehead. All these memories and wild imaginings were making me ill. Of course Martha didn't push her. Martha was a mouse.

'And your father?' I said, forcing myself to speak.

'Heart attack,' she said, a pulse throbbing at her temple.

Now I recalled his death. I'd still been at school at the time. The news had rippled around the village as news like that did. In his case it hadn't made much of a swell. He hadn't been popular, unlike my father whose funeral had been so full I'd been lost amongst the well-wishers. I had a sudden image of that awful day. Rita had chaperoned Mum, and Uncle Thomas and Donald had taken charge of me. I remembered being squeezed between the two of them in the church and later, at the wake, they'd argued, and I'd slipped away to Gabriella's room. Rita had found me, hours later, lying on the floor. I hadn't blamed Mum. She'd been a wraith by then, pale and thin, disappearing further and further into herself. She hadn't had the capacity to take me on as well.

I shook my head to clear my thoughts and bring myself back to the present. Still Martha didn't move. I spoke again to fill the silence. 'I'm dealing with a house clearance,' I said. 'Edward Lily. Lemon Tree Cottage. He's dead, but you probably heard that.' She nodded. 'I'll be in the village for a while longer. If you want to . . .' I stopped abruptly. What was I suggesting?

She looked at me, eyes blinking. When she spoke her voice was thick as if the words were sticking to her tongue. 'You never wanted to talk to me before.'

'What do you mean?'

'You didn't like me.' There was a hint of defiance in Martha's voice.

I studied her and my sympathy dropped. Her eyes were quick and sharp. She was slippery and sly. She'd always been like that. I looked away in distaste, all compassion gone. A line of sweat trickled down my side. My head was spinning. I needed to get home.

Moistening my lips, I groped for words. 'Why did it bother you what I thought? You only cared about Gabriella.'

She shot me a look so full of malice it was like a piece of flint piercing my skin. 'I blame you,' she said, her voice thick. 'You should have kept your sister close. If she'd been mine, that's what I would have done.'

I stared back at her, trying to understand. 'What do you mean?'

'You know.'

'No. I don't.' My voice was rising. 'Tell me what you mean.'

'All those men. And boys. Sniffing around her. Something was going to happen. It was obvious.'

'What the hell are you talking about?'

But she was gone, turning in one sharp movement and hurrying down the street, the mop head jiggling beside her.

I stared after her, blood banging in my ears. A new emotion rushed within me and this time I knew it was hate: a dark red hatred, rancid like rotting meat.

The world was tilting around me. Leaning against the shopfront, I waited for the nausea to subside. My face was burning hot. A heavy drop of rain splashed hard on my cheek. And then it came. A deluge. Slewing sideways, soaking me. But I didn't move. Because I was remembering another day in autumn, thirty years before, so different from this one, a golden day, sunny and warm. Such lovely weather for the time of year, that's what people had said, the kind of day when good things happened.

I gripped my hands, squeezing the memories home. Good things *had* happened. Mum had forgiven Gabriella. Her hair. She'd forgiven her for her hair. And the sun had been shining, and the birds had been singing and Mum had been making jam. And I'd found a feather on the way to school. And my glasses. What had happened to my glasses? They'd broken and Gabriella had smiled and we'd arranged to meet after school.

That day in autumn – the kind of unexpected sunny day when only good things happened. That's what people had said. But they'd been wrong. The precarious warmth and the shifting colours; the loosening leaves and straggling light. The beauty of the day had been too fragile. In the end, it had made no difference at all.

16

1982

'What have you done?' Mum's voice was tight with fury.

I jerked my head from my book. Gabriella stood in the doorway of the kitchen looking like she'd stepped from the pages of *Smash Hits*. It was her hair, jet black and backcombed. I opened my mouth to say she looked incredible and then thought better of it. This could be the worst explosion in Mum and Gabriella's battle and I didn't want to interfere.

'Get upstairs and wash it out.'

'It's permanent,' said Gabriella, tipping her chin in defiance.

Mum fastened her lips into a line and set down the bowl she'd been drying. She shook her head and turned away. Gabriella left the room.

It was Sunday, the day after Dad's birthday. I was off to church as usual with Mum. Gabriella was staying put. Dad had gone out early – I didn't know where, but I'd heard him say he'd be back before we left.

Plans altered. Mum made no movement to get ready for church. Instead, she busied herself preparing lunch, seasoning the beef, mixing the batter for Yorkshire pudding. She worked slowly, performing each task as if it took her complete concentration.

'Gabriella's dyed her hair,' she said, when Dad came home. Without comment, he went upstairs.

Later, and for the first time in ages, Gabriella ate with us. She'd smoothed her hair and tied it back. I guessed Dad had persuaded her to do that. Perhaps he thought it would minimise the effect, but there was no hiding the rope of black hair that slid down her back like a panther's tail. There was no disguising Mum's anger either which seeped through the walls and the floors and infected all of us.

Over the next week, the weather changed, becoming misty and cold. Any warmth left in the house was sucked into the chasm that gaped between Mum and Gabriella. And yet I sensed that Mum at least wanted to make up. Her mood was shifting. She was softening and she demonstrated her feelings with tiny gifts on Gabriella's plate. Extra butter on her toast. The cream from the milk swirled into her porridge.

On Sunday, the weather changed its mind again. Now the sky was clear blue, offering promises we knew it couldn't keep. In the garden, the plum and damson trees were full and heavy. And with the difference, Gabriella's mood improved.

We were out in the garden, gathering fruit, leaping to pull at branches, giggling when the boughs sprang back, sending sun-ripened missiles across the fence. I ran bare-foot, squealing at the sensation of fallen fruit squelching between my toes, while Gabriella bent double with her laughter.

Mum was grateful for our gifts. She put her arm

around Gabriella and whispered in her ear. Gabriella stopped short of responding, but she didn't pull away.

A few days later, we came down in the morning to find jam bubbling on the stove, its sticky sweetness infiltrating the cracks and cavities of the house. Mum was at the sink, sleeves rolled up. She hardly noticed as we passed through, grabbing our school bags and slices of toast from the rack.

Out on the street, the leaves had switched their wardrobe from green to burnished brown. And the wind, indifferent to their beauty, teased them from the branches, sending them swirling to the ground.

We passed Tom, pushing his cart, sweeping up leaves, lips moving in silent conversation with himself. Gabriella smiled at him as she always did and walked ahead, her body bowed with something sad – her secrets, I supposed. If only I could work out what they were. I wandered behind listening to birdsong, stopping to examine a magpie feather lying on the pavement. As I bent, my glasses slipped, and picking them up, I found one arm loose at the hinge. '*Madre mia*,' I said. It made Gabriella smile for a second time and when we got to the gates I took advantage of her softened mood and asked her to meet me after school.

'I can't,' she said, moving away.

'Why?' I called out, feeling disappointment gather. I longed so much for things to be the same as before and her smile had made me hopeful.

She turned and walked backwards as she spoke. 'People to see.'

I frowned. Who? What was she planning to do? I stayed quiet. She'd be annoyed if I asked her questions. Instead I clasped my hands and begged her, opening my eyes wide to make her laugh.

It worked. 'All right then, small person. Afterwards.'

Grinning, relief slid through me, easing the lump in my throat. 'Where? The shop? We haven't been there for ages.'

A dark look passed across her face. She was going to refuse. But she smiled again more sadly, and to my surprise agreed.

'What time?' I called out, but she didn't hear me. I shaded my eyes and watched until she'd gone.

After school, I walked alone to the House of Flores. It was still warm for October, warm enough to take off my coat and tie it round my waist. I hated my coat. It was blue wool, a hand-me-down from Gabriella. She had a parka. I couldn't wait until she'd had enough of that and it was mine.

When I arrived, Rita was standing at the counter with a new short haircut and it struck me how much younger than Mum she looked. Her face was smooth, while Mum's was marked with lines. 'Worry lines,' Mum had said, laughing. 'This one's called Anna. This one's called Gabriella. They get deeper as you two get older.'

Rita gave a big smile and a cheery hello. 'Kidneys,' she said, picking up a neat white packet and waving it at me. 'You'll take it to your mother, won't you?' I scowled back. Dad didn't notice. He hardly raised his head. He was polishing a silver knife. It had a handle shaped like a cobra. Rita left, and he was quiet, grunting when I asked him questions about the knife.

I waited for Gabriella, trying on a velvet hat with a feather, adding a shawl, black silk with tassels, and flouncing in front of a mirror. But it was no fun without Gabriella and now dusk was falling into darkness and the street lights were coming on. I paced the floor, fiddled with ornaments, wound up a clock, held it to my ear and listened to the tick. Where was Gabriella? What if she'd decided to leave after all, to run away from home?

Eventually, I left, mumbling excuses to Dad. I glanced through the window at the butcher's as I passed, and there was Rita in her overall now, serving behind the counter. She waved and I ignored her, keeping my head down, hurrying, my hands thrust inside the pockets of my coat. And all the time I was thinking about the suitcase, imagining Gabriella leaving the house.

Bursting through the front door, I found silence. No banging in the kitchen. No cheery *Is that you, girls?* Nothing but the beat of the pendulum clock in the living room. I dumped my school bag, waited for my heart rate to readjust and told myself not to be stupid. Mum and Gabriella had gone out. Maybe there'd been a problem at school, or they'd gone shopping at the last minute. I swallowed hard. My ideas were feeble and I knew it, but even so, there was no point worrying. It was better that both of them weren't here, rather than just Gabriella missing. I checked in the kitchen to be sure. The pot of jam was cold on the stove. There was no sign of tea. The side was strewn with dirty crockery. There was washing-up in the sink. What had Mum been doing all day?

She was in the living room staring at the blank telly. There was a scent in the air. Tobacco. But not Dad's. It was sweeter than that. A pipe. And the ashtray on the coffee table had been used. Maybe Donald and Uncle Thomas had visited. But they weren't here now and I couldn't imagine they'd have come and gone so quickly and without waiting for Dad. Besides, Mum looked too sad to have spoken to either of them.

'What's happened?' I said, kneeling beside her. 'Where's Gabriella?'

She looked at me as if she didn't know me until her face cleared and she smiled weakly. 'Nothing, dear. I've been feeling poorly. That's all. Aren't I silly?'

I took her hand, my eyes filling with tears. Had she been sitting here alone? I glanced again at the ashtray. No. Someone had been here. Who? A neighbour giving bad news? The doctor telling her she was ill? I pulled my thoughts backwards, telling myself not to be stupid. Mum had another headache. That was all. 'Shall I get you an aspirin?' I said, squeezing her fingers. 'Or a glass of water?'

She shook her head, and, rousing herself, patted my shoulder, saying, 'It's fine. I'll make tea in a moment.'

'Shall I help you?'

'No. Run upstairs and change. I'll be fine.'

Gabriella's door was ajar and I pushed it open. The curtains were closed and the room was dark and stuffy. The bed was unmade, pyjamas in a tangle on the floor.

I knelt down, my heart beating fast, and put my hands beneath the bed. Groping in the darkness, I grasped nothing; reaching further, my fingers brushed against the hard side of the suitcase.

Thank God for that. I sat back on my heels, grinning with the relief of it. Gabriella hadn't run away. Of course she hadn't. *You're my sister*, she'd said to me. *Nothing changes that*. Sisters stick together. Whatever problems Gabriella had, she'd never leave me. She'd probably phoned Mum to say she would be late, and stayed on at school to do extra work, or to help one of the teachers, or else she'd gone to a friend's house. I went back down the stairs. Mum would know where she was. And in the meantime, I was hungry and wanted tea.

Mum was standing at the bottom of the stairs look- ing up at me, her blank expression gone. 'What do you mean, where's Gabriella?' she said.

My smile faded. The front door opened and Mum spun round. Not Gabriella. It was Dad, his face pale and tired-looking. 'Charlie Ellis,' he said. 'In the pub shouting around. Lost his job. Death of a salesman all right.' He brandished the packet of kidneys. 'You forgot this, Anna. Kidneys from Rita.'

Mum looked beyond him. 'Is she with you?' she said.

He closed the door. 'Who? Rita?'

She grabbed his arm. 'Gabriella. Where's Gabriella?'

A crease of worry crossed his face. 'Isn't she here?'

'No,' said Mum, her voice rising. 'Anna came home alone.'

They both looked at me. 'She was supposed to meet me at the shop,' I said, my heart starting to pound.

'When?' said Mum.

'After school.'

'Why didn't you walk together?'

I hesitated. 'She was going somewhere first.'

'Where? Where was she going?'

'I don't know.' My voice was small.

'You must know, Anna. Think. Answer me.'

'Leave it, Esther,' said Dad. 'It's still early. She'll turn up.'

'But she might have—'

'No. She wouldn't. Stop it, Esther. There's no point. She'll be back. It's not late. Think about Anna.' They looked at me again.

Moments passed. 'I had a visitor,' said Mum and now her voice was muffled as if she spoke beneath a weight of thoughts.

Silence save for the pendulum clock and the rush of blood in my ears. I was right. Someone had been here. Who? Dad didn't ask and I guessed he knew. Beckoning me, he pushed my mother to the living room. 'Sit down,' he said. 'I'll make Anna a sandwich.'

I followed him to the kitchen. He put the kidneys on the table. Blood seeped through the packet like red ink on blotting paper. Jasper was sniffing the air, circling as Dad sifted through the mess of the morning, trying to find me something to eat. No bread. He made an omelette but cooked it for too long; it was rubbery and my teeth clicked on a piece of shell. I stopped eating and asked if I could be excused. He didn't reply so I left the room.

Mum was talking on the telephone in the hall, twisting the cord round her hand. 'That's right, Phyllis,' she was saying. 'I wondered if Bernadette knew if she'd been kept late at school.' Pause. 'I see. All right, then. Thank you. I'll try Nicola's mother. If you hear anything, will you ring me? Yes. I think she must have met someone. That's right. Thank you. Thank you. I'll let you know.'

I sat on the bottom step as Mum dialled another number, my body cold as I listened to the urgency in her voice. There was only one question in my head now. Where was Gabriella?

The hammering on the door woke me up. I struggled out of my dream and looked at the clock. Ten p.m. I was cold. I'd fallen asleep on top of the covers. I was wearing my school uniform. Why hadn't Mum come for me, told me to get ready for bed? I'd never been left like this before, and then I remembered. Gabriella hadn't come home. Maybe she was here now and they were too busy arguing to come and find me. Fumbling for my broken glasses, I pushed them on. The curtains were open. The sky was bright and clear, the moon almost full, only a slither missing.

I crept out onto the landing. Gabriella's door was open, as I'd left it, which meant she couldn't have come back, unless she was still downstairs. There were voices, though: my father, another man, and the sound of a radio, a person speaking and the man responding. I leaned over the banister. A policeman was in the hall, gripping his helmet under one arm. It was the local bobby. I'd seen him on the green chatting to the boys in the playground, or on the streets, doing his beat. He didn't belong in our house.

The policeman looked up and I stared back, my eyes sticky with sleep. Dad came to fetch me, walking slowly, his face grey, looking more worried than I'd ever seen him before. 'Gabriella still hasn't come home,' he said quietly, taking my hand and leading me downstairs.

'Where is she?' I asked, but Dad didn't answer.

'This is PC Atkins,' he said.

The policeman gave me a friendly smile. 'Hello, Anna. Sorry to disturb you. I need to ask a few questions. Is that all right?'

I nodded and pinched the back of my hand, trying to work out if this was real or just a dream.

In the living room, I sat on the sofa next to Mum. She took my hand and her skin felt cold. Like ice. PC Atkins sat squarely on the hard-backed chair with his helmet still under his arm. He leaned forward, bulky in his thick blue uniform, and spoke gently, while Dad stood silent behind him and kept his eyes fixed on my face.

As the policeman spoke, I answered in monosyllables. And as he persisted, and as my sleepiness disappeared, my monosyllables expanded into phrases, sentences, paragraphs.

He wanted to know exactly what had happened that morning, so I said about the jam, the feather and the leaves. I told him that my glasses had broken, and proved it by showing how I'd bandaged the arm with Sellotape. He took the glasses and inspected the damage, nodded gravely and gave them back.

PC Atkins was older than my dad. He had a long face with big sad eyes and saggy, folding skin. And a huge chin. I'd tell Gabriella. It would make her laugh. But then

I remembered I couldn't tell her. She wasn't here. I stifled a sob and shrank into the seat.

I answered more questions. We'd seen Tom. PC Atkins nodded sagely. He knew Tom. He asked if we'd spoken and I told him that we hadn't. Tom had disappeared in the other direction with his cart. Gabriella and I had arrived at school and we'd gone through the school gates together, and no, she hadn't seemed sad or depressed. We'd arranged to meet at the House of Flores, and yes, we planned to go there separately. No, I hadn't seen any strangers. And no, I hadn't seen her argue with any of her friends. And I didn't know where she was going after school.

PC Atkins cleared his throat and shifted his helmet to his other arm. I stared at him, wondering what he was going to say next, but he only fixed me with expectant eyes and Mum and Dad were looking at me in the same way.

'Thank you, Anna,' said PC Atkins, sitting back in his chair. 'You've been very helpful. Best try to get some sleep now, eh?'

Dad took me by the elbow and led me back upstairs. Kissing me on the forehead, he whispered he'd be in to see me later, and he left the room, pulling the door silently behind him.

A few minutes passed and there were footsteps on the stairs and murmuring outside my room. Tiptoeing to the door, I pressed my ear to the gap. It sounded like the three of them had gone into Gabriella's room. Drawers and cupboards opened and closed and I imagined PC Atkins going through my sister's clothes, flicking through magazines, looking under the bed and delving into the suitcase.

After a while they came out and I listened to them talking on the landing. PC Atkins said he was going back to the station. He said his sergeant had alerted the night shift already. A teenage girl was missing. The words froze in the air. Dad asked if they'd search the village. 'Twenty-four hours,' said PC Atkins.

I changed into pyjamas and sat on the bed thinking, going over and over the walk to school with Gabriella. Had she been sad? She was distant, but she'd been that way for ages. I switched off the light and lay in the darkness, staring at my digital clock; time moving forward, each second yet another moment without Gabriella. I pulled the blankets up beneath my chin and swung my mind back to the walk to school.

Had something happened? Frowning hard to help me concentrate, I traced every step I could remember, and everything I'd seen. No. Nothing unusual, except for my glasses. I touched the bandaged arm. It was comforting. I could close my eyes and see the scene again, my specs falling, my sister's laughter as she walked backwards into school.

I lay there for ages thinking, as the rain splattered softly against the glass, growing louder as time went on. And I waited for Dad, but he forgot to come.

The next morning, I woke knowing something awful had happened. I lay there thinking until in a sickening rush I remembered. Gabriella hadn't come home. Getting out of bed, I hurried onto the landing. The house was silent.

Gabriella's room was empty. Mum and Dad's bed wasn't slept in.

Feeling scared, I stole downstairs looking for my parents. I found Dad slumped in an armchair and Mum lying on the sofa, both of them wearing the clothes they'd worn the night before. Darkness crept over me. If my parents had been up all night, the situation must be serious. Why weren't they looking for Gabriella? What were they waiting for?

I paced the hall, pausing at the mirror. *Where are you?* I mouthed at my reflection. *Why didn't you tell me you weren't coming home?* Anxiety took over from Despair. My gaze fell on Gabriella's parka hanging on the stand. It had been warm the day before and she'd left it behind. She'd need it now. It was cold outside. I slipped on the coat and wrapped it around me, pulling up the hood. I was a chrysalis, bandaged in my sister's coat; nothing could touch me. If my parents weren't going to do anything, I'd do it myself. I'd search every place we'd ever been to until I found Gabriella. And then I'd bring her home.

I left the house, heading for Devil's Lane. After the rain the ground had shifted, exposing thick white roots like gnarly bones. The lane stretched ahead of me, endless and dreary. The hedges crowded in, narrowing the path. What would happen if I met a stranger, a murderer? There'd be no place to go except back the way I'd come; running, arms flailing, tripping over stones, the sound of fear rushing in my ears.

I pulled Gabriella's parka close about me, hauled myself over the stile and onto the green. The grass was like a swamp. I jumped over puddles, but the edges of my jeans were soon soaked and water seeped into the tops of my shoes. I squelched along past the swings, trying not to think about the worms rising to the surface of the earth. A couple of crows were busy pulling at the ground by the gate.

A boy, older than me, sat sideways on a swing in the playground, sipping from a can. Another two sprawled on the roundabout, smoking. Had they been here all night? My heartbeat sped up as the boys watched me with narrow, lazy eyes. I changed my course abruptly, increasing my pace and making for the gap in the trees.

The steps were slippery with wet leaves and I held on fast to the rail. The plants lining the slope had a rancid smell like rotting vegetables. In summer we hid beneath the willow tree at the water's edge, spying on passers-by. Now the branches were skeleton bones, dark and spindly and bare.

The lake was deep enough to drown in. It had happened to a girl one winter, when the water froze over, when she'd been skating. She wasn't the only one to go out on the lake, but she'd ventured the furthest and the ice had cracked beneath her. Mothers had used the tragedy to frighten their children, to keep us away. It hadn't worked on Gabriella. I could picture her now, stepping out, reaching the centre, grinning, breath frosting, giving a triumphant wave, hand painting a semicircle through the freezing air, while I stayed behind the railing, planning how I'd save her. I kicked a stone across the path. Why had she always taken risks? What had been the point?

I stamped along the path, shoving my hands deep inside Gabriella's pockets, playing with the scraps of paper and the dust I found there along with a pebble and a Bazooka Joe. I unwrapped the bubble gum and stuck it in my mouth, pulled out a bus ticket and examined it. It was a return to town dated a few weeks before. I had a vision of Gabriella in Our Price, mooning over the boy with the drowsy eyes.

Pushing aside my thoughts, I headed away from the lake and planned my route: through the woods and on past Lemon Tree Cottage, down the lane and back to the village. Amongst the trees, I stepped carefully, following the way I always went with Gabriella. The ground was soft beneath my feet, a yielding bed of bracken, and around me branches drooped as if reaching out to clasp me. I resisted the urge to stop and let myself be taken; instead I moved on, peering through the gaps in the trees, searching for my sister.

Once I thought I saw her – running ahead, weaving amongst the trees – but it was only sunlight glinting through the branches and the movement was the wind brushing its fingers through the leaves. And then I thought I heard her voice, the sound of her laughter, but it was only water flowing over stones in the stream, or silent birds finding their voices.

I was seeing ghosts. Wood sprites. Titania's fairies. Things in my imagination. Why would Gabriella be here? It was stupid of me to consider she'd be hiding in the woods. Folding the parka close around me, I stumbled onwards until I reached the path leading to the lane.

Someone was there. This time I was sure. A girl. Fair hair tumbling around her shoulders. I tried to call out, but the words were caught in my throat. I moved quickly, following the figure with the light-coloured dress that drifted as she ran.

Reaching the lane, she stopped and turned in one abrupt movement. I gasped. For a split second I thought it was Gabriella. Her face was pale. Her features small. Her eyes wide as she stared back at me. And as we looked at each other the world quietened. The rustle of leaves. The sound of my breath. Even the birds forgot to sing.

'Gabriella,' I said, but she didn't hear me because I spoke the name so quietly, the letters disappeared into the breeze. I stayed watching, paralysed with hope, not daring to make a sound in case I frightened her away.

The girl was the first to recover, swivelling and continuing on her way. I watched as she vanished into Lemon Tree Cottage, my stomach sinking with despair.

Of course it wasn't Gabriella. It was Lydia. Gabriella's hair was black now. She was younger too. And she'd never have worn a dress that flowed about her like a shroud.

I continued onwards, past the cottage, with only one glance at its dark walls. And as I reached the road and the tears stung and blinded me, I held my hands outstretched like a sleepwalker, as if I might grasp everything that came to me before it disappeared.

17

A piece of coal dislodged and slipped onto the hearth. I watched it smoulder. How much would it take to set the carpet alight?

If the house burned down, I'd go back to Athens and ignore my responsibilities. I'd forget these people who picked and pried and wanted to judge. They didn't need to say what they thought. I recognised it in their eyes. Like Mrs Henderson. And Martha who hadn't tried to disguise her dislike.

After the storm, I'd hurried home shivering, stripped off my soaking clothes and wrapped myself in a blanket. There was coal left in the scuttle, so I'd piled it into the hearth and lit the fire and fetched a bottle of wine.

Now, as I drank, I thought back to what Martha had said; the way she'd made me feel. She'd shown her true self, that was for sure, blaming me for losing Gabriella. It was as if Martha had never stopped thinking about her. Maybe she hadn't. I remembered how desperate she'd been to be Gabriella's friend. And for a while Gabriella had responded: encouraging Martha, spending time with her. And what about the letter? I closed my eyes as my mind ticked backwards. I sifted through the facts, unpicking them from emotions.

The village fête. Martha had talked about a man. He'd given Gabriella a letter. I hadn't believed it at first, preferring to think Martha was winding me up. Then I'd seen the letter in Gabriella's hands and I hadn't been able to deny it.

The coal burned. Taking my father's tongs from the set, I threw it back on the fire. Dad. The man whose heart had broken. I wished he'd kept it together for a little while longer, if only for me.

Later, I went out, closing the door softly behind me. I walked through the village, following the dim light of the street lamps, and the moon. Things looked different now, their colours stolen by darkness, leaving shades of black and grey. Houses crouched like tired old men, trees and hedges trembling in the cold air. I hunched into myself, flexing my fingers against the chill, pushing forward. It was my memories I wanted to freeze, to crack and shatter into a million pieces I could never recombine.

I was on Acer Street, my mind sharpening as I looked about me, remembering Tom, a ghost in the gloom clanking along with his road sweeper's cart, or Gabriella, dashing past to get home.

Now there was only silence, and the slow sweep of the wind through the trees.

Most of the houses had lights shining. Martha's was in darkness, a brooding block of stone. All I could think about was the smell inside: tobacco and flowers. A garden filled with roses and foxgloves and pinks. Martha must have inherited her mother's green fingers because the tiny stretch of grass at the front was clipped short, the border neat, soil turned over; fresh pots of flowers lined the path.

Where was she: in bed at nine o'clock, or downstairs

in the dark, staring at the TV? Was that movement in the upstairs window, or a trick of the eye, a fluttering of nothing?

All these years, she'd stayed in the village, living her life, going through the motions, her little routines. How pathetic and miserable that had seemed to me. Now I wondered, as I made my way home, had my life been any better?

I stayed away from the shop, feeling sorry for myself. More sympathy cards arrived from people I didn't know, telling me how much they'd loved my mother. The certificates I'd ordered came. I scanned each one of them and propped the envelopes with the cards on the mantelpiece, feeling no appetite for a family tree.

Eventually, I returned to the House of Flores and made up for lost time, working hard with Rita and Mattie, shifting Edward Lily's things, deciding what to donate to charity, to sell or leave with the shop. Some of it was useless: broken ornaments, scratched furniture, teapots with chipped lids. Other things told tales of Edward Lily, about his travelling, his interest in acquiring things. I lingered over a Russian samovar, the brass dull with age; a muted Afghan rug; a row of Indian elephants carved in ebony.

Dawn came, as I'd suggested. She spent a long time sniffing and dabbing her eyes and fussing around before taking a fruit bowl shaped like a fish. We exchanged phone numbers and I told her to drop in or ring if she wanted anything else. As she was leaving, David appeared. He'd changed out of his work clothes, and wore clean jeans and a blue shirt which creased across his body. 'Last check round?' he said, producing a bunch of keys and jangling them in front of me.

'What's left?'

'Some gardening tools et cetera in the shed, and a couple of boxes Dawn put together. Oh. And the chair.' He grinned. 'I could bring the boxes here, but if you want to come and check everything is in order,' he stopped and looked away shyly, 'I'd appreciate your company.' My colour rose as I nodded and turned, crashing into a green baize card table and cursing silently as I headed for the back room to tell Rita and Mattie where I was going. They said they'd take a break while I was gone and I suggested we meet again at two.

For a few minutes, we drove in silence. Then David mentioned the House of Flores and I found myself responding, talking freely about my father's business. I asked him about his career emptying houses. Was it pre- or post-Japan?

He paused, before saying, 'I was a history teacher first.'

'Why the career change?'

'My wife died.'

'Oh God. I'm sorry.'

'It's all right,' he said, swerving to avoid a pheasant. 'It was a long time ago and we had no children.' Did that make a difference, or was it something to say, a distraction, a ploy to put a stop to questions? I'd done the same enough times myself. But he was talking still, telling me about his wife. 'Beth was ill for a long time. I stopped work to look after her and I didn't feel like going back. I sold the house in London, went off to Japan – the cathartic bit I was telling you about – and when I returned, this came up, an acquaintance of an acquaintance, you know how it is. We did a bit of business together and then I started on my own.'

'Why here?'

'Pin and map, a bit like Japan.'

There was a long silence. I twisted the strap of my bag. David asked about my job. I told him about teaching in Athens, and, as if to justify myself with something more interesting, the travel articles I wrote.

'What about in England?' he said.

'I had a business. A shop in Paddington.'

'What did you sell?'

'Gifts, mainly from India.'

'Why?'

'I was travelling, brought back jewellery, scarves, things like that, sold them and then expanded.'

It had been my mother's idea. I'd come back from Delhi with silver earrings and bangles shaped like serpents with precious stones for eyes. 'Beautiful, Anna,' she'd said. 'You could sell these.' And so I had. I'd gone again to India, bought tapestries and carvings. I'd rented a market stall and when a shop had come up for let in Paddington, I'd looked around the neglected shell and had a vision.

Mum had lent me the money. I suspected Uncle Thomas had encouraged her. He'd been worried about the distance between us. 'Try,' he used to say to me. 'Reach out a little more.' He'd emphasised the *little* because he'd known no matter how hard I reached out to my mother, I'd never have grasped a thing.

'What made you stop?' said David, breaking into my thoughts.

'Money,' I said. 'Nobody wanted gifts from India in Paddington. Too hippy.' He laughed. 'Still, it lasted five years and failure gave me an excuse to travel again.'

'And what about the House of Flores? Are you planning to keep it open?'

'God no. I could never do that.' I spoke without thinking and gave him a sidelong look to see if he'd noticed, but he was staring ahead, concentrating on the road. I tried again. 'What I mean is, it would feel like going back.'

He glanced across at me. 'I know what you mean. There's no point. Although revisiting isn't a bad idea, before the final valediction.' He frowned. 'Is that the right word?'

I shrugged. 'Yes, I think it probably is.'

The cottage seemed lonely when I stepped back inside, and cold, though it was hardly surprising since all of Edward Lily's belongings had gone. I wanted to ask David how he felt, working in empty houses as the last of the memories were stripped away, but he was already heading for the living room with his crossword and settling in the chair.

I wandered upstairs, letting my fingers drift across the walls. The rooms were empty as David had said they would be. I stood in each one, absorbing their melancholy. I pictured Lydia, when I'd first seen her, staring out of the window. Had she wanted to escape or was she glad to be on the inside looking out? Years ago, I'd thought Gabriella was here, hiding out, or even imprisoned. My mind had been full of expectation and now that hope had gone. Perhaps that was the point. This was the final farewell, or valediction as David had said. The last visit to a house that had once been important to me for no other reason than fantasy.

Downstairs, a couple of boxes had been left on the kitchen floor. These must be the things Dawn had collected. Lydia's possessions. The things she and Edward Lily's sister had left behind. Crouching, I opened the lid of the first. There was a piece of material folded on the top. I lifted it out and discovered a shawl, black satin, with red roses. The shawl was faded and threadbare in places, and some of the tassels were missing, but it must have been beautiful once. And I remembered Lydia wearing something similar in a photo, standing on one of the bridges in the Plaza de España.

Holding the material to my face, I breathed in the scent. No hint of perfume, only the musty fragrance of the past. Leaving it on my lap, I looked again. More clothes. And now it seemed awkward delving through Lydia's old dresses and skirts. They were feminine, unlike anything I'd ever owned: gauzy and flowing, light-coloured and long.

In the second box were children's books, the titles the same as those that had stood on mine and Gabriella's shelves. I picked out Roald Dahl and Enid Blyton and classics: *The Railway Children*, *Little Women*, *Treasure*

Island. The books were well read, their pages turned down, with scribbles in the margins. I was surprised Lydia hadn't wanted these. Although realistically, I thought, was there any point in keeping them? My books were in the loft. I'd forgotten all about them until I'd looked there. Travel light. That had been my way of thinking. Still, I made a mental note to check these hadn't been left by mistake. I moved on, pulling out a wooden fan with a hand-painted figure of a flamenco dancer, a silk scarf, an embroidered handkerchief. Whispers from the past. Sparks from Lydia's life. The air was alight with them.

Footsteps in the hall made me start. Guiltily, I held my breath and listened. The front door opened. David must be going to the van. Now I was alone, the cottage seemed oddly silent and still. Turning back to the box, I imagined my father urging me on. *If you look hard enough, you'll find a fossil. If you prise it out gently, you'll discover it's a gem.* I touched the shawl again and held it to my face. A vivid picture of Lydia appeared and all of a sudden I understood why Dad had thrilled at every house clearance. Bringing people's lives back, for the briefest of moments. It was a way of cheating time. A way of finding out secrets too.

I stared at the rest of the things in the box: half-empty perfume bottles, a mirror with a dented frame, a heart-shaped jewellery box with pairs of tarnished earrings and a bracelet inside. Things that had belonged to a teenage girl abandoned now in the cottage. Dawn had told me that Edward liked to bring his daughter treats. Food because she didn't eat. Perhaps he'd brought her gifts too. A way to trigger an interest in life.

Whistling roused me and I hurried to the window. David was walking across the lawn, hands in his pockets. He gave a cheery wave. I smiled back, watching as he picked his way through the long grass towards the end of the garden and squeezed past a trellis, disappearing into the far section where the shed must be. Leaning forward, I squinted, feeling relief at the flash of his sleeve.

Shaking my head, I chastised myself for being dramatic and returned to my task. Most of the contents of the second box were spread out on the floor, but there were a few more books, a couple of china dolls and mementoes from Spain: a pair of wooden castanets, a postcard of the Madonna. I pushed my hand down the sides of the box for one more look. Feeling around, I pulled out a piece of card. Blank. Brown-spotted with age.

I turned the card over, expecting to see nothing, but there was a drawing. A portrait. A face. A chill crept through me. Could this be true? I closed my eyes and opened them again.

It was a picture of Gabriella. The face was fuller, the mouth not quite right, the hair not long enough, but it was her. I sat back on the floor, the cold from the stone seeping through my jeans. Shivering, I held the picture close, staring until my vision blurred. A question drilled through my head. Why was there a picture of Gabriella lying amongst Lydia's things?

A knock at the window made me jump. David was grinning at me, gesturing towards the back door. I stood up, trying to focus, but my legs were weak and I held on to the side as I stepped across and turned the key.

'Everything all right?' His smile turned to a frown. 'You don't look well.'

'I'm fine,' I said, forcing myself to reply. 'A headache.' I rubbed my forehead as if to prove it.

'I've got paracetamol in the van.'

'It's fine. Thank you. I just need to go.' I turned my back on him and crossed to the box, the portrait still in my hand. Kneeling, I put it back with trembling hands.

'You want me to take that?' He gestured to the box.

'I'll manage,' I said quickly. 'Can you take the other?'

'Course.' He crouched beside me and his arm brushed mine. I looked at him. Our faces were close, his eyes dark and interested. I felt the heat from his skin and I had a sudden urge to tell him what I'd found. 'Are you sure you're all right?' he said.

The feeling passed. I nodded and moved away, but I sensed David still looking at me, his disappointment clear. He must have known I was concealing something. Replacing the lid with a clatter, I closed down my emotions. Lifting the box, I made my way out of the house. Without commenting, David followed me back to the van.

As we drove, I rested my chin on my hand. All the while I'd been searching, not knowing what I'd find. I'd stalked the streets in the village, interviewed people, checked their alibis. I'd broken into Lemon Tree Cottage looking for Gabriella, convinced Edward Lily had spirited her away. But I'd given up. Even when I came back this time, I'd been reluctant to search again.

How stupid I'd been to doubt myself, to believe the clues had long gone. I should have known there'd be something that the police had missed. That I had missed. And here it was, buried in a box in Edward Lily's house. A portrait of Gabriella.

I closed my eyes, trying to make sense of its meaning, but no explanation would come.

18

1982

Mum was sitting beside the telephone, making calls. She spoke in a bright voice each time she explained that Gabriella was missing, her crisp words fracturing only at the end of the conversation.

For a moment when I passed her, she looked across, her face bright, seeing Gabriella's parka before she saw that it was me. Her face fell as I hung up the coat and I felt the misery of knowing that I'd raised her hopes. And then the guilt. I was the wrong daughter. It was only when she finished her call and yelled at me for going out, then immediately wrapped me in her arms, that I understood she cared.

It was Friday, but no one mentioned going to school. No one mentioned anything. I sat in the kitchen alone eating Rice Krispies from Gabriella's bowl. When I walked back through the hall Mum was still there. She gave me a sad smile and dialled another number.

Dad disappeared. I watched him from the window, leaping into his van and driving away fast. He came back an hour later, shaking his head, holding his hand out to my mother who had stopped making phone calls and was in the kitchen, sitting at the table, hands clasped as if in prayer. 'She's not there, Esther,' said Dad quietly. 'He hasn't seen her either.'

Mum breathed out slowly. 'He wouldn't have done. He was here.' I remembered the scent of tobacco, the unexplained visitor from yesterday.

'I know that, but still she might have gone afterwards.'

'After what? We don't know what she did.'

They suddenly seemed to remember me and stopped talking. Who were they talking about? Where had Dad been? I didn't ask, because the only answer I cared about concerned the location of my sister.

In the afternoon, PC Atkins came back. He stood in the hall, his radio crackling, talking to Mum and Dad. His boots clumped across the floor as they went through to the kitchen. The door closed with a gentle click and the sound of exclusion rattled inside my head.

It was thirty minutes before Dad came to fetch me. I timed it on the pendulum clock, fixing my eyes on the hands and my ears on the beat so that I wouldn't have to think of anything else.

PC Atkins smiled reassuringly. 'Hello again, Anna,' he said. This time I sat on a chair with my hands jammed between my knees while he squatted in front of me, his body creaking with the effort. My parents stood behind him like a pair of bookends. My mother's face was so white it reminded me of one of the figures I'd made out of leftover pastry and varnished with milk for the oven.

'You don't mind if I ask you a few more questions?' he said, taking out his notebook and flicking through the pages. 'I've been to Gabriella's school now, talked to her friends and her teachers, and I just want to know what you think about that.'

He started slowly, explaining what he'd found out. Gabriella had been seen in morning lessons and at break time. She'd eaten in the canteen and registered in the afternoon. She'd walked out of the gates with friends, but they'd separated and nobody could say where she'd gone. Pausing from time to time to check his notes, to shift his position, to look at me carefully with his sad eyes, he eventually cleared his throat. 'What about outside school? Has anything unusual happened?'

I moistened my lips. Martha's image came into my mind – her story about the man and the letter. I hadn't seen a man, but I had seen the letter. And I'd seen the way Gabriella had looked. 'Anna?' said the policeman encouragingly. 'What are you thinking about?'

I shrugged. 'She had a letter.'

He studied me carefully and scratched his chin. 'Letter?' I nodded. 'Who was it from?'

'I don't know. She was reading it at the fête.' Should I tell him what Martha had said?

'Might it have been from a . . .' PC Atkins paused and glanced at my parents. 'Boy?'

I thought about the boys at school. I didn't think Gabriella liked any of them so I shook my head. There was only the one in Our Price, but she'd never spoken to him. Not properly.

There was a moment's quiet. 'Tell me,' said PC Atkins, grimacing with the effort, 'did your sister ever talk about leaving home?'

I waited five beats, counting slowly in my head. 'No,' I said firmly. 'Never.'

There was silence as he looked at the ceiling and

frowned a little. 'Only, I found a suitcase under your sister's bed.' I gripped my hands more tightly between my knees.

He cleared his throat again. 'Did you know about that?'

'No.' My eyes filled with tears.

He looked away again and spoke to the wall. 'Was she unhappy about something? Do you have any idea why she might have packed it? Do you think she might have been thinking about meeting—'

Dad interrupted. 'No. If you're implying Gabriella had a boyfriend that she was about to drop everything for and run away with, that's ridiculous. Gabriella didn't have a boyfriend, did she, Esther?'

Mum shook her head.

PC Atkins kept his eyes on me. 'What do you think, Anna? Do you know if Gabriella had any special friends like that?'

I stared back at him, my tears starting to fall, and now Dad stepped forward. 'No, of course she doesn't. And I've already told you, Gabriella didn't have a boyfriend and she hasn't run away. She's not the type of girl to do that.' He paused. 'She probably packed the suitcase because she thought we were going to Wales. She didn't realise we'd decided not to go. Besides, if she'd run away, she would have taken it with her, wouldn't she?'

The policeman didn't speak for a moment. Then he said, 'Do you think that's right, Anna? Do you think she packed the suitcase for your holidays?'

I nodded slowly and whispered, 'Yes.'

He leaned forward to catch my answer and then got

awkwardly to his feet. 'Thank you, Anna. You've been very helpful. And I don't want you to worry about anything.' Turning to my parents, he said, 'Do you mind if I take another look round? It's just a formality. All the rooms this time, the loft, and do you have a shed?' They looked at each other and nodded.

On Saturday, I woke early to the sound of voices. At first I thought the policeman was back, but when I came downstairs, I found Grandma Grace, Granddad Bertrand, Uncle Thomas and Donald. They'd been summoned in the night.

They gave me weary smiles. Uncle Thomas patted the seat beside him, but I preferred to sit on the floor. I always sat on the floor with Gabriella. It would be odd if I didn't do that now. Grandma Grace filled the silence with her comments. 'Such a lovely baby,' she said. 'Everything just right. Such a sensible girl. She'll be back.' But her words were frayed and she soon stopped talking and leaned on her stick, lips moving in silent conversation with herself.

The morning crept forward. Dad hadn't shaved and his eyes were bleary as if he hadn't slept. He kept running his hand through his hair until it stuck up in clumps. Rita came round, led Mum upstairs and they sat in Gabriella's bedroom. Donald made endless cups of tea which no one drank while Uncle Thomas persuaded me to sit next to him. He stroked my arm as I leaned against him and kept murmuring the same thing: 'Courage, Anna.'

The adults exchanged words they thought I couldn't hear. The suitcase had confused everyone. Despite the logic that Gabriella would have taken it with her, the police believed it showed a mind capable of flight. I stayed silent. I had no intention of spurring their theory on. I knew Gabriella hadn't run away because she wouldn't have left without saying goodbye. Not to me. She was staying somewhere for a day or two, hiding out for a reason of her own. I accepted the idea as if she'd mentioned it to me; it was simply that I'd forgotten exactly what she'd said. I only had to think hard and I'd remember. I only had to wait and she'd be back.

At ten o'clock, Dad broke. He glared at all of us, his hair and eyes wild, and announced that if the police weren't going to do anything, he was going to search the village. He took Uncle Thomas and Donald and vowed to knock on everybody's door. By late afternoon he'd returned and the whole village knew my sister had disappeared.

Dad marched straight to the telephone and phoned the police. He was shouting, insisting that they searched for his daughter. Mum and Rita came down the stairs. Uncle Thomas took Dad outside. It was left to Donald to pat my shoulder and tell me everything would be all right.

Later, I peered through the front window at two police officers in our road. I watched them going in and out of gates and driveways, staying a few minutes at each door. My policeman (as I saw him now) arrived with another who introduced himself as DC Sayers. They sat together in the kitchen while I stayed in my room. I'd watched enough police programmes to know that DC Sayers was a step up from PC Atkins. To force it from my mind, I tidied my bookcase, taking all the books out, laying them on the floor and putting them back in alphabetical order. Some I'd inherited from Gabriella: *Malory Towers*, *The Famous Five*. These I laid on my bed. I was going to read each of them again. Nothing else until she came home.

As soon as the men left, I crept halfway down the stairs and listened to my parents talking once again. Scores of police officers were being organised to conduct a fingertip search. They were satisfied, apparently, that Gabriella wasn't the kind of girl who would run away. The vicar, her teachers, everyone who knew her had created the same picture.

I imagined the scene: a line of blue uniforms stooping low as they swept across the green, crouching when they found a ring or a bracelet, a set of keys, a glove. Except they wouldn't discover anything, I told myself repeatedly, because there'd be nothing there to find.

In Gabriella's room I peered through the window. The neighbours had come out and were gathered in the street. Every now and then one of them looked across at our house. A man, who I recognised from two doors down, was talking, waving his hands around. His wife had had a baby only the week before and Mum had sent me round with a pink fluffy bunny and a card. Even Mrs Henderson was there with her stupid son Brian. I opened the window and let the words float through. 'We have to do something,' said the man with the baby. 'If it was one of ours . . .' He dropped his voice and I didn't hear more. A woman holding a toddler hugged him closer. A man put a hand on her shoulder.

Leaning forward, I let my breath mist the glass. My body felt hollow as if nothing was inside me, no organs, no blood pumping, only the bones of my skeleton and the shell of my skin.

The group drifted home. I pictured them, and all the rest of the people in the village, locking windows, checking doors, sitting with their children, keeping them at home.

I kept a vigil by the window, keeping track of who came and who went. From time to time a neighbour ran down the street, the soles of their shoes smacking on the pavement. Other neighbours knocked on doors and disappeared inside. It was as if they were planning something we were excluded from, some kind of terrible surprise.

At midday, the doors opened. One by one, men and boys stepped out, turning as if under instruction, in one direction, and walking silently away.

Later, a gold Ford Cortina clattered down the road and stopped on the kerb opposite. Two men swung open the doors, stretched their arms and looked around them, their gaze falling longest on our house. They opened the boot and hauled out a tripod. Setting it up on the pavement, they levelled a camera straight at our door.

The doorbell rang. Dad answered, half shutting the door behind him, and when he came back he spoke to Mum who was waiting in the hall. 'The neighbours are searching,' he said. 'The whole lot of them, man and boy. They're on the green, helping the police.' My empty stomach churned. I put my hand there to make it still. Dad was trying not to cry as he took Mum's hand, and drew her close. And as they leaned against each other, the autumn sun, straggling through the arched window at the top of the door, made weak patterns on their skin.

Dad went off again, this time taking Uncle Thomas. Donald stayed to look after the rest of us although I could tell he didn't want to; he wanted to be out there, searching like the other men. He kept fidgeting, walking about the room. Eventually he disappeared and came back with loaves of bread, Edam cheese and pickle. He enlisted my help and we made stacks of sandwiches for everyone. He put me in charge of buttering the bread and piling on the pickle. Gabriella didn't like pickle, I wanted to tell him as I slathered it on. She preferred salad cream.

After dark, Dad and Uncle Thomas came home, shaking their heads. And then the family – Uncle Thomas and Donald, Grandma Grace and Granddad Bertrand – left, trailing out in silence with a promise to return the next day.

Jasper appeared and jumped onto my lap. I buried my face in his fur and prayed. *Please God. Let my sister come home.* And as I listed the extra chores I'd do, the services I'd go to, the old people I'd help, the Christian Aid envelopes I'd deliver, I tried to ignore Gabriella's voice in my head: *What's the point of praying when God doesn't reply?*

19

David and I were both silent on the journey back to the House of Flores. There were too many emotions twisting inside my head. I was afraid that if I spoke, I'd lose control.

I thought I'd seen every picture that existed of my sister – the photos they'd used in the papers; the snapshots we'd had at home. Now I'd discovered an entirely new image inside a stranger's house and I didn't know how to react.

From time to time, David gave me a curious glance and I wondered if he resented my detachment. There was nothing I could do. I didn't have the strength to take his feelings into account.

Still, I felt a tug of regret when David came into the House of Flores and I refused his offer to stay and help. He suggested meeting for a drink instead and I made an excuse for that too.

'It's all right,' he said with a rueful smile. 'It's not obligatory.' But he pulled out a pen and scribbled his number onto a scrap of paper before he left. 'In case you change your mind.'

I took the boxes into the back room. The clock chimed from its hidden place and I checked my watch. Two o'clock. Rita and Mattie were due. I pulled out the portrait and slipped it into my bag. By the time they arrived I'd gathered myself and a pile of paperwork together and was pretending to be absorbed.

They worked in the back room, sorting Edward Lily's clothes, his shirts and pinstripe trousers, linen jackets, hats and shoes. After a while, I gave up on the accounts and fetched the portrait.

The artist had captured Gabriella exactly, the way she looked to one side, the hint of a smile on her lips. The picture had been drawn by someone who knew my sister, or else had watched her, day after day. Dawn had said Lydia was strange. Withdrawn. A solitary girl with solitary pursuits. She'd been a reader. Had she been an artist too? Taking my address book, I flicked through until I found Dawn's number and made the call.

Dawn sounded out of breath. 'I was in the garden, pulling out weeds,' she said. 'Needs must, now I'm on my own. Is everything all right? Did you find Lydia's things?'

'Yes. Thank you.' I stopped and walked across to the window. From the back room, I heard Rita and Mattie discussing how to deal with Edward Lily's clothes.

'Good,' said Dawn. 'I wasn't sure what to do with them, because of course I couldn't carry them, and the man with the van said—'

'That's all right,' I said, interrupting. 'They're at the shop now.' I hesitated. My heart was beating too hard. I put my hand on my chest to try to slow it down. 'There's a drawing. I wondered where you found it.'

'Drawing? Oh yes. It was in the living room, on the empty shelves. I thought it had been forgotten so I popped it in the box.'

'Do . . . ?' I stopped again, and tried to breathe normally. 'Do you think Lydia might have drawn it?'

There was a pause. 'Well,' said Dawn. 'I don't know.'

'Did you ever see Lydia drawing?'

'I don't remember. I don't think so.'

'It's only . . . the portrait is very good.'

'Is it? Well, to be honest, I didn't really look. I was in a hurry to get the boxes sorted. The man with the van—'

'That's fine,' I said. 'Don't worry.' I waited a few seconds before I asked my next question, gathering my breath and speaking quickly to get the sentence out. 'What about Edward Lily? Was he an artist?' My voice was high and strange. I gripped the phone. Had Dawn noticed?

'I'd say it was more likely,' she said. 'All those paintings he collected, but I can't say I ever saw him doing anything like that himself. Perhaps he bought it. What makes you think it was either of them who drew it?' It was a good question and one I couldn't answer. So I thanked her again and told her to come in any time if she wanted to take another look through Lydia's things. I was going to keep them for a while in case Edward's sister or Lydia herself came back to claim them.

After the call, I considered more carefully the possibility of Edward Lily being the artist. I imagined him watching Gabriella so often he'd managed to capture her expression exactly; to draw her hair, her eyes, her mouth so precisely. I thought of the man in the photos, his books and his beautiful things. I thought of his wife. His daughter. If it was true, had they known what he was like?

Crossing the room, I stood before the Modigliani. The girl's eyes looked back. Defiant. Strange I'd never seen her like that before. I touched the glass gently with my fingertips, traced the narrow face. Gabriella. She was everywhere. In my thoughts and in my dreams, beside me now, staring outwards from this painting. And there was I, my reflection, staring back. Two sisters, trapped in one place.

That night I stayed awake, moving through the darkness in the house. Gabriella: my first thought in the morning, my last memory at night.

The discovery of the portrait had changed everything. The faceless shadow that had visited me in my dreams was real. Suspicion finally had a foundation. The figure had a face. And that meant something else. The police would need to know. The newspapers would dig up the story all over again. People would pick over the pieces, like crows on raw meat.

The realisation bore down on me as I paced. I'd spent years barely speaking of Gabriella, and it struck me now: so few people I'd ever met beyond this village even knew that I'd had a sister. When friends talked about their childhoods or complained about their families I was silent and they assumed I had no one. People told me that I was lucky. I didn't tell them otherwise. I looked at their family photos and showed them nothing in return. Now I would have no choice but to admit I'd had a sister. I would no longer be able to deal with things alone.

The thought gripped my throat, suffocating me. I needed air. Out in the garden, I stood beneath the damson tree, staring upwards through the thin boughs at the cold moon.

I remembered the day Gabriella disappeared. The loneliness, the desolation; how I'd made up stories in my mind to explain where she'd gone. I'd refused to believe her absence was absolute until I'd finally given in and accepted what everyone else had seen as inevitable. What choice had I had? I'd needed to get on with my future and put that other life behind me. Although I hadn't done that, had I? I'd only hidden the grief inside myself. And now perhaps this was the closest I could ever be to Gabriella, beneath the tree where we'd gathered fruit, feeling her breath in the wind.

20

1982

On Sunday, DC Sayers arrived alone. He was younger than my policeman with slick black hair, and a sharp, clean-shaven chin. 'Start from the beginning,' he told me, crossing his legs and leafing through a file. 'Take your time.'

We went over Gabriella's movements, talking on and on until my mind was spinning. I tripped over thoughts and forgot details, until again it felt like I was supposed to know; that I held the answer to where Gabriella had gone.

DC Sayers paused, licked his finger with the tip of his tongue and turned the pages in the file back to the start. 'Tom,' he said. 'You saw Tom. Did you speak to him?' I shook my head. 'Nothing at all? Did you wave, or call out, anything like that?'

I screwed up my eyes, trying to remember. 'She smiled,' I said at last.

'Smiled?' he said quickly. 'Gabriella, you mean?' I nodded. 'And did Tom smile back?'

'No, I don't think so. Tom never smiles.'

DC Sayers glanced across at my parents. 'And when you left him . . . What did he do?'

I tried to picture what had happened, but I couldn't recall. Yet this policeman thought it was important what

Tom had done. He was relying on me to know and I wasn't able to tell him. If only I could say we hadn't met Tom, maybe that would mean Gabriella would still be here.

'Is there anything else you can think of?' said DC Sayers, sighing a little now. 'You mentioned a letter, didn't you? To PC Atkins.' He paused and tapped small, sharp teeth with his pencil. 'Can you think of anything we might connect to that? Did you see your sister talking, for example, to a boy or a man you didn't know?'

I frowned. My mind was going backwards, ticking off each person I'd seen Gabriella with.

'Perhaps you didn't see them talking,' he prompted. 'Perhaps you only noticed them watching.' He uncrossed his legs. 'What I mean is, there might have been someone new around . . . maybe over the last few days . . . or weeks.' I moved uncomfortably in my seat and he leaned forward. 'Anna?'

'There's someone,' I said quietly.

'A man?'

I nodded. 'He lives at Lemon Tree Cottage. He stared at Gabriella, but I'm not sure . . .' I stopped and glanced at my parents. They were stony-faced, looking back at me.

DC Sayers squinted and re-crossed his legs. 'And just to be sure . . . what does this man look like?'

'He wears a hat.' I looked again at my parents, but still neither of them spoke, and suddenly I wasn't sure what they wanted me to do. I bowed my head with the despair of it all, and tried to blink away my tears, but they came anyway and rolled steadily down my cheeks. 'His name's Edward Lily.'

There was a chill in the room as if the temperature had suddenly dropped. Dad stood up. 'Enough,' he said.

'Is there something you'd like to add, Mr Flores?' said the policeman, his eyes watchful.

'Annie,' Dad said, holding out his hand to me. 'You don't need to stay.' He led me to my room. And that was what I wanted, to be alone, to lie on my bed and make Gabriella appear with the force of my imagination. But then I felt worse because Dad kissed my forehead and stroked my hair, and left me alone. And no matter how much I held her in my mind, I couldn't bring Gabriella back.

On Monday the search widened, spreading to the woods, but also to people's gardens and their outhouses: sheds, greenhouses, even chicken coops.

The men with the tripods were still there, but now they'd been joined by several others, smoking, or with hands in their pockets, talking quietly. Around them, the houses were silent, windows and doors drawn tight, curtains closed, lights off, as if the whole street had calcified like a row of Donald's fossils.

The reporters stayed all night – illuminated beneath the street lamp, smoking, their voices filtering through the partly opened window. Sometimes a neighbour confronted them – the man with the new baby. His wife came out once, hair loose around her shoulders, wearing her dressing gown and holding the baby wrapped up in a pink blanket. She yelled about common decency and respect, but all they did was take her photo and call after her as she retreated home.

The house was different without Gabriella. I lay in bed at night listening to the sighs and mutterings in the pipes and behind the walls. There was an emptiness, a stillness. Gabriella had created sound. I missed her conversation, her funny comments at the breakfast table, the way she needled Mum and wheedled her way around Dad.

I searched for the letter, but it was nowhere. Had the policemen already discovered it? Wouldn't they have mentioned it? Asked me if it was the same one? I looked for Gabriella's Walkman but I couldn't find that either. She must have taken it to school, hidden in her bag. She would have listened to her favourite songs as she made her way down the streets to meet me. If she'd ever set off to meet me. I lay on her bed, thinking about that, trying to fit into the dent in the mattress, in exactly the same way she'd done, and I played her records, softly, so that Mum wouldn't hear, and tried to fill the silence Gabriella left inside my head.

One week after Gabriella had disappeared, and the search had dwindled, I found a newspaper abandoned on the kitchen table. A picture of Gabriella appeared on the front page, a school photo taken last year. I traced her face, my breath coming in shallow leaps. There was a photo of Tom too, without his cart, and another of Mrs Ellis with a scarf wrapped around her throat.

Mrs Ellis was a witness. She'd been in the street at

five o'clock on the day Gabriella had disappeared. She'd been waiting for her daughter to come home after a late lesson at school. And while she'd been standing outside her house, she'd seen Tom and Gabriella talking. 'I didn't think anything of it at the time,' she said in the interview. And now Tom was under suspicion.

I threw down the paper. This was all wrong. I'd seen Tom push his cart onto the road to avoid a snail and cry when he scooped up a flattened hedgehog. I'd seen him stand still for ten minutes listening to a blackbird song. Tom would never hurt Gabriella. He'd never hurt anyone.

Over the next few days, I pieced together as much information as I could. I listened outside doors as the police reported to my parents, and read the newspapers I found stuffed down the side of the sofa, or hidden inside drawers.

Tom had admitted to seeing Gabriella on Acer Street at around five o'clock. She'd been alone at the time. He thought she'd said hello to him, but he really wasn't sure. He thought Gabriella had been with a friend after all, a girl of the same age, or it might have been a man, he really didn't know. He was confused. He often forgot things. Once he forgot his way home. His mother had called the police and they found him wandering in the woods. Another time he forgot his cart, left it by the side of the road. Someone stole it and took it on a joyride. It turned up in the lake. All those old stories were written in the papers.

Things changed again. Mr Sullivan, eighty-five, a well-known resident of the village (having lived in the house next door to Tom his whole life), and a regular member of the church, came forward. Well respected, always trusted, he was only a little forgetful which was why he hadn't been to the police before. Now he recalled that on the day Gabriella had disappeared, he'd been on his way to the chemist. He'd met Tom on the High Street soon after Mrs Ellis had seen him near her house. It meant Tom wouldn't have had time to do anything to Gabriella (not that I'd ever believed he had). Not only that, but Mrs Ellis added to her statement too, suddenly remembering seeing Tom leaving Gabriella and continuing on his way.

PC Atkins explained the story. He said there were too many unreliable witnesses. Too many contradictory sightings and times. And no evidence against Tom. Not a trace of human blood, or spit, or semen, or any other body fluid found anywhere near him or his cart, only a spot of rat's piss on the bristles of his broom. That was what was said, more or less.

And now Tom was no longer a suspect.

Nobody was. Not even Edward Lily. And I didn't know why. DC Sayers had been curious enough about him. Why hadn't he been mentioned again?

21

I called David the next morning. 'It's me,' I said.

'Who?' He spoke above the engine of his van.

'Anna.'

'Wait.' He cursed in the background before his voice came back. 'Anna. I can't speak for long. Are you still there? What is it? What's wrong?'

My resolve crumbled. I'd wanted to tell David about the portrait, but I had no idea where to start.

He was cursing again. 'There's a tunnel coming up. Listen. I'm on my way to Yorkshire. A one-off job. I'll be back late tonight. Can I call you then?' The phone went dead. I felt stupidly disappointed and then immediately relieved. It would be ridiculous to confide in a man I'd only just met.

What should I do? Call the police? The portrait had to be grounds for suspicion. But would it be enough to open an investigation that was thirty years old? I thought of Rita. If anyone would know what to do, it would be her. She was full of ideas and advice. Yesterday, I'd been too shocked to speak to her about the portrait, but now that I was thinking more clearly, it seemed obvious that she should be the one I told.

I took my bag with the portrait tucked inside, slipped on my jacket and DMs and opened the front door. It was cold and a fine rain was already falling. I grabbed an old-fashioned stick umbrella from the hall and stepped outside. A figure was standing opposite, on the other side of the road. Not again. Bloody Martha. What the hell was she doing here? Anyone would think she was waiting for me the way she was watching. She wore her raincoat, but she had no hood and even though the rain was coming harder, she didn't seem to care.

For a moment I was transported back in time. The two of us standing across from one another in the street. Martha had been crying. What had she said? Something about biscuits. That was it. It was a bizarre memory. I tried filling it in with a background, but all I saw was a crowd of people. Had it been the day of the reconstruction? I closed my eyes. I didn't want to think about that now. I didn't want to speak to Martha. I slipped back inside the house and closed the door behind me.

If it hadn't been so early, I'd have drunk a bottle of wine. Besides, I hadn't eaten. I pulled out a frying pan and a box of eggs and set to making an omelette. While I was busy, there was a knock at the door. If it was Martha, I didn't want to know. I carried on making my food, whisking the eggs, heating up the oil. There was another knock, louder this time. And still I ignored whoever was there.

Sitting down to eat, I found I had no appetite. I shoved the plate to one side and made coffee instead. While it was brewing, the letter box clattered and I made my way stealthily out into the hall. No one was hovering at the door. There were only a couple of letters on the mat. Two more cards from people I didn't know, sending their condolences.

Taking them to the living room, I placed them on the

mantelpiece. My eyes rested on the envelopes containing the certificates. I should file them before they got lost. Pulling them out, I scanned Dad's birth and death certificates. There was nothing I didn't know – parents' names, place and date of birth, cause of death. I took a moment to remember the day of his funeral. Images trekked through my mind, snapshots of Uncle Thomas and Donald dressed in black, my pale-faced, fragile mother, a fraction of who she'd been. And me, twelve years old, uncertain and small, perched on a pew that smelled of polish, staring through the lattice of my fingers at the pale coffin as people around me prayed for my father's soul and Gabriella's words sounded again in my ears. *What's the point of praying when God doesn't reply?*

Where *were* the original certificates? Taking a look around the room, cluttered still with the junk I'd pulled out from shelves and cupboards, I guessed they'd be here somewhere. Eventually they'd turn up. I'd been too impatient to wait.

I examined the wedding certificate. Groom: Albert Flores. Bride: Esther Button. The witnesses, the name of the church, the addresses. And the date: October 1966. I paused.

The story, the one recited over and over again by Grandma Grace. It was the romance of the year, so she'd said. The summer storm, my father summoned to clear the garden. Love at first sight. The wedding had taken place six weeks after. I'd known the story nearly off by heart, but I hadn't known the date. Not the day or the month. Only the year. I thought about that now. Had my parents celebrated their anniversary? If they had I could hardly recall. Perhaps they'd played it down, made their celebrations private, not wanted to draw attention.

A cold sensation began its slow ascent. Icy fingers nudging at my spine. Fact: October 1966. The date was solid, written out in front of me. Yet Gabriella's birthday was March 1967. I could hardly forget that. Fifteen years of birthdays: cine film of cakes and candles, piles of presents, chubby faces changing as we grew. Thirty more years of imagining how each birthday would have been – how Gabriella's face and body would have altered; who she would have shared the celebrations with; what gifts I would have bought her.

Clumsily I counted, my mind frozen up with thoughts. Mum must have been several months pregnant when she married. And yet she'd only known Dad six weeks. It had been a romance as wild and fast as the storm that had got them together – that was what Grandma Grace had always said. And I was sure Gabriella hadn't been premature. Everyone had said how lovely she was, everything just right.

My mother must have been pregnant before she met my father. The thought occurred to me before I could stop it, a jolt of an idea that I let settle inside my brain. I considered other more rational alternatives. But the only explanation was that Grandma Grace had been confused. My parents' courtship had been longer than six weeks. Six months maybe. Perhaps the storm had been in the spring, not the summer. They'd got married because my mother was pregnant. That was it. The whirlwind was more like shotgun. Grandma Grace's memory was wrong.

Or else she'd lied. But why would she have done that? And whatever the case, whether it had been the ramblings of an old woman or deliberate deceit, surely somebody would have pointed it out. No one had ever said that the storm hadn't been in the summer. Or that the six-week romance was wrong.

Gripping the certificate, I climbed up the stairs, mouth dry, mind reeling as I stopped outside Gabriella's room. I didn't want to think about this anymore. I wanted to rewind each new theory. Yet that initial explanation remained. 'My dad was not my sister's father.' I said the sentence out loud. Twice. Three times. Louder each time, listening to the ring each word made in the silence of the house, hoping to hear the hollowness of a lie, but hearing only the ring of certainty.

Why had my parents lied? Why had they denied Gabriella the truth about her father? Why had neither of them ever told me? Surely we'd both had the right to know the reality of the relationship between us. Not that it would have made any difference. Nothing would have changed the way I'd felt. Gabriella was my sister. Nobody could take that away from me.

I opened the door. The room was exactly as it had been the last time I'd been inside, just before I'd gone away to Greece. Mum had refused to change it over the years, although she'd never stopped me entering, and she'd always kept it clean. Uncle Thomas had said it was because she hadn't wanted to lose hope. If she'd packed away Gabriella's things, it would have been an admission that she wasn't coming back.

I knelt on the carpet. The suitcase was beneath the

bed. Mum had left that too, waiting for Gabriella to come home and unpack. I lay down, curled up on my side, remembering my sadness the day we'd argued, the spiral of fear when she'd told me she would go. I'd tried to stop her packing, but she hadn't listened, only shaken me away. Afterwards, she'd put her arm around me. I remembered her words exactly. *You're my sister. Nothing changes that.*

Eventually, I sat on Gabriella's bed, staring at the certificate I clutched in my hand. Of course I was her sister. Why had she even said that? And then it struck me. The rows, the bad feeling between Gabriella and my parents, the time she'd run out the room when Grandma Grace insisted on telling that tired old story – the romance; the lie. Gabriella knew we were half-sisters. And on that day, perhaps she'd hinted at the truth, tried to let me know that having different fathers didn't affect us. We were sisters. Nothing changed that. If only I'd pushed her to say what she'd meant. If only I'd asked her to explain.

Now I tried to clear away preconceptions of my mother, father, sister and myself. I wanted to start again, a blank canvas, laying out my thoughts and memories and looking at them afresh. But I was bewildered by the knowledge that had slowly begun to build. And I left the room searching for proof.

In my mother's bedroom, I studied each item of furniture, each picture, painting and ornament. What was hidden here? What secrets would make my suspicions fall into place? Sitting at the dressing table, I stared at my reflection in the glass. A few grey hairs stood out against the dark and reminded me that I was older than my mother had been when Gabriella disappeared. What would Gabriella have looked like now? Artists could age missing children using complicated software and family characteristics. How would they have aged Gabriella? Would they have made her look like a fair-haired version of me? Or would the distinctions between us, the different genes we possessed, have pushed us further apart?

I drew open drawers and closed them again. What was I looking for? What could I hope to see that hadn't already been found? Rifling through the jewellery box, I lifted up the pendant with its emerald stone. It reminded me of Mum's ring, the one she used to take out and admire from time to time, but never wore. I'd always thought the ring was so precious she hadn't wanted to lose it.

Where was that ring? I hadn't seen it since I'd been home. Mum had been buried with her wedding ring. I couldn't imagine ever getting married myself, and anyway, it should have been Gabriella's since she was the eldest. But the emerald ring. I wanted to keep that.

I spread the jewellery across the dressing table and searched through. No ring. I opened drawers again, suddenly desperate to find it. And there it was, tucked away in a box in a satin drawstring pouch. I slipped the ring on my finger. It was loose, but then my fingers had always been narrow. Mum had been so thin after Gabriella disappeared, hardly eating. Perhaps the ring had become too big for her too.

Going to the window, I admired the stone in the light. Outside, people were walking in the rain, holding their umbrellas at different angles like a Renoir painting.

I looked for Martha, but she'd gone. Instead, Mattie was wandering by. He stopped and took out his mobile, his face intense, reminding me of Rita. He saw me watching, grinned and waved in a wide arc. It was one of Rita's gestures.

Sitting back at the dressing table, the ring slipped off my finger and clattered onto the wood. I'd have it altered, but in the meantime, I'd keep the ring with the necklace. The two seemed to belong together. Had Mum bought them in the same place? Taking the box, I turned it over and scrutinised the words. The lettering was gold, too small to read. I reached for my bag and took out my glasses. Now I made out the words. *La Plata, La Calle Pájaro, Sevilla.*

A drumbeat of memory sounded in my head. I tried to concentrate on what I was reading, but a dark cloud had settled around my brain, making me sluggish, stopping me thinking. With an immense effort, I shook off the feeling and stared hard at the words. I'd read them before. One more wrench of my mind, and I'd recall where.

And then I did. I'd seen the address typed on the invoices in Edward Lily's house. I let the idea percolate in my brain. Why had my mother bought jewellery from his shop? Or had it been my father, buying gifts? I rifled through the jewellery again, examining boxes, but they were all imprinted with the names of shops in London. Was it a coincidence? This necklace and this ring?

Sounds from outside filtered in. A woman along the street was calling for her child. A trumpet sounded. Music practice. Far off a truck announced it was reversing. They were normal sounds. Normal life. They drew me back to the window. Mattie was still there, talking to a friend, gesticulating as he told a story. Rita again. I recognised her in the way he moved.

Downstairs, I resisted the urge to open that bottle of wine. Instead I sat at the kitchen table and ran my fingers across the wood, feeling the scratches of age. The kitchen hadn't changed much. Glancing around, my eyes rested on the food I'd taken from the cupboards. Tins of Campbell's soup – my mother's diet for the last few years. Old packets of rice. A forgotten packet of Vesta curry. And neglected jars of jam, covered in dust, the writing on the labels smudged and faded.

I knew without looking that each label was dated no later than 1982. Mum never made jam again after Gabriella disappeared. The fruit in the garden wasn't collected. Year after year it dropped and rotted, a rancid mess seeping into the ground. I hadn't gone to the fête again either, not without my sister. Only once, shortly before leaving the village for London, I'd made my way down Devil's Lane. I'd stopped short at the stile, heard the jangle of the merry-go-round and gone back.

Now I pushed myself to remember that last fête. The day had been marred by the incident with Dad. He'd hurt his hand – in a fight. That had been my assumption anyway, though Gabriella hadn't believed it. And there'd been another fight. Mr Ellis had been involved. And Gabriella had abandoned me on the merry-go-round. And what about the suitcase, and Mum's suspicions – telling me to spy on Gabriella? Or had that come before? I rubbed my eyes, trying to order my memories.

Stretching out my hand, I spread out the photos on the table. Edward Lily. Everything came back to him. And yet my parents had been so convinced he'd had nothing to do with Gabriella's disappearance. I slotted his arrival in the village into my time frame. The summer of 1982. A few months before Gabriella went missing. When our family had started to disintegrate.

And Lydia, such a strange girl. I'd been uncharitable saying she was mad. I'd adopted the language of the village. Everybody had called her that. Except my parents. They'd never gossiped like other people did.

I examined the photo of Lydia in Spain and lifted it close to my face: the hair, the look, the secret smile. She'd been a beautiful, mysterious girl. I took the portrait of Gabriella from my bag and laid it beside the photo. The artist was truly talented the way he or she had captured Gabriella's hair, her look, her secret smile.

My breath caught inside my throat.

I'd thought Edward Lily was obsessed with Gabriella even though she was young enough to be his daughter. And now I understood. I looked from the portrait to the photo. Sisters. No wonder I'd been drawn to Lydia so many times. No wonder I'd felt the connection with this photo. I'd even mistaken Lydia for Gabriella once, that day in the woods when I'd been searching.

Edward Lily and my mother had been lovers. In love enough to exchange gifts. An emerald necklace. An emerald ring. Lydia was Gabriella's half-sister. Edward Lily was Gabriella's father.

And my father. He'd known. I was certain of that. And he'd made up for it, loving Gabriella as much or even more than he'd loved me. Working hard every day, stitching together a perfect tableau: the four of us. An ideal tapestry of family life. How he must have despaired when Edward Lily arrived in the village and threatened to unstitch all that embroidered cloth. How far would he have gone to stop Edward Lily from taking what he loved?

And how far would Edward Lily have gone to claim Gabriella back?

22

1982

Dad was crouching by the damson tree with an unlit cigarette dangling in his hand. I hunkered down beside him and we stayed that way in silence for a while.

I wanted to ask him what the police were doing next. Who would they interview? Had they really given up on Tom? I was glad because I knew he was innocent, but I wasn't sure Dad thought the same. Eventually, I asked about Edward Lily. What had happened about him?

Dad looked at me steadily and for a moment I didn't think he'd reply. And then he spoke, labouring each of his words so they hung like lead between us. 'The police have interviewed him.' I gazed at the ground, waiting for more. Dad cleared his throat and continued. 'They went to the cottage and didn't find anything and, anyway, he has an alibi.'

I let the words settle in my mind. 'So he isn't a suspect.'

'He's innocent.' It was the end of the conversation.

Later that night in bed I brooded about Edward Lily. I closed my eyes and imagined him at Lemon Tree Cottage. He was standing at the gate as I'd seen him before, staring at Gabriella and me in the lane. And his daughter, Lydia, was floating through the house like a phantom with a cloud of hair. I shifted restlessly in my bed. If only I had that moment again, I'd change the future. Somehow. I'd walk in a different direction, take Gabriella away.

My thoughts switched to Tom. Dad was certain that Edward Lily was innocent, but what about Tom? What exactly had he told the police about Gabriella? Had he been as confused as they'd said he was? If only I could speak to him too before he got more muddled and forgot completely what he'd seen.

It was dark. I got up and peered through the curtains. The light was on in the kitchen, illuminating the front part of the lawn and the damson tree. At the edges, things were harder to pick out, the shapes of familiar bushes and shrubs made ghostly by the shadows.

I should go and see Tom now.

If only I was brave enough.

I'd been brave enough to go into the woods and dig up Martha's box. But that was different. That was daytime. This was late at night. I glanced at the luminous hands on my clock. Almost ten.

The light in the kitchen went out. My parents must have gone into the living room. I was tired. I wanted to sleep. But the idea kept at me. Scraping away. If I didn't go now, Tom would forget. I imagined him going through the motions of his life, watching the telly, eating his tea, following the rituals of his evening. Each movement clouding his memory.

I knew I had to do it. I had to sneak downstairs without my parents hearing, and out the back so the reporters wouldn't see me and then over the neighbours' walls until I reached the end of the row of houses.

Slowly I pulled on my sweatshirt, and made my way through the house, grabbing my coat, opening the back door and slipping into the night.

It was cold. Clouds drifted across the half-moon, extinguishing its light. There was a rustle in the bushes. A pair of gleaming eyes. But it was only Jasper, pleased to see me, mewing loudly and winding around my legs. I stooped and ran my fingers along his back – tiny bones beneath the fur, so vulnerable, so delicate, so easy to break. I breathed deeply, pushing away my fear as I heaved myself over the wall that divided us from the Hendersons', and jumped into their garden.

I landed next to the empty chicken coop, banging my arm on the roof. Mrs Henderson was in the kitchen washing up. She looked up. Had she heard me? Could she sense that I was there? I froze, watching her face distorted by reflection and her eyes searching, worriedly, through the dark. I stayed where I was, shivering, teeth chattering, until she went back to her task. But her lips were moving – calling to her husband, I guessed – and sure enough, there he was, his square bulk as wide as she was thin, standing in the background. I sprang into action, scrambling over their wall, running across the next lawn, bending low, to the sound of the new baby crying from inside.

At the end of the row of houses, I jumped onto the pavement. The street was shadowy and quiet in the dim lamplight. I'd never been out so late on my own and now it seemed as though the village was alien, every shape an enemy.

Tom lived in a narrow street close to The Eagle. In daylight, I could run there in minutes, but in darkness, with all confidence gone, my pace was slow. I started at sounds, imagining footsteps, shouts, expecting a hand on my collar and a voice demanding to know why I was there.

At last, I arrived at Tom's house – a stone-clad terrace. I waited at the gate but there was no movement, no light or sound. Clenching my teeth, willing myself to be brave, I stepped forwards.

The garden was thick with the dark. Keeping my eyes firmly on the path, I groped onwards, stopping only to listen. My breath. The rustle of leaves. The creak of a bough. A new sound – footsteps on the pavement. I crouched as a figure turned into the house next door. The doorbell rang. A rap on the glass. The light in their porch flared and Tom's house lit up.

My throat went dry. The door and the walls were covered in giant red letters. *Pervert*, they said. *Weirdo. Nutter*. An upstairs window had been smashed in. The windows on the ground floor had been boarded up. Had Tom and his mother gone away? Hope choked inside my throat. But I wasn't going to go home yet. Creeping down the path, I stood at the door; taking a deep breath, I leaned on the bell. Nobody came. I rang again and stepped back. I had to speak to Tom to find out what he'd seen. Next door, the light went out, but not before I'd seen the twitch of the curtains above me. I rang for a third time and the door opened.

It was Tom's mother. A short, solid woman with grey

hair and grey glasses and a face like a wizened orange. She stood blinking at me, whilst behind her, Tom hovered, his thin body stooping, his eyes large, like an owl, illuminated by the dim light that filtered from the room beyond.

There was kindness in the woman's eyes. And something else. Fear? I snatched at the kindness as I asked her to let me in. But as soon as I was through the door the tears came. Hanging my head, I let them fall unchecked. 'Poor child,' said Tom's mother, producing a handkerchief. 'How can I help you?'

I took the handkerchief and blew my nose, pulling out words at last, trying to explain how much I wanted to know what had happened when Tom had seen Gabriella.

There was a pause, and then: 'He's innocent,' she said quietly. 'People accept that. Now.'

'Can I speak to him?' I glanced at Tom who was hanging his head. 'I only want to know . . .' My words faded.

'You can try, child, but I don't think he'll reply.'

A car drew up outside. The engine stopped. A door swung open. Quickly, Tom's mother pushed the door shut and we were left in the semi-darkness. I clenched and unclenched my fists. I wouldn't be afraid. This woman was kind. Tom was kind. They would never harm me. Or Gabriella.

'Where did you see her?' I asked him quickly. 'Was she in Acer Street like Mrs Ellis said? Was she with someone?'

Tom glanced at his mother. They exchanged looks and she answered for him. 'He's confused,' she said. 'He thought he saw a man. He thought he saw a girl.'

I nodded. I knew that already. Which was it? A man, or a girl? 'What did the man look like?'

Tom shook his head.

'What about the girl?'

He shook his head again.

Now I wanted to grab Tom and shake the words out of him. Tom's mother must have sensed my feelings because her look hardened as she stepped forward, blocking me. 'You mustn't push him, child,' she said. 'He's too easily confused. But I know . . . I *know* he wouldn't have harmed your sister.'

I bit my lip. I needed to speak to Tom alone, but his mother was herding me to the door, wanting me to leave. I allowed myself to be guided. It was only when I was on the doorstep that she spoke again. 'I understand how you feel, child. I understand that you want to know, but my son has nothing to say. He's told everything he remembers to the police.'

I stared at her, feeling the sharpness of my disappointment. I didn't want to leave without learning something new. Closing my eyes, I imagined Tom and Gabriella passing each other in the street. I tried to picture her face. Was she friendly as she always was to Tom? Was she happy in those moments, looking forward to seeing me? I needed to fill in those blanks. Swallowing hard, I forced myself to ask: 'Did Tom say she was smiling?'

There was silence and beneath the folds of her wizened skin her eyes glistened. 'Please tell me,' I urged. 'Did Tom say if Gabriella was happy?'

She shook her head. 'I don't think so, child.'

'What then? How did she look?'

But his mother wouldn't answer. She only shook her head again and closed the door, mumbling that she was sorry.

A few days later, I found out that Tom and his mother had moved away, driven out by those in the village who hadn't believed in his innocence, despite what his mother had told me. 'Don't worry,' PC Atkins had said. 'We know where he's gone. Family in Colchester. If we need to, we can interview him there.'

But I'd had my chance. I'd never see Tom again which meant I'd never know how my sister had looked that day.

I went back to school three weeks after Gabriella disappeared. My friends surrounded me, pressing forwards, vying with each other as to who could get the closest, while Gabriella's friends were shadows, barely visible, huddling in twos and threes. And Martha. She was on the edge of it all. Her face tear-stained, her eyes huge and watching. I turned my back on her. I had no time for pity.

Mrs Green asked me to go to her office. I perched on the leather sofa reserved for visitors while she sat at her desk. She took off the glasses she wore on a chain, polishing them with a cloth, leaving them resting on the shelf of her bosom, before picking them up and cleaning them again. She kept clearing her throat and restarting her sentences. 'I'm so sorry, Anna . . . We're so sorry, Anna . . . The whole school is so sorry . . . We're all devastated . . .'

I waited while she pulled out a handkerchief from her sleeve and blew her nose. She tried again. 'Will there be . . . ? What do your parents feel about . . . ? A memorial service might be . . .' She stopped.

I stared at her. 'A memorial service?'

She rubbed her glasses vigorously. 'A service to remember—'

'I know what a memorial service is.' I spoke loudly. For a moment, I had the feeling I was outside of myself, looking down, and I marvelled. Who was this girl with the broken glasses and the grubby socks speaking so rudely to the head teacher she'd barely had the nerve to glance at in the past?

'We could have one at school,' she said, finally finishing a sentence.

'My sister isn't dead,' I retorted.

'I'll speak to your parents.' She shuffled a pile of papers on her desk and looked away. 'In the meantime, I hope . . . Please ask if . . .'

I left the room.

There was no memorial service. I knew there wouldn't be. My parents thought the same way as I did.

As well as Mrs Green, all the teachers, even those who'd never taught me, wanted to talk. Each of them had a different way of doing so. Mr Riley, the sports teacher, with his bluster. Miss Davidson, who taught geography, with her kindness.

Teachers stopped me, pulling me from corridors into empty classrooms to offer me advice or to ask me how I was coping. Some of them spoke in low tones about loss and uncertainty, never once mentioning Gabriella by name, their words spinning in circles. Others were silent, communicating only with sympathetic smiles, passing over me when they collected in homework, or asked for shows of hands. Perhaps they thought if they spoke they'd remind me of the terrible thing that had happened. If they were silent, I might forget. And they could too.

Soon, though, the attention stopped, and the hollowness inside me grew. Like the reverse of a cancer, it was an empty place, a chasm, pushing aside my organs, squeezing my heart into a smaller and smaller space, until I wondered whether it was there at all. I longed for a voice to fill that void, to shout at me, to tell me to sit up straight in class, to demand my overdue homework, or to touch my arm and say, *I miss Gabriella too*. Nothing happened. It was as if I didn't exist, and worse than that, as if my sister had never existed either.

In December my policeman came back. I was glad to see him in a funny kind of way. He was like a comfortable sadness with his mournful eyes hiding so successfully in the folds of his skin.

I listened outside the kitchen door. Dad talked too fast, complimenting the police on their persistence, their doggedness, their determination to find the culprit. Then came the excuses; the reasons why Gabriella hadn't been found. I pictured Dad silent now, with his head bowed and his arms slack. Mum was crying, a soft, persistent sound.

'There must be something you can do,' Dad said.

'We're doing our best. We haven't given up.'

'But you can't stop searching. Please. Tell me what else you can do.'

Covering my ears with my hands, I ran to my room. Where was Gabriella? Why didn't she come home? Wild theories marched through my mind. She'd self-combusted. She'd burst into particles and not one trace could be found. She'd run away to be a dancer in Russia. She was hiding out in a nunnery. She was a scientist in Antarctica. Each thought I had, I rejected, just as each path I'd followed trying to find her had come to nothing.

Outside, the wind lurked around the house, prising at the windows and the doors. I pulled out a notebook and wrote a heading, *Suspects*, and then Edward Lily's name underneath. But I didn't know what to write after that. Dad had said he was innocent, but why was he so sure? What if Edward Lily had hidden Gabriella in his cottage, or was, right now, trying to persuade her to leave and go with him to Spain? Or was she already there, learning flamenco, falling in love with dark-eyed gypsy boys? Or was she outside in the cold, longing for me to find her? Like Cathy in *Wuthering Heights*. Only Gabriella wasn't a ghost. I refused to believe that was true. And why would Edward Lily want Gabriella anyway? I shook away the obvious. Stories about kidnapped girls. The things I'd read in newspapers. The things people said.

My thoughts roamed back and forth as I picked through my theories, until finally, I threw the notebook down.

It was late evening by the time I emerged. Mum had forgotten to give me tea but I didn't care. Brave since my midnight trip to Tom, I grabbed the parka from its peg and went into the garden.

The wind had blown itself out now and the sky was

black and clear. The damson tree hunched in the moon-light like a tired old man, gnarly branches hanging as if it had given up the fight. I felt that way too, as I stood there shivering. In the distance an owl hooted; closer, a small shape zigzagged past. There was movement in the laurel bushes. The night animals were hiding, alert to intruders. Gabriella had never cared about danger, never been afraid. *So what?* I heard her saying. *I'll do it if I want to. Nothing frightens me.*

'Please God,' I whispered as I listened to the crack of the damson tree, the rustle of leaves, tiny paws on broken twigs. 'Please God, if anything happened to my sister, please say she wasn't afraid.' And as I thought of God I wondered, if she had died, had she been lifted upwards, taken to a different place, to heaven, like they said at church?

But when I looked up at the vast, dark sky, I couldn't contemplate my sister being lost there. It wasn't possible. I went back inside.

23

I leaned forward in the chair in Rita's living room and waited for her response.

'It's Gabriella,' I said.

No need to explain. I could tell from Rita's face that she knew. Still, she studied the portrait I'd thrust into her hands for a moment longer before she handed it back and asked me where I'd found it.

'In Edward Lily's things.'

Two spots of colour burned, one on either side of Rita's face. And now I understood. She knew the truth. Rita had been my mother's confidante; the keeper of her secret. And she'd tried to warn me – but not hard enough. In the churchyard, she'd hinted that my parents had hidden something and I should be forgiving. I hadn't realised what she'd been trying to say, but now I did. And acceptance tipped into anger.

'Why didn't you tell me he was Gabriella's father?' I said, my voice hissing as I spoke. She shook her head and there were tears in her eyes. I gritted my teeth. 'Where did they meet?' As if that detail mattered.

She spoke quietly, her face still flushed. 'In Edward's shop.'

'What shop? In Spain? My mother didn't live in Spain. Or did she? Is that something else I never knew?'

Rita shook her head. 'Edward had two shops, one in Seville and one in London – Piccadilly. Your mother worked in the office there. They fell in love.' She gave a small, regretful smile as she spoke.

I stared, incredulous. Rita spoke so calmly as if it was a simple fact. As if no other complications mattered. 'But he was married.'

'I know.'

'So why . . . ?'

'His wife, Isabella . . . It wasn't a happy marriage.'

I looked away. It was no excuse. 'Why didn't he leave her, if he was so in love? And what about when Mum fell pregnant?'

Rita grimaced as she glanced away. It was a guilty gesture. 'He didn't know, did he?' I said.

She shook her head. 'Not at first.'

'Mum lied and stole his child?' I said, accusing.

'It wasn't like that. It was considered . . .' Rita stopped and took a breath. 'Your mother was advised not to tell him.'

'Advised?' I said, raising my voice. 'Who by?' But it was obvious. 'Grandma Grace. It was her, wasn't it?'

Rita nodded and I visualised Grandma Grace with her determination and control, orchestrating the plan. Keeping her daughter away from an unsuitable married man with a suicidal wife and finding an uncomplicated, hard-working alternative. I imagined the scene. My good-looking, good-natured father arriving the morning after the storm. Grandma Grace offering him tea and then dashing up the stairs, two at a time, hauling her daughter from her bed, where she lay languishing, not because she had a stomach bug, and was too ill to work, but because she was suffering from morning sickness.

My grandmother had created the story about how they'd married in a whirlwind of love and romance. I pictured her sitting in the hard-backed chair telling the tale each time with more detail. She'd told it so often she'd begun to believe it herself, while the rest of them, her husband, my father, my mother and Uncle Thomas, had been complicit, staying silent, knowing it was a lie. And Rita. Had Donald known too? Had it only been me who had been deceived? Gabriella and me. And then just me.

I took a breath, trying to contain my resentment. Even after Gabriella had disappeared, nobody had told the truth.

'Did she love my father?' I said after a while.

'Esther?' Rita looked surprised. 'Yes, of course. No question. Your mother made a mistake with Edward. She was young and he was handsome. Albert was the best thing that happened to her. He knew about the baby but he loved her anyway. They both wanted the same thing: a steady life, a family.' She looked away and it occurred to me that perhaps that was what Rita had wanted too. Or maybe she'd been glad to lead the uncomplicated life that she'd had. No secrets of her own, she'd been free to guard the secrets of somebody else. And she'd done that brilliantly, I thought bitterly now, and left me completely in the cold.

I forced my mind back on track. 'So they agreed to deceive Edward Lily. When did he find out the truth?'

Rita closed her eyes. For a moment I thought she was going to refuse to tell me. But she rubbed her temples and began again. 'Edward contacted your mother. He was going to leave Isabella. She told him she was married with a child and that there was no future for them. He guessed, or she told him the truth about the baby. In any event, he agreed to leave her and Albert alone. Perhaps he felt guilty.'

'How old was Gabriella then?'

'She was a baby.'

The christening bracelet – silver inlaid with green stones. It matched the necklace and the ring. Had he sent it to Mum as a farewell gift? And yet he'd returned. Why had he done that?

'If he'd agreed to stay away,' I said slowly, 'why did he come back all those years later? What happened to change his mind?'

'Isabella died. Lydia was ill. I suppose that's what drove him to reclaim Gabriella.' She fell silent. I wondered how much she knew and how much she was guessing. But the fact remained, Edward had come back.

A shiver ran through me when I thought about the timing. Three months after Edward Lily had arrived in the village to claim his daughter, she'd disappeared. Tragic coincidence, or something else? But the police had interviewed him and they'd searched his cottage. And my father had said categorically that Edward Lily was innocent. He must have been sure. I wondered if the police had known that he was Gabriella's biological father.

Rita nodded when I asked her. 'Your parents told them.'

'Is that why he was exonerated?'

'No.' She hesitated. 'He had an alibi. He was with your mother for most of that day.'

I looked at her, startled. 'What do you mean?'

'No,' she said quietly. 'It's not what you're thinking. It wasn't like that. Their affair was over. Your mother was trying to convince him to leave the village. She knew Gabriella would find it hard to forgive her. And she thought it would be easier for you all to move forwards if he wasn't there.'

I shook my head in disbelief. 'She lied to Edward Lily. She lied to Gabriella.' I paused. 'And so did Dad. Do you think they would have told her the truth themselves one day?'

'I think they would have done. Only Edward took that chance away from them.'

When had he told Gabriella? How long had it been before she disappeared? Scenes chased through my mind – the arguments with my parents; Gabriella's anger when she ran from the room on Dad's birthday. And then other thoughts – packing the suitcase; my sadness as she told me she would leave. And the letters. 'Edward Lily wrote to my mother, didn't he? You were the one who found the envelope on the mat. You said it was from church. I knew you were lying. It was from him, wasn't it? What did it say? Was he threatening to tell Gabriella the truth?' I spoke angrily, but I didn't care. I wanted to wound Rita. To make her feel guilty.

'Not threatening,' she said, holding up her hands as if to defend him. 'Edward wasn't like that. He regretted giving Gabriella up. He begged Esther to let him see her.'

'And when she refused? Did he write to Gabriella too?'

'Yes. The police found that letter. But it was irrelevant because Edward had been cleared.'

I hunched forward and spoke deliberately, allowing my hostility to seep through. 'You said Edward was with Mum for *most* of the day. What about after that? He could have persuaded Gabriella beforehand to go to the cottage straight from school. He could have been planning to meet her there and to take her away. And then, when she refused . . .' I closed my eyes, not bearing to think anymore.

But Rita was shaking her head. 'I don't believe that. Nor did your parents, or the police.' She looked at me directly. 'Do you?'

I didn't know. Common sense told me the police must have investigated Edward Lily thoroughly before they dismissed him. I looked around the room, at a loss for what to say next.

The room was surprisingly modern. Abstract paintings covered one wall. Bright blocks of colour. Despite Rita's reliability, she was unpredictable. A contradiction. Perhaps that was why my mother had liked her. Rita appealed to the part of her that had been lost when she'd married. When she'd given up Edward Lily. The real romance of her life.

Now Rita took off her glasses with a sigh and rested them in her lap. Without them she looked much older and I felt a pang of guilt at the way I'd spoken. It wasn't her fault. She was my mother's friend and she'd been loyal throughout her life. Still, she'd deceived me and I didn't know if I'd ever forgive her for that.

'Why didn't you tell me the truth when the clearance began?' I said finally. 'There was no one to stop you, no reason not to make things clear.'

'I suppose I was afraid,' she said. 'I didn't want you to think badly of Esther.'

I thought about this. Here were new character traits I hadn't associated with Rita. Vulnerability. Indecisiveness. Perhaps I could understand that. So much pressure with all those secrets. But still I wasn't certain why Mum had accepted the clearance in the first place. Why would she have taken on the aggravation for a man who'd caused her all that trouble in the past? My mind reverted to my original thought. It had been her way to access Edward Lily's life, to discover if he'd had something to do with what happened to Gabriella. By the time he died, he'd been back in the village for almost a year. Maybe she'd had cause to be suspicious. It must have been a strange time for them both.

I broached the idea with Rita. She lowered her eyes as if weighing up whether to tell me or not. 'They forgave each other,' she said finally.

I hadn't expected her to say that. 'But he ruined her life.'

'Well, he didn't do that, Anna. Not exactly.'

Her chastising tone, her denial, made me bristle. 'No, but he messed it up pretty badly. How could she forget that?'

Rita looked at me as if I was twelve years old again

and she was my mother's friend, raising her eyebrows at something I'd done. 'That's what people do when they get old,' she said. 'They see no point in being hostile, not when there's nothing to be gained.'

I was about to answer resentfully when I thought about it again. I tried to see it from my mother's point of view. Perhaps forgiveness had been the only way to make sense of all that had happened. It was something she had the power to do. 'Did she go to his funeral?' I said eventually.

Rita nodded. And I felt my resentment collapse. My mother had been going through all of that while I'd been in Athens caught up in my own selfish life. If only she'd told me. I might have helped. If only Rita had stepped forward before.

'She must have guessed I'd find out eventually.' My voice was full of reproach. 'And you. Why didn't you tell me when the clearance began?' I asked again.

Rita looked away. She had no real explanation. And I wondered if I ever would have discovered the truth. If I hadn't found the portrait, who would have told me? Everyone was dead, apart from Rita. Maybe Rita would have kept quiet forever and I would have gone back to Athens knowing nothing about Gabriella and Edward Lily.

I should have been angry with my parents and yet, my anger was dispersing. Secrecy had been natural to their generation. It was how things had been. Parents didn't tell their children about illegitimacy, mental illness, divorce. It was their business, not ours, and who was I to say otherwise.

'I'm sorry, Anna,' Rita said. 'I really am. I didn't know what I should do. Old secrets. You get used to them.'

I sighed and looked at the portrait. Now I didn't see it as something fearful. It was only Edward Lily loving his daughter enough to draw her picture.

And yet it bothered me. Why wasn't there other artwork in his house, or art materials? It seemed odd. And if Edward hadn't drawn the portrait, who had? Rita had offered no suggestions either. I looked across at her paintings. Rita: well-organised, efficient, in control. Yet contradictory, unconventional too. Brought up in a family of butchers yet beautiful and elegantly dressed. A churchgoer. A reader of crime novels. Single. No children. An artist. What else was there to know about Rita?

'They're good,' I said, nodding across at the paintings. She smiled faintly. 'What else do you do?'

Rita frowned. 'What do you mean?'

'Portraits, landscapes, or just modern art?'

'Oh.' She laughed nervously. 'You think they're mine. Whatever made you think that?'

'You said you took art classes.'

She blushed. 'Ah. I didn't explain. I do life classes.'

'You paint?'

'No. I pose.' It took me a second or two to realise what she meant. She smiled sadly. 'Think Beryl Cook. You might get there.'

I blinked. For one crazy moment, I'd thought she'd drawn the portrait of Gabriella. How ridiculous I was. How useless.

And now silence rested between us. Neither of us seemed to know what to say. How could we move on from this point? More importantly, what would I do now that these threads had unravelled? Gabriella was my half-sister. A truth had been exposed, but it was a raw and unwelcome reality. I wanted to cover it back up. Stitch over the spaces with brightly coloured lies. Stop it from distracting me from the only thing I wanted to know. What happened to Gabriella?

The sky was darkening, changing rapidly. The wind picked at my clothes, burrowing through the gaps as I trudged along Devil's Lane. The familiar pieces of information I thought I'd known had been gathered up and scattered. And yet, I reflected, as I hauled myself over the stile and walked across the green, what had changed? Rita was my mother's loyal friend as she'd always been. Edward Lily was innocent as my father had said. Gabriella was my sister.

The steps down to the lake were slippery. I held on fast to the rail and shivered beneath the tunnel of trees. I trod carefully along the path which was flooded in places, choked by dank foliage, wet with mud. The lake stretched out before me, a green slick of slime covering the edges, clusters of yellow leaves and broken branches floating on the water.

The police had done a fingertip search of the lake in a last-ditch attempt to find Gabriella. It was after the reconstruction and the dozens of useless sightings that had come in that day. She'd been spotted in Oxford, Southampton and Hull. She'd been seen alone, with a twenty-something man, with an old couple, with a dog. The furthest sighting had been in Sweden. The closest came from a clairvoyant who said her body lay in a shed on the edge of the village.

Letters had arrived from well-wishers: parents whose children had died, believers who told us to trust in God. And young people who'd run away from home, who'd talked about abuse and neglect, or simply the fact that they hadn't fitted in. All the runaways had said the same thing. They had no intention of ever going home.

My parents had kept those letters. I'd found them bundled in the sideboard, tied up with a ribbon. I'd read them all one night, when my mother was asleep, just before I'd left for London.

A solitary swan drifted across the lake. I imagined its feet paddling madly out of sight. It was such an effort to glide like that, such an effort to keep on going. I'd given up years ago when I'd stopped searching for Gabriella. And now I knew I'd failed again, the only mystery I'd solved being one I hadn't even known was there.

As soon as I got home, I gathered my emotions and tucked them away and laid everything out on the table: the portrait of Gabriella, the scrapbook, my notebook, the photos of Lydia I'd found in Edward Lily's desk.

A gust of wind flicked through the open window, ruffling the pages of the scrapbook. If I believed in ghosts, it would be a message. If I believed in a deity, it would be a sign. But I had faith in nothing like that, not anymore. I only had my intuition. The answer was here. Had my mother thought that too? And if she hadn't given up, why should I?

Inside were articles from different newspapers which

showed the same photo of Gabriella time after time. I read about Tom's ever-changing story, the way he'd been hounded from the village even though his innocence had been proved. I read from the point of view of the witnesses, the well-wishers, the shocked residents in the village. Nothing was concrete. Nothing was proved. What had Mum hoped to find?

I shut the scrapbook, feeling suddenly lonely, and glanced at the clock. Five o'clock. Was David back from his trip? Had he gone to the pub like he often did? Maybe I could claim that drink he'd offered. Grabbing the laptop, along with the scrapbook and my bag, I made a decision. If he came in, I'd pretend I was working, rather than waiting for him. My cheeks burned at the childishness of my idea, but even so, I hurried out the door.

The pub was empty apart from a few men at the bar who, from the way they propped themselves up, looked as if they'd been there all day. I avoided eye contact, ordered a glass of wine and took it to the table by the fire.

I returned to the scrapbook and carried on reading from where I'd left off. There were more interviews with shocked people from the village. There was a photo of a group of mothers waiting for their daughters outside the school, and another of people streaming into church. I peered closely, identifying those I knew.

The last few pages of the scrapbook made my heart miss a beat. Here my mother had attached different articles relating to girls who had gone missing around the same time as Gabriella or later. I picked one of the girls at random. Her name was Claire, she was thirteen years old and she'd gone missing in Dartmouth in 1984. I typed the details into Google and found the same photo my mother had cut out and stuck inside the scrapbook.

The girl was dark-haired and plump and lived miles away. She and Gabriella had nothing in common apart from being missing teenagers. I scrolled onwards looking for more information. Claire had been found – dead in a ditch. Raped and shot through the head. The police had investigated farmers with their shotguns and eventually they'd made an arrest. The girl's teacher. There was no explanation of how he'd got the gun.

I typed in more names from the scrapbook, and scanned the reports. Each of the stories was different, and all of them had been solved, save for a blonde girl with a fringe from York called Victoria Sands who'd been raped and strangled in 1982. Her body had been found in a river. The girl's picture was familiar and I remembered hearing the story on the news.

I studied the details again. Her family had been quite ordinary – her father an accountant for a stationery firm, her mother a carer in an old people's home. Were they still alive? Quickly, I googled their names and found more recent articles. The mother had died years before, but the father still lived in the same house in York. He refused to move, he'd told the reporters. His memories were there. There'd been a brother too, but there was no information about him. Only a photo taken in the eighties of a sad child of ten or eleven, in a mini-suit and a tie, staring at the camera.

I held the picture close and recognised the look in his eyes. It was the dazed expression of a sibling not understanding why his sister had disappeared. How had he coped on that day? Had he listened to his parents talking with the police – not understanding, only wanting his sister to come home? Had he heard his mother weeping through the night and been afraid? Had he spent lonely vigils at his window making up stories about where his sister had gone?

And when the body had been found, had it been a relief for the family – a way to find peace – or an agonising wrench knowing the rest of their lives would be infected by the memory of what that man had done?

A single day had determined their lives would never be the same. As mine hadn't been. Or this boy's. He understood more about me than anyone else I knew.

I focused again on the stories. Parallel cases. Is that what Mum had been searching for? Yet there had been no real similarities since most of these crimes had been solved. And all of the bodies had been found. Perhaps Mum had been drawn to the fact that these girls had gone missing. They had parents who understood her pain. Like the boy who understood mine.

And yet. Parallel cases. How far had the police investigated? I typed *unsolved murders* into Google and trawled through them. There was one in 1983. Marian. Aged fourteen. She was from Glasgow and had been raped and strangled. There was a reference to some similarity with the death in York, but the investigation had been abandoned. The girl had been from a children's home and the article made a lot of the way she'd been dressed

– the length of her skirt and her make-up. The police had said she'd probably run away and they'd found her coat at the bus station. I rubbed my temples, scratching my face with the ferocity of the movement.

Scrolling onwards, I looked for similar stories. All through the rest of the eighties there was nothing, or nothing similar at any rate. I was starting on the nineties when David appeared. Flushing, I closed the lid of my laptop and placed it hastily on top of the scrapbook.

David wore dark trousers, rather than his customary jeans, and a light blue shirt that had been ironed until sharp creases showed on the sleeves. He carried a smart jacket and his hair was combed flat in a style which didn't suit him. I wanted to reach out and ruffle it up.

'I've been trying to find you,' he said, running his fingers through his hair and spoiling the look himself. 'Are you all right?'

It took a moment to realise what he was talking about. 'Ah. Sorry about the phone call. It wasn't important.'

He raised his eyebrows but didn't comment, going instead to the bar and bringing back a glass of wine and a pint of beer. Sitting down, he folded the jacket neatly and placed it on the seat beside him. 'Are you working?' he said.

'What?'

He leaned across and tapped the lid of the laptop. 'Writing.'

Catching a whiff of his lemon aftershave, I nodded, and before he could speak again, I asked him about his trip. He described what he'd been doing – helping an old lady in Leeds with a house full of antique furniture and cats downsize to a flat in Ripon.

There was a lull as David sipped his beer and I gazed at the fire, my mind dragging back to the scrapbook on the table between us. The mention of Ripon had made me think of the girl with the fringe in York.

'So everything's going well?' said David, breaking the silence. 'With the house clearance I mean.'

'Absolutely.'

He put down his glass and raised his eyebrows again. He wasn't stupid. I'd rung him out of the blue and then denied there was anything wrong. I distracted him, describing items from the house clearance he'd already seen, asking his advice about the best dealers to approach. Eventually, I became aware that my voice had taken on a higher tone. I was talking too much and too quickly. I was repeating myself. I drank more wine. I'd let David think alcohol was the reason.

'Another?' he said, pointing at my second empty glass. I shook my head. 'Food?' He looked at the bar.

'I've eaten,' I lied. I needed to go. David's eyes were full of sympathy and knowledge. I stood up too quickly, stumbling as I tried to grab my bag and my laptop at the same time.

'Don't forget this.' He held out the scrapbook and my legs buckled. Two large glasses of wine on an empty stomach was the reason I gave myself. I'd be fine once I was home. I only had to make it out the pub.

'Wait,' said David as he took my arm to steady me. 'You look terrible.' He spoke softly and I caved in, dropping back into my seat. And then he was talking again, telling me about when his parents had died, one after the other, in the space of a year and how hard it had been for him and his brother. My eyes filled with tears. 'Hey,' he said, leaning towards me and laying his hand on mine. 'I didn't mean to upset you. I only think you're brave, dealing with all of this on your own.' His voice dipped. 'You've lost a lot. Maybe I can help.'

I shook my head. He had no idea of my loss. 'You can't do anything.'

'Try me.'

I breathed out slowly. Was this the right time to speak? Was this the right person to tell? My stomach turned over with the thought of it. All these years of silence. What would it be like to break that?

'Anna,' said David gently.

My heartbeat quickened. 'It's my sister,' I said.

He frowned. 'Your sister? God. I'm sorry. I assumed, since you were here on your own, you didn't have one.'

A silent tear rolled down my face. 'I don't,' I whispered. 'Not now.'

David's expression changed as he watched me. It was a slow understanding like the unravelling of dawn. 'Tell me, Anna,' he said.

And so I did. I told him things I hadn't told anyone in my life. I told him how beautiful Gabriella had been and the fun we'd had. I told him about our grandparents and Uncle Thomas and Donald. I told him how one day my sister had gone; in an instant she'd disappeared. And how hard I'd tried to find her even when everyone else had given up. And I explained how I'd frozen my feelings, but that now, everything had begun again. The house clearance, the portrait, Gabriella's father. That old desire to *know*.

By the time I'd finished talking, my tears were coming steadily. David was shaking his head, not knowing what to say. He pulled out a tissue and offered it to me, his eyes full of sympathy. The men at the bar looked across curiously. I shouldn't have said anything to David. What did he think of me now?

'You do know you couldn't have prevented whatever it was from happening,' he said at last.

I wiped my eyes and shrugged. 'I sometimes think if I'd heard something or seen something, I might have stopped it, saved her. Or maybe if I'd done things differently, it might have changed the course of events.'

'What do you mean? How could you have changed them?'

'If I'd got up five minutes later; if we'd walked instead of run to school; if she'd worn her hair differently; if I hadn't dropped my glasses.'

He nodded. 'You mean the butterfly effect.'

'Yes,' I said, staring at him with hope. 'Yes, I suppose I do.'

He sat back in his chair. 'You can't think like that. You'll drive yourself mad.'

'I already have.'

'I know but . . . small differences – at least ones like you're describing – can't change really serious events. I don't believe it.'

'I know. You're right. It's just . . .' I pressed my fingers to my temples.

'It's the not knowing, isn't it? I understand that, in my

own way. When my wife first got ill. I knew there was something wrong, but she wouldn't tell me, not for months. If she had, maybe she would have been saved. And you know,' he said, looking beyond me as he spoke, 'grief never goes away. You can disguise it or turn your back on it, but when you look closely, when you turn around, it's still there.' He paused. A man laughed at the bar and David gave a wry smile. 'Grief is an unwelcome guest. The only thing you can do is let it live alongside.'

We stopped talking, both gazing down at the table, lost in our thoughts.

'What about the portrait?' said David after a while. 'Would you show it to me?'

I scrabbled in my bag, drew out the picture and laid it in front of him. He looked without speaking for a few moments before he spoke again. 'She was very beautiful,' he said.

I smiled. And we sat with the portrait between us, in a reverent kind of silence. And along with the sadness, I experienced a warmth, as I acknowledged it was the first time I'd truly shared my loss with anyone.

24

1982

A crowd had gathered at the school gates, pointing at the cameras and the lights as if the crew had come to film a show. I pulled up my hood. It smelled of Gabriella's perfume and her hair.

The police were staging a reconstruction: Gabriella's last journey. My parents said it was too late – more than two months since she'd disappeared. The police had been distracted, following the wrong suspects, and now the time had gone. I'd left Mum at home knitting a scarf with furious concentration while Dad was working in the garden, digging up non-existent weeds.

The road was blocked. No cars. And the crowd dropped into silence. Now there was only the ghostly trundle of a road sweeper's cart as a lookalike Tom walked past. People followed behind the camera crew, who in turn followed behind and around and in front of a girl. She looked like my sister. She wore a school uniform and had ribbons in her hair, but she was taller than Gabriella and less graceful and she moved differently.

I wanted to catch up with the impostor, to tap her on the shoulder and say no, she didn't walk like that, it was like this, and her pace was faster. I wanted to demonstrate, even though I knew I could never copy Gabriella. She was like a gazelle when she moved, upright, long legs stretching. But the girl was too far ahead of me and there were too many people in between, jostling and shoving, craning their necks to see, so I stepped away.

Shoving my hands into my pockets, I felt the stitching tear. And when the stragglers had cleared I saw Martha on the opposite side of the road. She spotted me too and after a moment's hesitation, half ran towards me, her hands outstretched as if she was groping in the dark. And when she reached me, tears streaming down her face, she opened her mouth to speak, but nothing came out, only a strangled sound, like a sick animal.

I felt dislike and disgust and pity all bundled together as we stood looking at each other, neither of us knowing what to say.

'Biscuits,' she whispered at last.

'What?'

'I bought biscuits.'

What was she talking about? Did she think I wanted biscuits? Did she think biscuits would make me feel better, like Rita thought tea would fix Mum, and Grandma Grace thought stories would make us forget, and neighbours brought food thinking we could eat?

Did Martha believe that now Gabriella had gone I'd be her friend instead? She'd tricked Gabriella. She'd taken advantage of her good nature. Well, my nature wasn't good. It was terrible, and now, a new emotion – white and hot and furious – was burning me inside.

Martha was blubbering, her voice choking. She wore a scarf in her hair and this time I wanted to rip it out because it was Gabriella's and I didn't want to lose anything else of my sister's. I forced my hands to stay by my side and screamed at her instead. 'I hate you, Martha Ellis. Everyone hates you. Don't ever speak to me again.' I turned my back and walked away.

In the evening, I was watching the news when a photo of Gabriella came on the screen. It was the same picture they always used. And then they showed images of a whole lot of girls who'd gone missing in the last decade. A fourteen-year-old from Cornwall. A sixteen-year-old from Dundee. The girl from York. Another from Glasgow who'd disappeared from a children's home. Yet these girls had been found. Murdered. The media was trying to connect them. Were they suggesting that this had happened to Gabriella too, and that it was only a matter of time before her body would be found?

I dug my fingernails hard into my palms trying to make my imaginings go away. 'Bullshit,' said Dad, appearing at the door. 'Fucking bullshit.' He switched off the television and slammed out the room.

That night the dreams came: swooping demons that grabbed Gabriella with their talons and took her down to hell. I woke screaming. Nobody heard me. Nobody came. I slept with the light on, but the images wouldn't go away.

The reconstruction produced nothing apart from a bunch of crank calls. There were no new witnesses coming forward and eventually no stories in the newspapers. There were only the facts. Gabriella was fifteen. She was going to meet her sister in her father's shop. She hadn't arrived. That was it. No one saw her being bundled into a van or dragged into a house. No one saw her at all. It was as though she was invisible.

Silence stretched. The pendulum swung. And then it stopped. Nobody remembered to wind the clock. And with that, it seemed, everything else was forgotten. When the family came round Donald forgot to fill his pipe. Uncle Thomas forgot to make jokes or do magic tricks. Grandma Grace forgot to speak and even Granddad forgot to snore. Only Jasper made the best of things, winding his body around me, filling the room with his purr.

Rita came most often, but she no longer brought crime novels or parcels of bloodied meat. She brought lemon puffs and boxes of Milk Tray and Turkish delight and pots of honey. She wanted to sweeten the sadness away, but my mother ate none of it. And I thought of Martha with her talk of biscuits and I remembered how angry I'd been.

The two of them, Mum and Rita, sat in silence. Sometimes when I went into the kitchen, thinking no one was there, I found them, heads bowed, Rita's hand covering Mum's on the table. I felt left on the outside again. Only this time it wasn't my parents and Gabriella I was watching.

If only it was. I'd deliver a million church leaflets, go to a million church services, walk a million times around the village.

It was Christmas. Uncle Thomas and Donald arrived but Granddad Bertrand was too ill to travel so he and

Grandma Grace stayed at home. My parents tried. They forgot the decorations, but they bought me presents: books, a T-shirt, a video. Uncle Thomas gave me a magic set and Donald a piece of fool's gold the size of my fist. I put the magic set in my cupboard and the fool's gold in my box of special things.

Uncle Thomas and Donald cooked the food, but the turkey was too big and the potatoes were too hard and they forgot the stuffing and the cranberry sauce. Nobody cared. Nobody ate. Nobody pulled the crackers. Donald cleared away the plates and threw the food in the bin.

In the afternoon, Rita came for the Queen's speech. She brought three blood-red poinsettias and a bowl of clementines. 'From the ladies at the church,' she said. 'You shouldn't mind them. They only want to show they care.'

And while we watched the Queen talking about seamen rescuing people from the Falklands eight thousand miles across the ocean, and as Donald took the plants and set them around the living room, and Uncle Thomas placed the clementines on the table, where the orange clashed with the purple-tasselled cloth, I wondered why, with all those guns and ships available, nobody had bothered to rescue Gabriella from wherever she had gone.

On New Year's Day the phone rang while I was still in bed. Dad ran to answer it and his voice rose through the house until it filled every space.

I looked over the banister. Mum was standing beside

him, gripping his arm, shaking her head each time he spoke.

'I'll be there,' said Dad, and in five minutes he was gone, slamming the front door behind him.

'They say they've found Gabriella's bag,' Mum said later when she came to find me. She sat on my bed and held my hand, hardly able to look at me. Her fingers were strange, loose and light like they belonged to a broken doll.

'Where?' I asked in a small voice.

She moistened her lips. 'At the railway station.' I frowned, and she said, 'Yes, I know. Why didn't they find it before?'

Dad told us afterwards that the bag had been hidden behind a bin in the waiting room. There was no purse so the explanation given was that she'd abandoned the bag and taken her money to buy a ticket.

'But nobody remembers selling her a bloody ticket,' said Dad, pacing the carpet as he spoke. 'So why the fuck do they think that?'

Eventually, PC Atkins brought the bag back to us, his sorrowful eyes closing as he passed it across with a sigh. From his pocket he produced an envelope. Was it the missing letter? PC Atkins handed it to Mum whose face paled as she looked at the front. Glancing at Dad she nodded, and in response he reached out his hand and rested it on her shoulder. It was only at the door when they were showing PC Atkins out that the three of them spoke again, their voices so hushed it was impossible to hear.

*

Later, we unpacked the rest of her things and laid them out on the table: school books, cassettes, copy of *NME*, red lipstick, gold eyeshadow, purple scarf. Walkman.

'That settles it,' said Dad, holding it in triumph. 'Gabriella didn't run away. She would never have left without her music.'

A chill slipped down my spine as I stole a look at my parents. Mum's eyes were wet. Her lips parted. And now that Dad had spoken, triumph had drained from his face and been replaced by fear. Was he thinking the same as I was? Gabriella wouldn't have run away without her music, but she wouldn't have done anything else either. She wouldn't have caught a train, a bus or gone for a walk without it. She wouldn't have given it up for anything.

25

The larger pieces of furniture had gone now. All that remained were boxes and a pile of paintings leaning against a wall.

I worked quickly, searching one more time. I wanted to be sure. No more pictures of Gabriella. No art equipment either. I flicked through the paintings. They were framed prints, a mix of traditional and modern, and nothing that resembled the portrait. I was now satisfied that Edward Lily wasn't the artist. But who was? How would I find that out?

I'd been in the House of Flores since dawn and by the time I'd finished searching and was locking up the shop, the village was awake. Men and women dressed for work waited at the bus stop, or hurried to the station. The cafe was full for the breakfast shift. I joined in, ordering coffee from the girl with the magpie hair.

The night before, I'd left David in the pub, although he'd wanted me to stay. He'd made me promise to ring him if I needed to and I'd been glad to do that. When I'd got home, I'd drunk as much wine as there was in the house and collapsed on Gabriella's bed.

I used to do that when I was small – creep into Gabriella's room crying after bad dreams. She used to ask me what they were about but I never said. How could I have done when they were about me protecting her, releasing her from funeral pyres, fighting usurpers with clashing swords? And yet, I would think, as I lay there and listened to her breathing and the murmur of the TV downstairs, wasn't it the wrong way round? Gabriella was the oldest. Shouldn't she have been protecting *me*?

And if I'd told her about those dreams, would she have listened and been warned? Would she have avoided whatever it was that had taken her, and been with me now, drinking coffee, telling tales about her job, the one she'd fantasised about: a writer for *NME* or *Time Out*? Maybe she'd have children – a set of mini-Gabriellas skipping along the thorny path she'd spectacularly beaten down.

I finished my coffee. I had to move on. What next? Who else could I speak to? If Uncle Thomas had been alive, I'd have gone to him. And then there was Donald and his sudden disappearance to America. Had he died or was he still a geologist? I remembered Uncle Thomas finding an article he'd written about dinosaur finds in Montana. So they must have been in contact for a while. Maybe I'd find him online.

I sighed. What a lonely, pathetic figure I cut sitting in the window of a cafe, attempting to dredge up names of people from the past. I could barely think of any school friends, not ones I'd feel comfortable contacting anyway. I'd not so much drifted away, but vanished on a tidal wave.

As if to remind me, a group of teenage girls barrelled past the window. One of them stumbled and almost fell against the glass. Our eyes met as she righted herself and she smiled shyly. The girl was dark, her hair in plaits. Nothing like Gabriella. Even so, my heart beat a little faster as she hurried to catch up with her friends.

A woman in a belted raincoat walked past. Martha. I drew back instinctively, full of the sense that she was following me again. But the woman hurried on and I realised it wasn't her. Martha had said what she'd wanted to say. *You should have kept your sister close.* Well, she was right about that. If only I'd insisted on waiting for Gabriella that day after school. If only I hadn't left her on her own.

I finished my coffee and pressed my palms against my eyes. I had choices: go to the police, show them the portrait and ask them to reopen the investigation; give up on everything and go back to Athens; speak to the only person I could think of now who'd known my sister at school.

Dragging on my jacket, I shoved back my chair and stood up. I'd try one more time to uncover the truth before I went to the police.

I knocked on Martha's door. Moments passed. Stepping back, I scanned the windows searching for a shape, then knocked again more loudly, and pressed the bell. Still no answer, or stir from anyone inside.

Hitching my bag on my shoulder, I wandered around the side of the house. There was a gate that opened with a creak and a gravel path leading to the garden, edged with rose bushes and splashes of colour from trees with scarlet leaves. I rapped on the back door and tried the handle. The door pushed open and I closed it again quickly, backing away and almost falling over a ceramic pot. As I righted myself, a face peering across the fence made me jump. It was the old lady next door, her short white hair combed flat against her head. I smiled politely. 'I'm looking for Martha, but she doesn't appear to be home.'

The woman stared at me blankly. 'What do you want her for?'

'Just a social visit. But it doesn't matter. I'll come back later.' I walked away but was halted by her voice.

'Are you a social worker?'

I stopped. 'No. Why?'

'Martha doesn't get visitors. Only social workers.'

I nodded as if I knew what she was talking about. 'Well. Never mind. If you see Martha, perhaps you could tell her Anna Flores came to visit.'

'Anna Flores.' There was a new interest in her voice. 'I know your mother. She's always been good to me. She visits sometimes.'

'My mother . . .' I stopped and looked away, disconcerted. 'I'm afraid to say she passed away.'

The woman's face clouded. 'Oh dear. I am sorry to hear that. I am really very sorry to hear that. I would have come to the funeral if I'd known. I don't hear things these days. I don't speak to people. Housebound.' She held up a stick as if to prove it.

'Martha knew,' I said gently. 'Might she have told you?'

Her expression soured. 'Martha doesn't speak to me or anyone. She's strange, like her mother.'

My interest was piqued. I walked a few steps closer to the fence. 'How long have you lived here?'

'For always. I was born here.'

'Really? That's incredible.'

She smiled at me. 'Isn't it.'

'I'm sorry. I don't know your name.'

'It's Eliza Davidson.'

'Well, it's lovely to meet you Mrs Davidson.'

'Miss. But please call me Eliza.'

'Thank you.' I paused. Who was this woman? The name was familiar. Miss Eliza Davidson.

'I used to teach your sister.'

My skin tingled. That's how I knew her name. 'Gabriella?'

'Yes. I taught her geography.'

'So you remember . . .' I paused.

She produced a handkerchief and blew her nose. 'Yes, I do. Your poor mother. I don't know how she survived.' She looked at me. 'Or you, my dear. Or you.'

I blinked hard and looked away for a second. 'Do you recall,' I said, hesitantly, 'that day?'

She knew what I meant. She blew her nose again and dabbed her eyes. 'Yes, I do. I remember it very clearly indeed. How could I forget such an awful thing?'

'Mrs Ellis said she saw Gabriella. Did you see her too?'

She shook her head. 'No. I didn't. And I told the police that when they interviewed me.'

'What about Martha? Did you see her?'

She shook her head again. 'Not then. Not after school. Only later.'

'Later?' I prompted.

'She was on the front steps, crying. She'd been to the shops, I think. She'd bought something. I can't remember what it was.'

'Why was she crying?'

The woman shrugged. 'Who knows? It was quite usual to see that little girl sitting on the steps. Her parents used to lock her out. They were awful people. Both of them. It's no wonder Martha turned out the way she did. But that day she was there for longer. I remember it was quite dark by the time they let her in. I was putting the bins out. Late. And she was still there. Awful people.' She looked around and over my shoulder as if she might see them still. 'He killed her guinea pig.'

I started. 'What?'

'He killed her guinea pig, battered it with a hammer. It was after he lost his job as an electrician. He was angry. Even more angry than he'd been before.'

'Oh my God. How awful.' I covered my mouth as I remembered. The damp earth, the smell of the dead, the taste of the bile I vomited onto the ground. I'd been convinced it was Martha who'd done that. I'd left no room for the idea it might have been someone else. How stupid I'd been. How jealous and stupid.

'Did you see it happen?' I said.

'No, but I heard Martha screaming about it. That scream. It was worse than her mother's. I called the police several times, you know. He used to beat his wife; everyone knew that. Do you know what the police did?'

I shook my head.

'Nothing. They said it couldn't be proved. Unless there was a complaint from Mrs Ellis, nothing could be done. She always defended him, you see. Lied about it. Said she'd fallen down the stairs. The usual.' Eliza sighed. 'I saw that with the girls at school. So many of them did the same. They were too afraid, you see. They thought if they told it would make things worse.'

'Like Martha.'

'Exactly like Martha. The only time there was any peace in that house was when he was away with his job.'

'That must have been a relief for his wife. And for Martha.'

She nodded. 'Indeed. They should have taken the chance of those times to leave him. But they didn't. The house was quiet for a few days, but as soon as he was back, it all began again.' There was silence. 'Well then,' she said at last. 'I'd better go inside. Mind out for Martha. She isn't right. None of it's her fault. But she isn't right. And, my dear, I'm so sorry about your mother. So very sorry.'

I waited until Eliza's door banged shut. I was wondering exactly how angry Mr Ellis had been. Angry enough to beat his wife and child, angry enough to kill an animal. What else had he been capable of? I glanced behind me and back up at the windows of Martha's house. Might he have been angry enough to kill a girl? I took a step towards the door, my mind whirling.

26

1982

'And what do you want?'

My heart banged in my chest. 'Please may I ask you some questions.'

Mrs Ellis opened the door wider and peered at me. She wore the same grey cardigan, with a scarf wrapped round her throat. Her face was white and there were dark shadows beneath her eyes. She contemplated me for a moment, gnawing her lip and looking me up and down, and I saw myself through her eyes: a small girl in an oversized parka and broken glasses. 'What about?' she said, her expression unchanging.

'Gabriella.'

There was a pause. 'You'd better come in.'

I stepped inside and edged around the boxes in the hall. The sweet scent of pinks was missing, and now the house smelled of stale tobacco and burnt food. She ushered me into the living room where Mr Ellis slouched in his armchair as he had before. Only this time, he was awake and reading the newspaper, his stomach spilling over his trousers, his bare feet stretched out and resting on the pouffe. He glanced at me with bleary eyes as I made my entrance and sat on the sofa while Mrs Ellis swivelled and left the room, her worn-down slippers flip-flopping as she walked.

The last time I'd been here I'd been with Gabriella. I laid my hand on the fabric of the seat she'd touched and stole a look at Mr Ellis, but he was staring at his newspaper as if I wasn't there. I shifted my gaze to the print of the insects. All those beetles, flies and ants. Why would you have such a horrible picture on your wall? Shuddering, I looked back at Mr Ellis, letting my eyes travel down his body. His bare feet were veined and white, the toes like fat maggots – huge, wriggling maggots. My gaze moved sharply to his face and now he was looking back at me, his mouth twisted in a grin.

I clenched my fists, reminding myself why I'd come. Just because the police had scaled back the investigation, it didn't mean I was going to give up too. I'd gone back to my book of suspects and made more lists: friends, family, neighbours, shopkeepers – everyone Gabriella had ever spoken to. I'd interview them, take advantage of my status as victim. I was the missing girl's sister and people had to listen.

Mrs Ellis came back with a cup of orange squash and a garibaldi biscuit. She sat, unmoving, on the edge of an armchair. I counted to five. 'I'm trying to find Gabriella,' I said. And now my heart was beating so hard I thought she must be able to hear. Speaking in a rush, words spilling out into the room, I asked her to describe what she'd seen the day my sister disappeared.

She sniffed. 'I've already told the police.' She glanced at her husband. 'But I suppose I can say it again.' And she repeated what I knew – how she'd been waiting for Martha and she'd seen first Gabriella and then Tom pushing his cart and mumbling to himself. 'In that *mad* way of his,' she added maliciously.

'What about Gabriella?' I prompted. 'Did she seem . . . scared?'

She gave me a sharp look. 'Scared?' She shook her head. 'Oh no, oh no. Not scared.' She gnawed her lip. Mr Ellis turned the page of his newspaper. 'She was quite the opposite. Quite bold.'

Bold? What did she mean? My legs were weak. If I wasn't sitting, I'd crumple. I looked down to steady myself. The carpet was dirty and stained. It couldn't have been vacuumed for months.

There was a sound in the hall, a sigh, a brush against the wall. Was Martha there, listening to what we said?

'Why was Martha late?' I said.

'Martha?' Mrs Ellis seemed wrong-footed. She frowned as if trying to remember. Her face cleared. 'Art.' She rolled her eyes and glanced at her husband. 'Extra lessons. What a waste of time.'

Mr Ellis turned another page.

The second person I interviewed was Mr Sullivan, Tom's next-door neighbour and the witness who'd come forward. He was an elderly, never-been-married, childless type of man who might have fitted the dark, fallen angel profile of my imaginings except he had silver hair and a shiny pink face. Not only that, but he *had* been married. His wife had died after a year. 'We were childhood sweethearts,' he told me mournfully. 'I've never looked at anyone since.'

Mr Sullivan provided milk and custard creams. When I asked him about Tom, he declared that the people who had accused him of the crime were short-sighted and looking for a scapegoat. 'Your parents excepted,' he hastened to add.

As for the teenagers who had persecuted Tom, he described them as mindless thugs, wicked young people with no morals like so many other young people these days. 'Yourself excepted,' he said.

'Do you think Tom will come back?' I asked, dunking a biscuit in my milk.

He shook his head. 'I don't think so. The last thing I heard, he and his mother had gone off to Colchester permanently. You can't blame them, can you? After what those hooligans did to their house. All those nasty words and implications.'

Nodding, I tried to look wise and asked politely if he thought Tom had got another job.

'I doubt that very much, don't you? Mud sticks. Probably on social security by now. Queuing at the dole office with the rest. Taxpayers paying. Thanks to them.' He used his thumb to indicate the direction of Tom's house so I assumed he meant the hooligans. 'Let's hope they find them and cart them off to borstal.' Again I assumed he meant the hooligans, not Tom and his mother.

I saved my most important question for last. 'What do you think happened to my sister, Mr Sullivan?'

He stopped and scratched his head. 'Young people do unpredictable things,' he said, blinking hard. By that, I assumed he favoured the idea that Gabriella had run away.

Tom's neighbour on the other side – a pepper-pot-sized woman, with a sick husband and an absent son – confirmed and agreed with everything Mr Sullivan had said. She gave me home-made currant buns and a strawberry flavoured Sodastream and, after answering my questions, kept me for another hour talking about her sick husband and absent son.

After that round of interviews, I was none the wiser. I didn't spot a new suspect amongst the pepper-pot family and Mr Sullivan seemed unlikely – though that night the swooping demon in my imagination metamorphosed at the point of entry into the earth's atmosphere and became a slender, gliding figure, rather aged, with pale eyes that flickered, a fuzz of silver hair and a packet of custard creams. He glided on past Gabriella as she walked home from school. Neither of them saw the darker shadow creeping against a wall. It wasn't Mr Sullivan. The next morning I scored a line through his name.

I worked my way through the neighbours. One day as I was coming out of a house a few doors down from us Dad appeared. We stood facing each other, either side of the garden gate. 'What are you doing?' he said as his glance slid to the notebook I was clutching.

Pushing my glasses back to the bridge of my nose, I said, 'I was asking questions.'

'About what?'

'Gabriella.'

His face paled. 'What kind of questions?'

I held my notebook defiantly. 'I've been asking everybody. I've been making lists of suspects and ticking them off.'

'That's not for you to do, Anna. That's for the police.'

'Well, the police have given up,' I said roughly. 'They aren't looking for her. Nobody's looking for her now.'

'Even so, you shouldn't go knocking on people's doors. Not after everything that's happened.'

The pulse on his temple was throbbing, but still I couldn't stop. 'Somebody's got to do something,' I snapped. 'The police do nothing, you and Mum do nothing. The neighbours talk about it. They think she's run away, or been murdered, or been kidnapped, but they don't care. I'm the only one who cares.'

There was silence. A front door opened and closed quickly. Was it Mrs Henderson interfering? Or stupid Brian spying again?

'Even so,' Dad repeated, his voice deathly calm. 'You need to stop.'

I stared at him. Rage firing inside my mind. I opened my mouth to tell him he couldn't prevent me from doing what was right for my sister, but he held up his hand, halting my words.

'Go home, Anna,' he said. 'And don't do this again.'

I wanted to reply, but one glance at his stony eyes made me think better of it. Slipping through the gate, I led the way back to our house.

It was the day after my falling-out with Dad and we were having tea. Mum was ladling Campbell's tomato soup into bowls. She sat with us, although I knew she wouldn't eat more than a few spoonfuls. I hadn't seen her eat much in weeks. She'd taken to playing with her food, pushing it around her plate, lifting a forkful to her lips and putting it back down. Her face had become gaunt, and she tied her hair in a tight band that pulled at the skin on her face.

Now she was stirring the soup, faster and faster. 'Mrs Henderson paid me a visit,' she said at last. 'She heard you two arguing in the street.'

'It's nothing,' said Dad, placing his hands flat on the table.

'It can't be nothing otherwise she wouldn't have come.'

'Leave it.'

'How can I? The whole street knows by now.'

'*Madre mia.*' He thumped the table. 'Who cares what people think?'

'I care,' said Mum. 'I don't want them talking about us and Gabriella, and . . .'

He swept his arm across the table and a bowl smashed onto the floor, red splashing across the stone.

Mum stood up. 'You need to keep yourself together.'

'Why?' He slammed his chair backwards and grabbed the side of the table with his strong, thin fingers as though he wanted to upturn it. 'What's the point?'

There was silence. Mum looked at me. 'Leave the room,' she said. And I did. I crept out and stood in the hallway listening.

'What's the point?' Dad said again.

'Because Gabriella will need us.' There was a pause. 'When she comes home.'

'She won't come home.'

Silence. I leaned against the wall and closed my eyes. Dad had always said that Gabriella hadn't run away, that she'd be back if only the police tried harder to find her. Why had he stopped believing that? It was my fault. I was the one who had put bad ideas into his head. And now I wanted to go to him, to lay my hand on his arm and say I was sorry. Gabriella hadn't been murdered. Her absence was temporary. She would come back if only we could find her. If only we could persuade her.

But Mum was speaking, her voice low and urgent, telling him not to give up hope, to take back control, that the police wouldn't look for Gabriella if he stopped telling them to try. Mum was the one in charge now. Not Dad. And while I yearned for him to fix us, to build a time machine, to reverse events, to bring Gabriella back, I knew now that he never would. He'd lost his power to make things right.

It was the last time Dad raised his voice. After that, he stayed in the shop for long hours. He came home to plates of cold food left on the table. I sat with him, but he didn't look at me. He chewed until he'd had enough and scraped the rest into the bin.

Towards the end of January, it had been snowing lightly and Dad had lit a fire. He was reading the newspaper; at least, he had it open. In reality his gaze was fixed on the far corner of the room. Mum was knitting. A ball of blue wool lay on the floor beside her armchair; it jerked as it caught, and she yanked it with impatience.

Lying on the rug, I was reading 'Leda and the Swan'. *A sudden blow: the great wings beating still.* I was repeating the lines inside my head, not understanding, but trying to memorise them anyway. *Above the stagger-*

ing girl, her thighs caressed; By the dark webs, her nape caught in his bill. I closed my eyes, conjured the patterns of the letters and the words; repeated the same line again and again. I checked to see if my memory was right, and when I finished, moved on. *He holds her helpless breast upon his breast.*

There was a low moaning sound. At first I thought it was the wind in the chimney, or the keening of an animal outside.

The knitting stopped. 'Albert,' whispered Mum.

Dad had dropped the paper. He was holding his head in his hands and staring straight at me as if horrified by something I'd done. And I realised, I'd been saying the words of the poem out loud. And in an instant, their meaning clicked and I understood what my dad was imagining. My sister, held down and savaged by an animal. Not a swan, but a man. The same man I'd imagined as the Devil.

27

The kitchen smelled of bleach. Curtains closed, it was shadowy and quiet. I walked across the floor, footsteps tapping, seeing how old-fashioned the room was, stuck in its original time: green-painted cupboards, pull-down tabletop with a single chair. There was a vase on the window ledge, with a rose, but its petals were soft and drooping; one had already fallen.

The place was pristine with the sides scrubbed and the old sink chipped but gleaming. No clutter. The strands on Martha's new mop were already wearing and when I bent to open the fridge, there was nothing inside but the scent of antiseptic, a carton of milk and a piece of ham.

How sad Martha was. My eyes rested on a plate laid out on the table with a knife and fork ready alongside; a solitary cup and saucer, a single teaspoon. Worse than sad. It was humiliating. I shouldn't be in her house. And yet, as I stood in the room staring about me, I couldn't leave either. It was Mr Ellis I was here for now.

I stepped out into the hall. It seemed strangely large in comparison to how I remembered it. Before, there'd been boxes piled up at the front door narrowing the corridor to the living room. We'd had to squeeze past them as we'd followed Mrs Ellis. Now there were no boxes, no furniture, no piles of shoes or coats.

In the living room there was an old TV set, a clock on

the mantelpiece. A sofa. An armchair. The pictures had gone from the walls. The sideboard had been emptied and cleaned. Where were the things this family had collected over the years? Where were their memories?

Going to the foot of the stairs, I hesitated. No movement or sound. I made my way up, the sound of my footsteps deadened by the thread-worn carpet.

My heart quickened as I opened a door. It was dark. The curtains were drawn. I fumbled for the light switch and gasped. I'd expected the room to be as empty as the living room. Instead it was a perverse kind of shrine. Filthy, cobwebbed and thick with grime with clothes littering the floor. The bed was unmade, the sheets twisted and yellowed. A pile of cardboard boxes, spotted with age, slumped against the wall. And the place stank of mildew and damp, so strong I had to stop myself from retching. Covering my nose, I walked across the dirty carpet. An empty beer bottle lay on its side covered with dust. A belt snaked on the floor as if it had been whipped off and thrown down a moment before. There was a pile of magazines. I bent to look at the top one and straightened quickly. Pornography. I turned away, revolted. I shouldn't be surprised. A man like that.

Stepping away, careful not to touch anything, I opened the lid of one of the boxes. Inside were reams of yellowed paper, dusty boxes of pencils and pens. Why did Mr Ellis have them? A hangover from his job, whatever that had been, or stolen property? That wouldn't surprise me either.

This place was disgusting. I should leave, go back home and come again when Martha was here. Stepping out the door, I closed the room up and stood on the landing, breathing hard, trying to shake away the smell.

Martha's door was open. Guiltily, I went inside. The room was like a child's: the single bed, the dressing table. And it reeked of paint. One wall was whiter than the rest. I looked at it closely. It wasn't a wall, it was a cupboard. Martha had painted it shut; thick, uneven layers, still tacky to the touch. Why would she do that? It didn't make any sense.

I pulled open drawers. Her clothes were folded neatly, her underwear rolled into balls. Unable to stem my curiosity I poked and pried with shaking hands in every corner. I found nothing that told me anything I didn't already know. Martha was obsessed with order and cleanliness. A stark contrast to the neglect in her parents' room.

I stood for a moment listening. No sound. The house was silent. I moved towards the wardrobe. It was old, with scratched surfaces and doors that creaked. Martha had few clothes to hang in there: plain dresses and skirts. Beneath them was a single suitcase: an old-fashioned, brown box. Kneeling, I pulled it out and slowly unclasped the buckles.

Inside were piles of paper and card. Drawings and paintings. Martha's artwork. I dragged out a sheaf of them, my heart beating hard. There were sketches and sketches of Gabriella. I shuffled through them frantically, held them close to my face, one after the other, gazing horrified for several moments, trying to understand. In each picture, Martha had captured my sister exactly: each mood, each expression I'd known.

I searched through with trembling hands. Martha had been good at art. She'd won the school competition, hadn't she? What had she drawn? A portrait of a man. So talented. An amazing artist. And these portraits were incredible too. How closely she must have observed Gabriella to get the detail right.

And now the smell of paint filled my nostrils. The scent was overpowering. Why had Martha painted the cupboard door shut? What was she trying to hide? I ran downstairs, stumbling on the way. In the kitchen I grabbed a knife. Back in the bedroom I slid the blade into the crack of the door, slicing again and again until the paint flaked. I prised it open. My body shaking with the fear of what I'd find.

There was nothing. Nothing but cobwebs and dust. And an old bowl. Cracked in two. I turned away, my heart still speeding.

Martha stood in the doorway with her fists clenched and her eyes wide, watching me.

28

1982

One cold February morning, when I'd been awake for most of the night, I took out my notebook and scanned through the lists of suspects. Time and again, my eyes returned to the top of the list. Edward Lily. What if I interviewed him?

Dressing quickly, I grabbed a few biscuits for my breakfast and hurried out the house, cutting through the green and the woods to get to Lemon Tree Cottage. When I arrived, the windows of the cottage were open and a vacuum cleaner droned from inside. Dare I knock on the door? Walking past and down the lane, I ate ginger nuts as I considered what to do.

The roof of the cottage next door seemed worse than ever. Great gashes had been ripped into the thatch. It gave the house a creepy feel as if it had been under attack. The woman who lived there was by the washing line, a peg in her mouth as she stretched to hang up a sheet while her little boy sat on the ground batting his fists on the cloth.

I didn't think about what I was going to say until I clicked the gate open and stepped onto their path. The woman turned at the sound and, taking the peg from her mouth, studied me suspiciously. 'You're not selling anything, are you?' she said. I shook my head. Of course not. 'Or wanting something for the church?' More likely, but

I shook my head again and added a resounding 'No' to be sure she understood.

She nodded gravely. 'So how can I help you?'

Putting on my most adult voice, words came out unplanned. 'I was visiting your neighbour, but there's so much noise, vacuuming and suchlike' – I sounded like Grandma Grace – 'they didn't hear the doorbell.'

'Doorbell?'

Oh God. Please say they had a doorbell. I hadn't thought of that.

'Maybe it doesn't work. Have you tried knocking?'

I nodded firmly. 'Yes, I have.'

'Well,' said the woman, using the peg and fishing out a couple more from the pocket of her apron. 'In that case you'd better wait until the noise dies down.' As if to demonstrate the opposite, the child yelled.

I stayed where I was, trying to think of a question to ask. Failure, together with the appearance of the woman's dungaree-clad husband wielding an axe, made me leave. Mumbling thanks, I headed back to the gate as the man crossed the lawn in the direction of a wood shed.

The woman watched me silently until I was on the lane. 'They're going away,' she called after me.

Crack. The man split a log in two.

'Oh?' I tried to seem casual. 'Where?'

'Spain, I imagine. Leastways, that's what he said. Although . . .' The child got tangled with the washing. She leaned to pick him up and settled him on her hip. The man stopped chopping. I waited a moment or two longer before I prompted her again.

'Although?'

'The girl might not go with him.'

My heart beat faster. 'What girl?'

'His daughter. According to Geoff' – she nodded towards her husband – 'she's staying here. Well. When I say here, I mean England.'

Geoff gave a grimace of acknowledgement. I looked at him curiously. How did he know?

'Heard it in the village,' said the woman. 'You know the gossips. Must be true.' She smiled in a way that made me think she wasn't serious.

I asked when they might be going. 'Tuesday,' she said, leaning awkwardly to pick up the empty laundry basket. 'Lunchtime.'

Before I went home, I took another look at Lemon Tree Cottage. It was quiet now. Windows closed. No sign of the person who'd been vacuuming. No sign of anybody at all. My heart thudded. What if Edward Lily was spreading rumours about going back to Spain and leaving Lydia in England? What if he was pretending the cottage would be empty so that nobody would come? My sister might be a prisoner, locked up in a cellar or an attic room. You heard about these things on the news. People locked away for years and never found until one day they escaped or a neighbour or a friend became suspicious and broke in.

I formed a plan. It was Sunday. I'd bunk off school on Tuesday afternoon when Edward Lily should be gone and come back. No one would notice. And if they did, they'd let me off, like they always did. Making allowances for the missing girl's little sister.

*

When Tuesday came, I got ready as usual. Having breakfast, packing my bag and shrugging on Gabriella's parka,
which I'd adopted now. I spent the morning at school –
pleased for once that no one took any notice of how
quiet I was in class – thinking about what I would do
when I got to Lemon Tree Cottage. What I might find.

At lunchtime, I ate macaroni cheese quickly. Passing
Martha on my way out of the canteen, I avoided her gaze.
We hadn't spoken since I'd shouted at her. I was sticking
to my word; I never wanted to speak to her again.

Heading for the gates, I walked as if it was normal to
leave at this time. But as soon as the school was out of
sight, I set off with a tremendous sense of anticipation
and excitement. I was sure I'd find something at the
cottage – a sign at least that would help me understand.
Or else she'd be there – Gabriella. I pictured her standing
at the window like Lydia had done, watching for me on
the lane. Now I dashed up the hill like Hermes – as if I
had wings on my feet. But I wasn't a messenger, I was
Odysseus – on a quest to find my sister.

As I grew closer and reached the brow of the hill,
my nerve failed. What if there was nothing to find? What
if my chase was useless? I had no other ideas. No other
leads to follow. By the time I arrived at the cottage, my
heart was pounding with dread. I hovered by the gate.
The sun disappeared behind a cloud and the cottage
dropped into shade. Time ticked on, the sun came back
out and the silence was broken by a blackbird. Gathering my courage, I stepped forward into the gloom and
took the path around the back of the house. The birdsong stopped abruptly and I had a sudden feeling of

being in a different world, where living creatures weren't welcome.

The back garden started broadly and tapered towards a group of fruit trees. I skirted the house, gradually getting closer to the bricks and mortar, the drainpipes and windows, like an animal stalking its prey. Soon I was touching the walls, running my fingers across the rough surfaces, trying to sense what was inside.

All the windows were shuttered except one. At the back of the house was a flat-roofed porch supported by two thick, wooden uprights, and above that, there was a small, rectangular window. It occurred to me that if I could pull myself onto the porch, I'd be able to see into the first floor of the house. I looked around for something to stand on. There was a water butt cast away on its side on a flower bed by the fence. It was made of thick green plastic. I was sure if I turned it upside down, I could climb on and it would take my weight. I rolled the barrel across to the porch and settled it into position beside one of the wooden posts.

The light was failing and there was a chill in the air that raised goosebumps on my skin. But I wasn't ready to go home, even though I might have to walk back in semi-darkness, along the lane and past the fields. I told myself it would be worth it as I climbed onto the barrel, steadying myself, holding on to the post for balance and gripping the rough surface of the flat roof as I hoisted myself until one elbow was there. Hauling myself upwards, kicking my feet as they lifted from the barrel, I was suddenly on the roof, crouching like Jasper, ready to spring, though I didn't feel nearly as agile.

Breathing slowly, I edged to the side of the house. Was the flat roof strong enough? I imagined it giving way beneath me, one leg falling through and me left hanging on to the window ledge – stuck, with no one knowing where I was. Gingerly, I crept forward.

I pressed my face against the glass, hands cupping my eyes. Now I was looking onto a small, dim landing – the midpoint on an L-shaped staircase. Another short flight of steps rose to the main landing where there was a bookcase against the wall, crammed and untidy. All of a sudden, as I was staring at the books, I sensed movement – something bright and fluttering, a piece of clothing, someone looking back at me.

Surprised, I backed away, only remembering at the last moment that I was on a roof. Stopping myself, I scrambled downwards, hanging, searching with my feet for the barrel, realising it was falling away. My heart was thudding as I let myself go and landed on the ground, perfectly, amazingly, legs bent, arms forward and balancing, like a gymnast. For a second I wanted to climb back up. Was it Gabriella I'd seen? That was what I'd come for, wasn't it? To see if she was here. But now there was a sound. A window opening? Footsteps on the stairs?

I fled along the darkening lane and out onto the main road. I kept on going, my feet pounding the tarmac, dodging an oncoming car that blared its horn. Athlete. Marathon runner. It was as if I'd inhabited Gabriella's body. Or she mine. I ran home without stopping and burst through the front door.

Mum was coming out of the kitchen as I stood in the hall bent double, gasping for breath, all heroics gone.

And when I looked at her, I realised how selfish I'd been, going out without telling her. Mum always hated that.

I waited to be scolded for my scratched arms and torn clothes, at the very least to be sent to my room; but Mum was looking at me as if she hardly saw me. Had she even noticed I'd been gone? And now my ankle hurt from what I thought had been a perfect landing, and the pain was crawling, upwards, through my body. Yet there was worse pain on Mum's face. She seemed ten years older than she had the last time I looked, and her hair, I noticed, was more grey than fair. I stifled the sob that was trying to escape, let my shoulders sag and my head droop. She touched my shoulder. 'Your tea's on the table,' she said quietly. I gave a miserable nod before trudging to the bathroom to wash my scratched and muddy hands.

The water was soothing. I closed my eyes and considered what I'd seen. The flutter of a skirt or a dress, perhaps a scarf. Bright orange. It had been a person, but I hadn't seen a face. I'd been too afraid and quick to escape. What if it had been Gabriella waving for me to stay? What if I'd deserted her?

That evening, I went through the motions of my routine, mumbling responses to my parents. All the while I was telling myself there was only one way to find out the truth. I'd have to return to the cottage.

The next day I left the house for school as usual before slipping back and dumping my bag behind the bushes in the front garden. Setting off again, I pulled up the hood of the parka, felt the scraggy fur against my face and the pang of what was missing: Gabriella's scent. It was disappearing, displaced by mine.

This was my last chance. My last theory. There was no one else to ask and nowhere else to look. I had no plan, but even so, when I arrived at the cottage I knocked. No answer. I lifted the mat, looked behind the empty milk bottles. People left their keys in the most obvious of places. Not Edward Lily. There was nothing by the back door, either, although the shutters on one of the ground-floor windows had been drawn back. Pressing my face to the glass, I looked into a small, cluttered kitchen. I had to get inside. Where else would someone hide a key? Above the door. I stood on tiptoe and ran my fingers along the ledge, felt cold metal and pulled down the key in triumph.

A moment's hesitation. What if Edward Lily hadn't gone away? What would he do if he found me inside his house? Would he call the police – or worse? Taking a deep breath, I gripped the key and fitted it into the lock.

As soon as I stepped into the kitchen and scanned the room, I sensed the presence of a woman – a warm, perfumed smell of flowers. There were cups on the draining table, wine glasses too. I moved across and opened the fridge. There was a bottle of milk, the silver top pierced, the contents half gone. I sniffed it. Fresh. There were sausages on a plate, vegetables, a bottle of opened wine. And the Aga was still warm. The neighbour was wrong. Edward Lily hadn't gone away. He was here with Lydia still.

I tiptoed out into the hall and listened. No sound. Not even the ticking of a clock. The carpet was thick and muffled my footsteps. A large table stood by the door beside a stand with a wax coat hanging from one of its hooks. There was a pile of letters on the table including a large brown envelope, thick enough for a magazine or a brochure. I looked at the postmark. Oxford. If Edward Lily was here, he would have opened these letters. Yet someone must have taken them from the mat.

Outside, the gate clicked. I froze. Footsteps on the path. I backed away, preparing to escape. The letter box clattered as a leaflet was pushed through. The footsteps retreated and I relaxed.

Living room next. The curtains were drawn and it took my eyes a moment to adjust to the gloom. The room smelled of woodsmoke and tobacco. For a second I paused, taken back to the day Gabriella had disappeared. The ashtray, the visitor in our house.

I looked around me. The furniture was solid: a straight-backed sofa, a chintz-covered chair, a velvet chaise longue. A wooden pipe rack. There was a coffee table marred by a spiral of tea stains. Over the fireplace hung a mirror with a gilded frame. Around the room were vases with flowers left dying, a sorrowful yucca plant, an elaborate bronze urn, wooden icons of saints, painted in blue and gold, and beside the fireplace was a carving of a giraffe.

There were a few magazines left on the arm of one of the chairs and a brochure was open on top. It showed a photo of a huge old house. It reminded me of Saint Barnabas. And yet this place looked more like a hospital. There were nurses in some of the pictures. And private rooms with beds.

The staircase paused on a small landing as I'd seen before. I stayed there for a moment looking out the window. Nothing stirred. The garden was desolate. The sky grey. I crept up the second flight of stairs. The idea that Gabriella was held in the cottage against her will was fading but I needed to be sure.

The first door on the landing was ajar. It was a small room with a double bed that almost filled the space. A lamp with a bronze base and a leaf-patterned shade stood on the bedside table, and a bright orange robe lay across the foot of the bed. This must be the flash of colour I'd seen through the window. I lifted the robe to inhale the scent. It was fresh and unfamiliar. It smelled of flowers. Roses, perhaps.

Now there was a noise: the sound of a gate slamming. My heart hammered. Swinging around, I dropped the robe and ran from the room and down the stairs, arms outstretched for balance, body banging against the walls. I flew out the back, desperate to get away, not caring about the noise I made, or why I'd come in the first place, leaving the door swinging as I heard voices and the sound of a key.

Out on the lane, I picked up my pace, forcing myself to run without looking back. And as I fled a second time from Lemon Tree Cottage disappointment gripped my chest and squeezed my insides. Gabriella wasn't in the cottage. It wasn't her scent, or her voice. It wasn't her clothes lying on the bed. It wasn't her hands touching the things in Edward Lily's house, or her lips drinking from his glasses.

I slowed my pace and limped down the hill, tears

brimming. Was this the end of my investigation? Where else was I supposed to look?

In the village, a group of boys were heading towards me on the narrow path, their hands wrapped around cans of beer. There wasn't room to pass them. I'd have to step onto the road. But I held my ground. I didn't care. And as they looked at me with their sullen faces, I lifted my chin, and glared from beneath my hood. They could say what they wanted. It didn't touch me. I was on a quest to find my sister. Their importance had shrunk. I was strong and they were weak. I was afraid of nothing.

They lowered their eyes and stepped off the path, making way for me, and I suddenly realised why – nothing they said, or were prepared to do, could be worse than what they thought had been done to Gabriella.

For the first time, I doubted that she was hiding out. Maybe people were right. Something terrible had happened to my sister and she was never coming home.

29

Martha opened her mouth to speak, but nothing came out. I took one moment to look at her before I spoke, to take in the whole of her, to capture the anger that was building inside me.

'Why?' I said finally, indicating the portraits.

Martha stared back, silent still. I wanted to take her shoulders and shake the words out of her but I forced myself to stay calm.

'Why?' I repeated. 'Why did you draw all these portraits? Why did Gabriella even let you? Answer me, Martha. I need to know.'

Now she reacted, dropping her head, her shoulders slumping. 'Because she was kind. She was the only person who was. She came here and we talked. She *listened* to me and I told her things.'

'And she let you draw her?' I hardly believed it and yet I remembered the vivid sting, the time I'd seen Gabriella leaving Martha's house, the feeling of betrayal. How often had Gabriella visited Martha? Far more times than I must have known.

'It's not so terrible, is it?' said Martha. 'I was good at art, wasn't I?'

I looked at the portraits. There was no denying it. Martha was incredibly talented.

'But why did you give the portrait to Edward Lily?'

'I didn't,' she said sharply. 'I wouldn't have given him anything.'

'Why?'

'He was no better than anyone else.'

'Wasn't he?' I spoke sharply.

'I *told* you. Men and boys. All after Gabriella. It was never going to come to any good, was it?'

She looked away and I followed her gaze. I'd been so taken up with the portraits, I'd forgotten about the cupboard I'd forced open. Now she was registering what I'd done. 'You had no right to do that,' she said, her voice raised and angry. She pushed the door closed. 'Who do you think you are?'

'I had every right,' I spat back. 'I'm looking for my sister.'

'You won't find her.'

I took a step forward and she flinched. Her face was white, her eyes glittering. What was she afraid of? Turning to the cupboard, I grabbed the handle.

'Leave it,' she snapped.

'Why? What have you been hiding?' A sealed door and a broken bowl. Why would Martha paint the cupboard shut? I dropped my hand. A terrible idea was forming in my head, slithering into my consciousness. Lowering my voice, I forced out the words. 'Was somebody locked in there?'

'It's not your business.'

'It is my business. Did your father lock Gabriella in that cupboard?'

'No!'

282

I moved across and spoke into Martha's face. 'You're lying. My sister was a prisoner. He locked her in there, didn't he? Then what did he do?'

I grabbed her wrist and pulled her closer. I was imagining Gabriella captured. Had she called out? Had she hammered on the door? I followed the flow of her emotions: the disbelief, the fury, the closing in of terror, the desperation when she realised no one was going to come.

Martha was breathing heavily. I loosened my hold with disgust. She was like an animal, helpless and pathetic.

'How long did she stay inside the cupboard?'

'Stop saying that,' said Martha. 'He didn't lock her in there.'

'Then why did you paint it shut?' I persisted. 'What are you trying to hide?'

'It wasn't her,' she said, staring back.

'What do you mean?'

'It was me.'

There was silence. 'You?' I let out my breath. 'Why?'

'Three days,' she said, ignoring my question. 'He kept me there for three days. Can you imagine what that was like?'

She crossed the room and sat on the bed. I watched her, my arms hanging uselessly by my side, unable to move or speak. Martha afraid in the darkness, not Gabriella. A peculiar kind of relief. A peculiar kind of dread.

Eventually, I moved across and knelt at her feet. 'Tell me,' I said, forcing myself to be quiet. I put my hand on hers. It was like bone, with the barest covering of skin.

For a second she let it lie there, and then swiftly, she pulled away.

I sat back, trying to find a different way. 'Tell me,' I said again.

She closed her eyes and spoke. 'He used to be kind.'

I thought of what Eliza had told me. 'Was that before he lost his job?'

'He was an electrician,' said Martha, smiling as if proud of the memory. 'He used to let me play with his toolbox. I was his little helper.'

'And then?'

The smile disappeared. 'He was a salesman.'

There was silence again. 'And what was he like after that?'

'Drunk. Friday nights to begin with. Then every night. And when he came back, he raged around the house.' She closed her eyes as she remembered. 'Staggering on the stairs, peeing in the bowl, hitching up his trousers, hauling at his zip, buckling the belt.' Now she looked at me. 'Have I told you about his belt?' She didn't wait for an answer. 'He put it round her neck and pulled it tight. You want to know about my father? I would've killed him if he hadn't died. I would've drowned him when he was old, pushed his head down in the bath, or smothered him with a pillow. I would've done it, I swear, as soon as he was too slow to catch me with his fists.'

My blood turned cold. 'Whose neck?'

'My mother's.'

'And you?'

'No.'

'And Gabriella?' I whispered.

She slowly shook her head.

'Then who?'

Martha covered her face with her hands and I knew better than to push. I studied her for a few seconds more, willing her to speak, but she was crying, fat tears splashing onto the bed. I stood up, feeling helpless, blood racing as I tried to understand. If Martha wouldn't say, I had to find another way of finding out the truth.

I went back to her parents' room and stood in the doorway looking around me. The atmosphere was dark and brooding, like the demon in my dreams. Something was hiding. Secrets. In the cracks and crevices of the walls. I was so close to understanding. I only had to look harder and I'd know.

Stepping across the belt and the magazines, the scraggy carpet and the rug, I headed for the boxes. I touched their sagging sides and read the labels on their lids. There was the name of the company: Rawlinson Supplies. And the addresses of shops and businesses in different towns across the country. The destinations of a travelling salesman. Glasgow. Warrington. Sheffield. And York.

I read the names again, struggling to understand. It was as if my brain was working in slow motion. *York*, I read.

The belt. I kicked it over. A buckle slumped into sight. It was shaped like an eagle, its metal tarnished with age.

York. The word rang like a death toll.

Martha had followed as soundless as a ghost. I looked up and a coldness swept through my chest.

'Sometimes I think I see her,' she said.

An image came. A blonde girl with a fringe. The girl murdered in York. 'Victoria Sands?' I said in barely a whisper.

Martha made an impatient gesture, shaking her head. 'No. I see *her*. In the street, or by the lake. And here – footsteps, running through the house. Do you hear her? Do you see her?'

I shook my head. 'It's not possible.'

But I knew she was right. I saw Gabriella everywhere too.

'What happened to her?' I said. 'If he didn't strangle her . . .' I paused. 'Did he do something else?'

She looked at me, and despite everything, surprise lit her face. 'No. I told you. He didn't kill Gabriella.'

I exhaled with a sudden guilty relief. There was still hope. I took a giddy step towards Martha, stretching out my hands as if I might grasp the truth. She jerked backwards. 'Why did you come back?' she asked. 'Now I have to live it all again.'

'What do you have to live again, Martha?' I spoke softly. 'Tell me.'

She gave me a curious look, as if thinking something for the first time. 'You're just like those women, aren't you?'

'What women?'

'Those ones that made me go to church.'

'Church?'

'Yes. They thought I was lonely when my mother died.' She gave me a sly look. 'Why would I be lonely? I went once. That was enough. They gave out pamphlets about Christ and how he saved us, and took our sins, and would forgive us for what we'd done as long as we embraced him and repented. They probably thought they could save me too.'

'Save you from what, Martha?'

'You'd like me to tell you, wouldn't you?'

I kept my voice low and steady. 'Tell me what?'

'The how and the why.'

'Yes, Martha,' I said. 'I'd like you to tell me the how and the why.'

'The *why*'s easy – have you seen a butterfly in a spider's web?'

'Tell me!' I said, my voice rising. I was twelve again, my glasses bandaged, the book of suspects in my hand. 'What do you know, Martha? Tell me about the day she disappeared. Did you see her?'

Martha wasn't listening. 'I can almost hear it,' she said. 'I can almost smell it.'

'What can you hear?'

'Screaming.'

'What can you smell?'

'Flowers.'

I waited, my heart beating so loudly it must have echoed around the house. 'Tell me,' I said. 'Tell me about that day.'

A frown creased her forehead. I imagined the pictures forming in her mind, the sequence of events. She'd stayed for an art class after school. She'd walked home in the semi-darkness. Had Martha's arrival on Acer Street coincided with Gabriella's?

'What time did you get home?' I said.

Martha screwed up her eyes as if trying to remember.

'I don't know, but I knew my mother would kill me because I was late. She'd lock me out.'

'Is that what happened, you were locked out?'

'I sat on the wall,' she said.

'What wall?'

'Along the street.'

'You stopped because you were afraid to go home?'

She narrowed her eyes. 'I stopped because I saw the man.'

'What man?' Now my words sounded far away as if I was in a dream.

'Edward Lily.'

I breathed deeply, counting in my head, before I spoke again. 'What was he doing?'

'Talking to Gabriella.'

'Did you hear what they said?'

She nodded. 'They didn't notice me at first.'

'What? What did they say?'

She paused. 'He said he loved her. He said he wanted to be with her. I thought . . . I thought he was trying to . . .' She broke off.

'Did you know he was her father?'

She stared at me and shook her head. 'No. I thought . . .' She stopped again, her face flushed. She must have believed the worst of Edward Lily.

'He was her father,' I repeated and watched as the knowledge took its hold. 'What did Gabriella say to him?'

'I don't remember. I don't understand. Why didn't she tell me he was her father?'

'Why would she?' I said. 'She didn't tell me.' I crossed

my arms, trying to hold my emotion in, gripping my elbows, digging nails into my flesh. 'Try,' I said. 'Try to remember what Gabriella said.'

She shook her head. 'I can't.'

'Please, Martha. It's important. What did Gabriella say?'

She pushed her palms into her eyes as if trying to force the memories back. 'She said she wouldn't leave her family.'

I breathed again with relief. 'What else?'

'She said she didn't want to hurt anyone. And . . . and she gave him one of my portraits. The one I'd given her as a gift.'

Why? To apologise for rejecting him? As a substitute for her? 'Was he angry?' Martha shook her head. 'And what about you? Were you annoyed that Gabriella gave him the portrait you'd drawn?'

Martha looked away. It was true. She'd been angry and jealous . . . like me.

'And Tom?' I said at last, my heart pounding. 'Was he there too? Did he walk past while they were talking?'

Martha nodded.

Tom's ever-changing statement. His forgetfulness. Had he seen Gabriella with a man or with a girl? The answer was he'd seen her with both. He'd been telling the truth all along.

'What did Edward Lily do? Did he hurt her?'

She shook her head. 'He walked away.'

'And Gabriella?'

'She was crying.'

I brought my voice down to a whisper. 'What did she do?'

'She came to me. Can you imagine that? She *wanted* to be with me.'

'What happened then?'

'I took her home.'

'You took her home,' I repeated.

There was silence. I pictured Gabriella crying and vulnerable, led away by Martha, the person she'd helped and championed. But now the tables had turned and Martha was helping her. She'd seized her chance and taken my sister into her house once again. How she must have loved bringing a friend home, like any ordinary girl, with ordinary parents, in an ordinary house. But Martha wasn't ordinary, was she? She'd had a terrible life with a murdering father and a beaten mother.

'She was a bitch.'

The blood rose and thumped in my head. I stared at Martha. 'What the hell do you mean?'

'She sent me for biscuits.'

I looked away, confused. 'Gabriella?'

'My mother. She was a bitch.'

Images flickered: this abandoned bedroom, the anti-septic kitchen, the sterility of the living room, all personality gone. The Ellis grave with the defiling marks across the stone. She hated her father. Had she hated her mother too? She'd seen her die. My God, what had that been like? The thought crept in again. Did she push her mother? I rubbed my eyes, pressed my palms into the sockets. Martha hated *both* her parents. Her father was a monster, that was clear, but her mother was a victim in this. Wasn't she?

Martha was quiet. I leaned forward and let my hand rest on hers. She looked at the contact with surprise and this time she allowed it.

'What happened when you went inside?'

'She didn't have her scarf,' said Martha, lifting her fingers and touching her throat.

'Your mother.'

'Yes. And she was angry. Angry with me for being late and for bringing Gabriella home.'

'But Gabriella had been before and your mother hadn't minded.'

'No, but . . . the bruises. They were . . .' She paused.

'Had your father . . . ?'

'Yes. He'd beaten her the night before, and Gabriella kept looking at the new bruises and saying she had to go home. I tried to get her upstairs, I did, but the bitch persuaded her to go into the living room. She said she'd make her a drink. I didn't know what to do.'

And now I imagined how Gabriella had felt when the door had closed and she'd seen Martha's mother. The hall must have seemed darker, narrower. She must have looked about her and questioned why she was there. She must have wanted to come home to Mum and Dad. To me.

I clenched my fists, opened them again. 'And your father . . . Was he at home?'

'No,' said Martha bitterly. 'He was in the pub. He was always in the pub.'

I concentrated on levelling my voice. 'So what did you do?'

'We sat on the sofa.'

'What did you talk about?'

She smiled, remembering. 'Gabriella told me not to say anything to anyone about the man. She trusted me. And I forgave her for giving away the portrait.'

Her eyes closed with the effort of speaking. I forced myself to take her hand again and squeeze it. 'Tell me, Martha. What happened next?'

'She said she needed to go. She said she was meeting you at the shop and she was late.'

It was true. I'd been in the House of Flores, peering into the darkness waiting for Gabriella to come. If only I'd gone to look for her. If only I'd met her at school.

Now Martha spoke with malice. 'I might have helped her if she hadn't mentioned *you*. I might have led her out the house and taken a clip around the ear for letting her go.'

I released her hand, clamping my mouth shut. I mustn't be angry, or stop her from talking. I'd take anything from Martha if she'd tell me what she knew.

'She never would have found out if they hadn't kept the newspaper.'

I stared at her. 'What newspaper? What did she find out?'

'The one with the picture of the girl. The one from Yorkshire. The one he killed. It was on the sofa and Gabriella picked it up. And then *she* came in. *Put that down*, she said. But it was too late. Gabriella was looking at the picture and staring and I saw what my mother had written on it. *Bitch*, it said. Scrawled there. Right across the page.'

I felt myself swaying, imagined collapsing on the filthy floor. I anchored my feet and forced myself to speak. I was so close to understanding now. 'So what did your mother do?'

'She got her bag.'

'Her bag?'

'She got her purse and took out the money and gave it to me. She told me to go and buy biscuits. She said we couldn't have Gabriella over and not give her any biscuits.'

Biscuits. The hairs on my arms rose. 'What did Gabriella say?'

'She said she wasn't hungry. The bitch didn't listen. She told me to buy more squash. Milk too. She told me to take my time and that she'd entertain my friend. She pushed me out the door. The bitch pushed me out the door.'

'Martha,' I said, struggling for control. 'Tell me what happened after that.'

'I had no choice. You don't understand. I thought it would be all right. Ten minutes. Nothing could happen in ten minutes, could it?' She looked at me with pleading eyes as if willing me to reassure her.

'And the newspaper article? Had Gabriella guessed?'

She nodded. 'Yes. But I thought if I got back quickly . . . and then, when I got outside I saw him.'

'Who?' I said urgently.

'*Him*. He was coming back from the pub.'

My head cleared as realisation hit me. Mr Ellis, violent and unpredictable, in the same house as Gabriella. Why had Martha denied his guilt? Why was she protecting him?

'I should have gone back inside,' said Martha. 'But I was scared. So I ran as fast as I could.'

Martha was looking beyond me now, her eyes flickering as if she were watching herself, chasing through the streets. 'I bought biscuits,' she said. 'I didn't buy the squash or the milk. I wanted to save time, you see.' She looked at me, her eyes appealing. 'But by the time I got back it was too late. I tried to tell you. Don't you remember? I told you about the biscuits.'

I looked away, trying to hold back the sob that was rising in my throat. For now I remembered that day; when I'd rejected Martha, bawled at her in the street. I'd thought she wanted to be my friend, but I'd been wrong. She'd been trying to tell me about Gabriella.

And since I'd been back, she'd watched me again, followed me, desperate to confess. And what had I done? I'd spurned her once more – stopped her from telling the truth.

30

1982

The moment I got home from Lemon Tree Cottage, I knew there was something wrong. Rita was in the hall, her face white. 'Where's Mum and Dad?' I said, trying to push past.

She shuffled awkwardly, blocking my way. 'I'm sorry,' she said, her voice serious. 'I've got some bad news.'

'What?' I stared at her.

'Your mother's had to go to the police station.'

My stomach shifted and joy shook loose. A grin spread across my face. They'd found Gabriella. She'd come home like I'd always known she would. I stepped forward and opened my arms, all negative thoughts gone. Rita was the bringer of the most amazing news and I wanted to hug her.

But even as I was falling forward, she was shaking her head, gripping my arms and holding me back. 'I'm sorry, Anna. It's not good news.' I felt a cold sweep of fear. 'It's your father. He's . . . missing.'

'Missing?' She nodded. The cold turned to ice and I shivered. I spoke, but my voice sounded thick and far away. 'No,' I said. 'That isn't true.'

'Anna, you must stay calm.'

I gritted my teeth to stop them chattering. Rita was lying. I hated her. I tried to get past, but she wouldn't move. I shoved her with both hands and she staggered, yelping as she fell against the wall. She was nothing but a fat, filthy liar. I ran up the stairs, two at a time, leaping to get away from her.

'Anna, come back,' she called.

I didn't answer. My dad hadn't disappeared. He wouldn't have left me. Not now, not after Gabriella had gone. Not ever. I charged into my bedroom and threw myself onto the bed. Rita was a bitch. An evil bloody bitch. A bastard. A fat, filthy liar. I thought of the worst words I'd ever heard and put them together with her name. All she wanted was to ruin our family. I sat up. That was it. She'd taken Dad away and hidden him. What if she'd taken Gabriella too? What if Mum was next?

I shoved my head into my pillow and sobbed. I didn't want to be alone.

And Rita was there again with her arms around me. She was dragging me up, twisting my body and pressing me against her chest. I gave in – let myself go limp. And I cried as she stroked my hair. 'Where is he?' I sobbed. 'Why has he left me?'

'They'll find him,' she said, soothing me.

But I didn't believe her. I'd learned already. Nobody came back after they'd gone.

The next day, we stayed inside the house, the three of us. Mum had come back late in the night. I'd heard the front door and the sound of whispering, and later still, soft crying from her room.

Rita took charge, making meals that none of us ate; saying things that nobody answered. In the evening, they trooped back in: Grandma Grace, Granddad Bertrand, Uncle Thomas and Donald.

It was Uncle Thomas who finally told me what had happened. He said a woman had found my dad, in a copse, in the woods beyond the green. She'd been walking her dog in the early morning and called for an ambulance and the police. They said he'd had a heart attack. Why had he gone there? Had he been searching for Gabriella, one last time?

For ages, I had an almost uncontrollable urge to meet this woman, to question her on exactly what she'd seen, because while I didn't know, I could only speculate about the position of Dad's body, the look in his eyes, the details that I dreamed about.

I resisted the desire and in any case I didn't know where she lived. I set off to the wood instead, searching for a copse. And as I walked I remembered, Gabriella sitting on Dad's shoulders, the two of them talking about the names of the trees, and the way the sunlight shone through the branches at different times of the day; and me lingering behind, listening, searching for a pine cone, an insect crawling on a leaf. Where was Mum? She didn't appear in these scenes. She must have been at home, cleaning the bathroom, hanging out the washing, preparing our food, making jam; or perhaps she was out on a jaunt, dressed up and turning heads in Covent Garden.

Eventually, I found a copse and stopped, for no other reason than it had a fallen trunk where I could sit. I threw clods of dirt and stones at the trees around me until my arms ached and my face was streaked with mud and tears and my throat was sore with shouting Dad's name. And then Gabriella's name. Because it was always Gabriella.

As for Mum, when Dad died she forgot to function. She stared at the wall saying nothing, went out for walks in the rain, opened and closed cupboards without taking anything from them and didn't feed herself or me. We relied on the kindness of neighbours who made soup and stews that mouldered gracefully in our fridge.

Rita organised the funeral. The day passed in a blur of best clothes and serious faces. Mum drifted through the motions, her face ashen, her body wraith-like. Uncle Thomas looked after me. He held my hand in church and packed me in between him and Donald in the pew.

The house filled with well-wishers, buzzing round my mother where she sat. Uncle Thomas and Donald disappeared. I spotted them talking in the garden beneath the damson tree. Donald had folded his tall, thin body, until he was speaking right into Uncle Thomas's face.

I left them to it and circled amongst the guests. Occasionally somebody remembered me and pressed a biscuit or a sausage roll into my hand. I piled up the offerings on the sideboard. (The next day, I found a crumbling edifice of the remains.) In the end I disappeared to Gabriella's room and stayed there until Rita found me.

It wasn't so difficult when I went back to school for the second time. The head teacher made another attempt to talk to me in her office, both of us perched on the leather sofa, but her fragmented sentences were even shorter and the meeting lasted minutes.

At home, my grandparents came regularly, although each time they appeared, my mother treated them as if they weren't in the room; as if there was no one there, including herself. But they kept on coming, clinging to their visits, Grandma Grace, her face greyer, her body frailer, choosing the straight-back chair. She talked, but her voice was hesitant and there were no more stories about love, while Granddad Bertrand faded further into the upholstery, until one day, he got his wish and wasn't there at all.

The House of Flores stayed closed. I overheard Mum and Rita talking about it. At least Rita questioned. Mum shook her head and shrugged her shoulders. 'I don't know,' she kept saying.

Eventually, Uncle Thomas turned up with a single suitcase, like a travelling salesman. Donald had left him. He'd gone suddenly, taken a post in a university in America. Uncle Thomas handed me an envelope as soon as he walked through the door.

Donald had written a letter and wrapped it around a fossil fish. The fish was millions of years old, nearly as old as he was, he joked. In the letter, he said he was sorry and that these things happened and that no one could predict them or prevent them. He hoped I wouldn't forget him. He certainly wouldn't forget me. I put the fish and the letter in the shoebox and closed the lid. I was getting used to people leaving.

Uncle Thomas sold his shop in north-west London, which hadn't been doing so well since Donald had left, and took over the House of Flores. He had plans, he said: a special shelf for magic tricks, an homage to Houdini with photographs and replicas of the chains and locks he used. No doubt there was whispering in the village about this new set-up. People thinking there was something *Hamlet*-like about the arrival of my father's brother, the funeral baked meats coldly furnishing the marriage table and all of that. I knew there was no chance of a wedding between Uncle Thomas and my mum, but at the same time I received the news with mixed feelings. I was too old for his magic tricks. Besides, I didn't feel like being amazed. I'd had enough of the unexpected.

Still, I got used to having him at home. He filled part of the void. His gestures were large and his voice was loud – his deep-throated cough replaced the quiet clearing of the throat that had been Dad's way. Everything he did was vigorous. He had a habit of brushing his teeth anywhere in the house. He walked around with his toothbrush foaming, down the stairs, along the corridors, finding a sink, or a basin, in the bathroom, or the kitchen, to spit in. He wore holey socks and stretched jumpers and smelled of Old Spice. He left the scent lingering in the house.

I avoided the shop, but I liked to sit on the floor in the living room, with my arms wrapped around my knees and Jasper beside me, and listen to Uncle Thomas talk. He'd taken to sending me off for chips which we both ate straight from the wrappers before he lit his pipe – a habit he'd adopted since Donald had gone. I watched him tapping the bowl out in the ashtray, filling it again, tamping down the tobacco as he spoke about the past. I loved his stories, the ones Dad used to tell me too: the way they moved from place to place, how they fought, together, wielding sticks, beating off the bullies they encountered, who didn't want newcomers on their patch, who objected because their mother was Jewish and their surname was Flores. I wanted to hear tales of resilience and victory, to counter the tales of loss and despair.

But as Uncle Thomas seemed to grow to fill the space of our house, Mum shrank even further into herself. She didn't eat, despite Rita's coaxing, and she grew thin and silent, not caring even about the fruit in the garden which she left all through the following autumn until the trees were wretched with their overburdened boughs and then bereft as one by one the rotten plums and damsons dropped.

About a year after Uncle Thomas arrived we were watching the news when Gabriella's photo appeared on the screen. A girl in Ireland had disappeared; there was no obvious connection, but still the media brought up the details of Gabriella's case. The girl's family heard from her six weeks later. She'd started a new life in Canada. Nobody explained how she managed to get all that way on her own.

Another time there was a missing girl in London who turned up fine – there she was smiling into the camera, arms wrapped around her thirty-something boyfriend's neck, apologising for the distress she'd caused. And the girl with the fringe. They showed her face each time even though everyone knew how it had ended for her. And the girl from Glasgow. The one with no family to miss her.

Uncle Thomas folded the paper, or switched the

channel as soon as these stories came on. 'Let's have chips,' he'd say brightly while my mother stared at the screen from the door. And when I agreed, he'd slip me a ten-pound note that he produced with a tired flourish from behind my ear.

One time, I stopped at the grocer's for ketchup. The shop was crowded, but the hum of conversation halted when I appeared. It was only for a moment, and then it took off again, the ladies and Mrs Henderson droning on, an endless buzz of gossip.

'Is it on the market yet?' someone said.

'He's not selling,' said Mrs Henderson. I sensed they were back on Lemon Tree Cottage, and the seed of dis-like I had for the woman took root inside my belly.

'But they left ages ago, didn't they?' said the someone again. 'Don't they live in Spain?'

'Not her,' said Mrs Henderson.

'Who?'

'The daughter.' I tightened my grip on the glass neck of the bottle of ketchup I'd picked off the shelf. 'He shipped her off, I heard. To a home.' She lowered her voice. 'She is mad after all. And they don't last long in a village, do they? People like that.'

What did she mean, *people like that*? Outsiders I sup-posed. People who didn't fit in. I pictured the cottage and how lonely it was and how empty it would be with no one inside. Maybe the creatures from the garden and the fields would come in, the mice and the deer and the jack-daws from next door. Maybe if I ever went there I'd find a badger in the fireplace, a family of voles in the fabric of the cushions and gaping holes in the roof from the birds pecking their way through.

I paid for the ketchup and left the shop, turning my back on the gossiping women. I didn't think I'd go again to Lemon Tree Cottage. The flash of orange I'd seen was fading in its importance, and even though the place remained vivid to me, and I thought its walls veiled a host of secrets, I didn't think those secrets would tell me where my sister had gone. And that was all I wanted to know.

It was quiet on the streets. No more journalists pouncing on neighbours for inside stories; no more crowds of mothers out in the village stalking their daughters. I trudged along Acer Street, and as I walked, it was as if I was stepping in Gabriella's footsteps, following the route she'd taken that day. I brushed my hands against a laurel bush, along a wall, across the bark of a tree, and my fingertips tingled as I wondered if Gabriella had touched those places too.

Martha was sitting on her doorstep. My beautiful sister was gone, presumed dead – a body, cold and lonely in a faraway place. And here was Martha as if nothing had happened. Old anger surged. She must have felt it too because fear skidded across her face and she was on her feet, pushing on the front door, banging at the letter box, but no one was letting her in. She'd been locked out, and she was crying. My anger collapsed and my heart slowed, and I wondered how it had been when Gabriella's heart had stopped – if it had stopped. How would I ever know?

31

They came and searched the house. It was as though they might find Gabriella hiding in a corner. Why didn't they start in the garden? That's where she would be. It's what Martha had said as she'd sat quietly and confessed what she knew.

And while they searched, I stood outside the house, hands thrust into my pockets for warmth, praying they'd find her and then praying they wouldn't. Eventually, they moved the hunt into the garden. They came and went, people with digging equipment and a tent; men and women in white overalls carrying bags. I was disconnected: I wasn't a part of this alien scene. Only the brief nods of the police officers and their sympathetic grimaces reminded me that I was.

Slowly a crowd gathered, but they knew not to come close. Once again I took on the role of the missing girl's sister, and I had the right to keep my distance. There was only Rita with her hand on my shoulder. She'd always been with me, through every tragedy of my life.

It didn't take them long. Martha had told us exactly where the body had been buried, beneath the roses. Of course it was; no wonder they'd bloomed so well.

It was the silence that told me, the abrupt cessation of sound. No more thuds of metal on mud, no more grunts and murmurings. Even the wind seemed to blow itself out – as if the world had taken a breath.

And then came the release. The noise began again, the voices of the men and women, louder, and more urgent. Not that they could do anything for Gabriella now.

Martha had come home with two packets of biscuits. That's what she told me. But the door had been shut and locked. She'd hammered and hammered on the wood with both fists; she'd called through the letter box, and sunk onto the step to wait. Eliza Davidson had poked her head out from next door and asked if there was anything wrong. Martha hadn't answered and Eliza had gone back inside. It had happened before, after all, and the police had done nothing to help.

When Mr Ellis had let her in, Martha had found her mother lying down, eyes staring, body rigid, grey-faced like a slab of stone. Martha had shaken her, tried to make her say what had happened to Gabriella. She'd screamed and she'd shouted, begging to know the truth, until Mr Ellis had come, his face wild, his breath stale with drink. He'd been frightened, Martha had seen it in his eyes. His victims hadn't been so close to home.

He'd slapped Martha to shut her up and he'd dragged her away, threatening to kill her if she didn't pipe down, until eventually she'd slipped away and searched the house, silently going from room to room. She'd tiptoed into the garden and stood there as the rain had begun to fall. And she'd seen the fresh earth and known what that meant and had given a howl that had brought her father out.

This time, he dragged her back into the house and locked her in the cupboard, in her own kind of tomb.

He'd thrown Gabriella's school bag in with her and given her food that Martha had refused to touch, and he'd left it there until she'd smashed the bowl against the wall. And he'd beaten her with his belt. But still he didn't say what had happened to Gabriella while Martha had been exiled in the street.

Three days later he let her out. By that time, Gabriella's disappearance was common knowledge, the hunt was on, and the fresh earth had been stamped down and covered over with rose bushes. And the rain had washed evidence away. Nobody noticed when the police questioned the Ellis family. Nobody noticed when they searched their shed. Why would the family be suspects? Mr Ellis had an alibi. He'd been in the pub when Gabriella had last been spotted. He'd been involved in an argument. There were plenty of witnesses to that. Including my father.

Mrs Ellis had gathered up her strength. She'd told the police about Tom. They did that. Killers. They came forward before anyone else. They stepped into the limelight without being asked, giving information. The wrong information. The kind of thing that could skew an investigation and send it spinning so far in the opposite direction it might disappear from sight.

'It was your mother,' Mr Ellis had said to Martha after he'd let her out the cupboard, when he'd sat her down and stood over her, belt in his hand, ready to strike.

'No,' Martha had said.

But Mr Ellis had nodded. 'Yes. Itchy fingers round that girl's neck. Jealous bitch. Your mother didn't want me to get there first.'

And still Martha hadn't believed him. Not until he'd dragged her mother in to prove it. 'Say it, Dorothy. Tell Martha the truth.' And she had done. She'd stood, head bowed, cowering in front of her husband, and admitted to killing Gabriella.

Finally, Mr Ellis had whispered in Martha's ear. 'But it was your fault. You brought your little friend home and if you ever tell, I'll come and get you. Even when I'm dead.' He'd cut through the air with his fingers. 'Snip. Snip. You know what happens to little girls that tell lies.'

Later, he'd taken Gabriella's bag from its hiding place in the cupboard. He'd taken out the purse and got rid of it, burying it in the woods. He'd forced Martha to take Gabriella's bag to the station and to hide it behind the bin. Martha was less likely to be seen. The way she crept about the village, she was invisible. And once the whole family was implicated, Martha could never tell the truth.

When the police found Gabriella, I slipped away. There had been a lingering frost. The hedges were bright with crystallised webs and the paths dusted with white powder as if some cold magic had been performed overnight. I tramped along the streets, walking up the hill in the direction of the green.

I passed the church, stopped at the lychgate, looked across at the new mound: my mother buried alongside my father. Already there were new bunches of flowers to replace the old. Grief rose and I swallowed hard, waiting for it to break. A crow called and another answered. The wind picked up and scattered the autumn leaves.

The path narrowed as I left the village, where the houses were large and sprawling, contained on all sides by walls and high hedges as if they'd spread uncontrollably if they weren't. I picked my way down Devil's Lane, my mind ticking as I remembered why it was called that. Here the houses took a step backwards until they were out of sight. Hedgerows, threaded with blackberry brambles, rose on both sides. Fields edged into view, wide stretches of furrowed land. Crows hopped, pecking at the frozen ground.

The lane ended abruptly with a broken stile. I balanced on the wonky step, looked across the familiar expanse of green, bordered by bushes and trees. At the far end was the massive, spreading cedar tree marking the gap to the lake.

A woman was walking her dog in the distance. I placed my hands flat on the splintered stile, climbed over, and jumped onto the grass, landing awkwardly in a dip in the ground. I clocked the direction of the dog walker, and walked the other way. I wasn't in the mood for condolences or references to the past.

And yet, I thought, as I plodded onwards, my boots sinking in the wet grass, how could I avoid it? The past was a ghost, gone in essence, but ever present, lurking in the background with its queries and its doubts. And when I reached the woods, I sensed it around me: in the sigh of the trees, the flow of the stream; in the air above and around me and the earth beneath my feet. And there was Gabriella, one last time: weaving amongst the trees, with the autumn sunlight slanting through the branches

308

and the mist drifting at her feet; and her laughter fading finally and escaping on the breeze.

Rita came to the house. She let herself in and found me lying on the floor in Gabriella's room. She gathered me up and took me downstairs, and made strong, sweet tea.

I was sitting in the garden beneath the damson tree wrapped in a blanket like an invalid when David came. He smiled uncertainly at first. 'I'm sorry I wasn't there,' he said.

'How would you have known?'

'You should have told me.' He reached for my hand and I didn't pull away. 'In the future maybe you could rely on me a little bit more.'

'I've got some boxes that need shifting,' I said, enjoying the warmth of his fingers holding mine.

He grinned. 'No problem. I'm a man with a van and I can shift anything.'

My eyes filled with tears. He squeezed my hand and looked away. We both knew nobody could shift the weight of what I was feeling now. Even so, I asked him to be with me when the police gave the results of the post-mortem.

The coroner declared it had been too long for the exact cause of death to be known. The passage of time had eroded all evidence. Martha's statement was examined. She stated again that her mother had strangled Gabriella before her father had touched her. It was a case of cheating him of another victim. They said we could only imagine what had happened in that house when Martha had been away; those final details of how Gabriella had died; the final moments of her life.

The detective constable assigned to me came and gave me the news. (He reminded me of PC Atkins in a funny kind of way. He had that same slow manner, that same tired kindness.) He told me that when the police had searched Martha's house more thoroughly they'd found the newspaper article about Victoria Sands, the one that Mrs Ellis had defiled. It had been hidden, taped beneath the wardrobe. They found another article, too, crammed beneath the mattress. This time it was about the girl from Glasgow. The child who'd had no family to miss her. The articles were like bizarre boasts. A catalogue of crimes.

I watched Victoria's brother talking about his sister's murder on the news, thanking the police for finally solving the case, hoping now that his remaining family would find peace. I remembered the photo I'd seen of him when he was a boy. Large, lost eyes, wondering where his sister had gone. And I had that same wrenching connection, the knowledge that the two of us were tied by an understanding of how it was to have a sibling disappear.

Martha had been right to rejoice that her father had died. Who knows how many girls he would have killed? Or perhaps there had been others – girls with no one to notice; no one to report them missing.

We kept the funeral small: Rita and David and a few ladies from the church. I chose a white coffin for Gabriella's delicate bones and we sang hymns and listened to

Siouxsie and the Banshees. We tried to do things that everyone would have liked.

And we tucked her up close to my parents' grave. It rained again. The bottom of my skirt got soaked from the long, wet grass, and the scents were strong in the air: the tang of the rain, the earthy soil and the lilacs I laid on the grave. I wore my DMs and denim jacket proudly this time. Not appropriate? *So what?* I could hear Gabriella laughing.

Martha was there for the burial. She stood with her posy of red roses, close to her parents' defiled grave. No wonder she'd done that. I imagined her through the years, chiselling away at their names, trying to erase them entirely. Who could blame her after they'd taken her only friend away?

Maybe, eventually, I'd go and see her again. In the meantime, the social workers were keeping a close eye. Even Eliza visited, struggling on her stick, trying to appease her guilt for not having done more when she'd seen a young girl crying on a doorstep.

And then, when I'd thrown the first clod of earth into the grave, the villagers came, filing silently into the churchyard to say goodbye to the lost girl from so many years before.

After the funeral was over and the wake done, I spent my time alone, mourning my sister, walking through the village until I realised that I wasn't avoiding memories as I had done previously; instead, I was seeking them. There was the gate we'd swung on; the wall we'd walked along; the drive marked with Gabriella's handprint in cement.

One time when I was in the graveyard, putting more flowers on my parents' and Gabriella's graves, I wandered across to Edward Lily's and placed a spray of lilies there too.

The church door opened and Nicholas emerged, motorbike helmet under his arm as usual. He noticed me watching, waved and came across. 'Hello, Anna,' he said, gently touching my arm. 'How are you?'

'I'm getting there. Thank you for asking.'

He nodded and together we stood side by side looking at Edward Lily's grave. There were no flowers apart from mine, and a few weeds had found their way through the stones. I leaned down absent-mindedly to pull them out. Who in the village would do this after I'd gone? Rita perhaps. She'd promised to look after my parents' grave. And Gabriella's. Maybe she'd tend Edward Lily's as well.

I thought of Lydia. Why hadn't she been at her father's funeral? Not dead, according to Dawn, since the aunt had mentioned her. Was she in a home as we'd discussed, or perhaps she was ill? She would surely have been there otherwise.

'Do you remember Edward Lily's funeral?' I asked Nicholas.

He shook his head. 'Before my time, I'm afraid.'

'I was thinking about Lydia.' I gave him a sidelong look to see his reaction, but he was only waiting, interested in what I was going to say. 'You know about Edward Lily's connection with my family, don't you?'

He nodded, his cheeks turning pink.

'Lydia was missing from his funeral. I was wondering

where she was, what happened to her. I heard Edward put her into a home. She had a mental illness, I believe. It seems a cruel thing to do, to abandon your daughter like that. Do you think it's true?'

Nicholas considered. 'I can't say, Anna, but it's possible to find out. I'll speak to Lawrence.'

'Lawrence?'

'The vicar who was here before me. He would have organised Edward Lily's funeral. He's retired now.'

'Would you speak to him? I'd be so grateful.'

Nicholas reddened again. 'No need. I'd be delighted. I'll telephone him this afternoon and see what he has to say.'

I thought of something else. 'Lydia has an aunt – Edward Lily's sister – but I don't know where she lives. Perhaps Lawrence might know? I could write to her.'

'Leave it with me.'

'Thank you.'

We both looked at the grave again and stayed in silence until Nicholas left.

Lawrence was away for a few days – a fishing trip, so his wife said. Impatient, I tried to find out information from other sources. Rita had said that our point of contact for the house clearance was the solicitor, but maybe she had the sister's address as well. She didn't, but suggested I asked at Martin and Martin. *Client confidentiality*, I was informed by the prim secretary when I rang. No surprise there. I asked her to pass a message on. Perhaps the solicitor involved would call me back.

While I was waiting to hear from either Nicholas or

Martin and Martin, I tried investigating in a different way. David stepped forward and offered his help. We searched social media but found nothing. We looked for relatives of Edward Lily on ancestry sites, but there were none living, apart from his sister, a nephew and Lydia, and I had no information about Isabella. Her story was hidden in Spain.

I visited Dawn who recounted her memories of Lydia. She told me about her life as Edward Lily's housekeeper; how Robert would weed and cut back the bushes and the trees; and how Lydia would spend hours wandering in the garden of Lemon Tree Cottage, or staring from the window at the fields beyond.

Picturing Lydia in the garden, I recalled how neglected it had been. Robert hadn't done much of a job. I imagined a younger Dawn flirting with him, distracting him. It wasn't hard. Dawn was only seven or eight years older than me.

A new idea came. I tried it out. 'Did you clean the cottage when Edward was in Spain?'

She nodded. 'He wanted the place to feel lived in, and besides, he sometimes came back.'

'So you went to the house when it was empty, you and Robert together, to clean and do the garden?'

She nodded again and blushed. Mystery solved: the ashtrays, the food and the wine, the rumpled covers on the bed. I'd stumbled on a lovers' den that day when I'd explored the cottage, looking for Gabriella.

Dawn took out her handkerchief and blew her nose, covering up her burning cheeks. Had Robert been in the bedroom waiting for her? I imagined their faces when they heard the noise of scrambling on the porch, and Dawn's shock at coming out, in her orange gown, to see a child's face. How often had I dreamed about that piece of fluttering cloth?

I allowed myself an inward dash of irritation towards this woman: the intruder that had wasted my time. And then I allowed myself to forgive her. It didn't matter anymore.

Lawrence returned from his fishing trip. Nicholas came to see me, and handed me an address and a telephone number. 'Edward Lily's sister. Her name's Elizabeth. She lives near Oxford. She says you can call or write and ask her what you like.'

I took the piece of paper with a nervous feeling. What exactly did I want to find out? The thought of speaking directly filled me with anxiety, so after a few attempts, I wrote a letter and spent the next few days with Rita completing the final details of the house clearance. I contacted an estate agent and asked for a valuation. It was time to put the shop on the market. It was time to think about what I was going to do next.

The envelope was on the mat when I got home from the House of Flores. I looked at the unknown handwriting and my stomach flipped. I knew it would be from Elizabeth before I'd even opened it. Kicking off my shoes and shrugging off my jacket, I made my way to the kitchen where I sat at the table to read. The letter was long, three pages, the tone immediately warm. 'I was sorry,' Elizabeth wrote, 'to hear about your sister. So sad, never to have met my niece.'

I blinked away tears and read on. Elizabeth had known nothing until her brother had visited shortly after Gabriella's disappearance. He'd confessed his affair with my mother, the birth of their daughter, and begged Elizabeth to look after Lydia, saying he couldn't cope. Elizabeth had a son with his own special needs and she'd cared for them both. I was glad to know that Edward hadn't abandoned his daughter in a home, but I thought of my mother and her cousin Mary and I didn't judge him for the decision that he'd made.

'Lydia has a form of psychosis,' Elizabeth wrote. 'A personality disorder possibly inherited from her mother. Sometimes, when things aren't quite right in her life, she feels vulnerable, but she's learned to recognise those moments, and she manages them, going voluntarily into care. She felt that way when Edward died and she's in the care home now, but I know it won't be long before she's back with me. My niece is strong and independent. She's an exceptional person.' I nodded as I read her words. I might have guessed that. Gabriella had been the same.

Elizabeth continued, telling me about Edward's will, explaining how she was the executor and trustee. She said Edward had left the proceeds of the sale of Lemon Tree Cottage, its contents and everything else, to Lydia and Elizabeth's son in a trust, which meant that after Elizabeth was gone, Lydia would always have enough money to pay for her care.

'My husband was executor and trustee, too,' she wrote. 'But now he's passed away, I need to appoint a new trustee. Someone who Lydia can rely on after I'm gone.' I reread her words. Was there a question hidden between those lines? She hadn't met me. Perhaps she could tell from my letter that I'd do my best to help.

Finally, Elizabeth asked me to visit her. 'We have so much to catch up on,' she wrote. And she gave me the address of the place where Lydia was temporarily living in case I wanted to meet her, too.

Sighing, I folded away the letter and considered how wonderful Elizabeth must be. The kind of person who made sacrifices, who took on other people's children. Someone like my father. I sat for a long time, thinking, missing my family, focusing on who they'd been, bringing each one of them back to hold in my memory, if only for an instant.

Later, when the light had dropped and my grieving was exhausted, I crept upstairs to Gabriella's room. The window was open. Outside clouds glided, passing across an imperfect moon; the wind sighed and muttered, catching its breath in the branches of the trees. Voices. Ghosts. I thought I could hear them, urging me to carry on.

'I miss you,' I whispered into the darkness as a breeze reached in and caressed my face.

I miss you. Did an echo travel back?

Turning on my side, I found the pillow wet with tears. I was weeping, one more time – for the way my childhood had ended; for the death of my parents.

And for the day my sister disappeared.

It was a lovely, cold November day. The sky was bright blue with wisps of cloud like sea surf.

I drove down the gravel drive and parked outside the building. In the sunshine, it seemed less severe than I'd imagined, stretching in a semi-circle, surrounded by green. There was an oak tree rising to one side and a fountain that reminded me of the photo, the one in the Plaza de España.

A woman strolled across the lawn, arms linked with an elderly man. I watched them, imagining he was Edward Lily. And I thought of you, Gabriella. And wished that you were with me.

David had wanted to come, but I'd refused. I'd hired a car and driven myself. This was still too personal to share with him. Perhaps if things went well . . . I let my imagination wander. I'd have more time soon. I was going to sell the House of Flores. A buyer had come forward. I was glad about that. I was giving up my life in Athens to concentrate on writing, and with the money from Mum, I might open a gift shop. David had told me it was about time he moved on too. He'd hinted about us spending time together. It was possible. It was all possible now. Rita had been glad to hear the news.

I climbed the steps, clutching my bag. The entrance hall was quiet. There was a reception area with armchairs and low tables with magazines and books. A cat strolled across the carpet. A woman dozed in a chair. She wore a flowery dress and a cardigan, her hair was pinned in a bun and when the cat jumped onto her lap, she woke, laughing, delighted. I smiled, thinking of Jasper.

A voice called from the desk. 'Can I help you, madam?'

'Yes,' I said. 'I'm looking for Lydia. I rang a few days ago. She's a relative.'

The words sounded strange on my lips. I expected this person to think so too, to question me, ask for some kind of authentication, but she only nodded and held out a gold-tipped pen. 'Sign here, please. I'll take you through.'

I signed and gripped my bag as I followed her out into a corridor. 'Does she know I'm coming?'

'Of course. We always tell our residents in advance – give them a chance to refuse. Not everyone wants to be bothered.'

'Did you tell her my name?'

She looked at me directly for the first time. 'Yes, although I'm not sure how far she registered it.'

'I don't suppose she's used to having many visitors.'

'On the contrary,' said the woman. 'Her aunt came and her father, and so did his friend.'

My heart gave a lurch. 'Friend?'

'Esther.' She looked at me curiously. 'Esther Flores. I assumed she was a relative of yours.'

Our mother had visited Lydia. I shouldn't be surprised. Rita had told me she and Edward had made their peace. How betrayed Mum must have felt when Edward came to find you, Gabriella. When he told you the truth. And yet, she forgave him. She came to see his other daughter – Lydia. Was it a penance for denying a child her true father? Or was it because it was the closest she could get to you?

'When was she last here?' I asked, avoiding any explanation.

'Late summer. I remember it clearly, a lovely, sunny day. They sat outside, you'll see where. Lydia's there now.'

For a moment, I felt angry again. Why *hadn't* Mum trusted me with any of this? And then my anger rose and fell and drifted away. That generation. They had a right to their secrets – although I vowed that from now on, I wouldn't have any of my own.

In the garden, I looked around trying to identify Lydia amongst the scattering of people. A figure sat alone on a bench wrapped in a shawl. Her hair was loose, light-coloured and floating, like a cloud about her face. And as we moved closer, there was no mistaking. She had the same frailty I'd seen in the photos; her neck was slender like the stem of a flower; her face, though lined, was as pale as stone; her cheekbones pronounced. The beauty hadn't gone. And she had light-grey eyes, shaped like almonds, serious and sad. Like yours.

Tears rose. I had no idea what to say. How could I express the emotion I was feeling, or talk about the damage of the past? How would I explain who I was, the connection the three of us had?

I was aware that the woman was talking, leaning down, touching Lydia's arm, speaking too low for me to hear. And when Lydia looked up, I saw a hint of curiosity in the almond-shaped eyes. It came and went, so quickly you might not notice if you weren't already acquainted.

But I was. I felt that I was, anyway.

There was silence, save for a blackbird trilling in one of the trees. Lydia tilted her head as though she was listening. And I knew what I would say. I'd tell Lydia about you. I'd tell her all the most wonderful things I remembered – about the love and the laughter and the special things we did. I'd tell her how one day you were there. Then you were gone.

I took Martha's portrait from my bag. It was a beautiful picture, drawn with love. The blackbird stopped its song. The wind took a breath. Lydia stared at the picture and for a moment I thought she wouldn't respond. But then she looked at me, and with your eyes, Gabriella, she smiled.

Acknowledgements

I would like to thank my agent, the brilliant Sophie Lambert, for believing in *The Missing Girl* from the start. She gave me the confidence to think that success was in my grasp and her creative input, guidance and advice has been invaluable.

Thank you also to the team at C & W, and especially to Jake Smith-Bosanquet for his skill in foreign rights, and to Emma Finn for all her support. Many thanks go to Carrie Plitt for ensuring the book has the perfect home in audio.

I am incredibly grateful to Sam Humphreys for her superb editing and insightful advice on how to make this novel stronger. I knew from our first meeting that I wanted to work with Sam. Huge thanks to Josie Humber, Laura Carr, Katie James and the rest of the team at Mantle who helped create this book, and thank you to Emma Draude and Frances Gough for their fantastic support with publicity. I'm immensely proud to be published by Pan Macmillan.

I am indebted to all my Curtis Brown Creative class-mates for their friendly and honest feedback; to Rufus Purdy and especially to Anna Davis whose perceptive comments sent me down a better path. I am grateful also to the talented Erin Kelly, for her wonderful teaching on the course and all her excellent and good-humoured advice on being a writer since then.

Acknowledgements

Thanks to writer Morag Joss for her brilliant workshops as Creative Writing Fellow at Reading University. I still take heed of her nuggets of advice. To Alex Birtles, Jan Dacre, Caz Frear, Helen Hathaway and Maddy Read-Clarke – thank you so much for taking the time to read early drafts and for giving me such a great response. To Russ Aitkins for his ideas and suggestions relating to police procedure back in the 1980s. Any mistakes are most definitely my own. And to Jack Rogers who gave me ideas about legal procedure. Apologies if I went off track.

Thank you to all my family and friends who have supported me along the path to publication, and especially to my wonderful friend and early champion, Jenny Noël who passed away before this book was published.

All my love and gratitude goes to my beautiful children: Stephen, Amelia and Olivia, who have spent so many years putting up with overcooked dinners and a distracted mother who's always in a different world.

Thank you to my lovely, patient husband, Derick, who has rescued those overcooked dinners, made me endless cups of tea and never lost faith in my ability to achieve my dream.

And finally, I would like to remember my parents, who patiently read my early attempts at detective stories, who supplied me with shelves full of books, who took me on endless trips to libraries and who never had any doubt that, one day, my dream of being a writer would come true. I miss you still. This book is for you.

READING GROUP GUIDE

1. How has the disappearance of Gabriella affected Anna throughout her life? Why has this effect been so profound?

2. Family relationships are central to the novel. What are the various family dynamics that feature? What is the effect of the secrecy and lies?

3. What do you think the time-slip structure adds to the book? Did learning more about Anna's past change your view of Anna in the present?

4. How would you describe Gabriella's character in comparison to Anna's? Did the fact that you knew she would go missing have any effect on your reading?

5. In what way is Anna an unreliable narrator? How does this affect the reading of the novel?

6. How does each member of Gabriella's family deal with her disappearance? What does this tell us about their character?

7. The 'Missing Girl' of the title could apply to several of the women throughout the novel. Discuss.

8. Were Anna's parents right to shield her from their secrets? Did Anna have a right to learn the whole truth eventually?

9. Were there any characters you were surprised to find yourself sympathising with? And what made you sympathise with them?

10. How do you feel about the ending of the novel? How has Anna changed? Do you feel there is hope?